D0870198

FORGIVENESS

at

SKELETON COVE

The Adventures of Rogan Chaffey Series
Book #2

Laura L. Morgan

Forgiveness at Skeleton Cove
The Adventures of Rogan Chaffey Book #2

©2022 Laura L. Morgan

All rights reserved. This book or any portion thereof may not be reproduced or used in any manner whatsoever without the express written permission of the publisher except for the use of brief quotations in a book review.

Scripture references are taken from the New International Version.

This is a work of fiction. Names, characters, businesses, places, events, locales, and incidents are either the products of the author's imagination or used in a fictitious manner. Any resemblance to actual persons, living or dead, or actual events is purely coincidental.

print ISBN: 978-1-66787-177-6
ebook ISBN: 978-1-66787-178-3

DEDICATION

To my three amazing daughters: Erika Huestis, Allise West, and Rylee Knight. You are all women of noble character and make me such a blessed Mama.

ACKNOWLEDGEMENTS

To my husband, Trent: for blessing me with so much support and for always encouraging me. Thanks for letting me bounce ideas off you, and for helping guide parts of my story. You're my go-to for any outdoor knowledge I need to learn or verify.

To my daughter and son-in-law, Erika and Josiah Huestis who I can call and ask how Alaskans do or say things. Some of your life experiences spark ideas for my stories. You're doing a great job raising six wonderful children (soon to be seven!). Thanks for taking me on a crazy ride out across the ocean to get my cover photo shot. I still regret not getting a video of the dog flying in the air when we hit the wave. Thanks, Erika, for the chapter drawings 1, 13, 14,15, and 16.

To my daughter, Allise West, an excellent surgical circulating registered nurse who has a huge, giving heart. You married a great guy in Sean, and we are beyond excited with the news of your first child and are looking forward to more of our adventures together. Thank you for your chapter drawings 2, 4, 11, and 20.

To my daughter, Rylee Knight, for being my first Beta reader every time. Your feedback on and enthusiasm for my stories helps spur me on. I love how we have fun together with the idea of Sasquatch. You and Forrest are going to be wonderful parents and we can't wait to hold little Miss Opal when she arrives. Thank you for your chapter drawings 5, 7, 9, and 10.

To my artistic and story-loving granddaughter, Jayel Huestis. I am so excited to use your drawings for chapters 6 and 19 as artwork for this book. Great job!

To more granddaughters, Keturah and Rahab Huestis, for being great cover models. You are Alaskan to the core and you both love adventures in God's country.

To Marta Swanson who told me about her experiences at Survival School. Thank you! It was the perfect event for this book.

Thank you to my Beta readers for your time, valuable insights, and feedback: Rahab Huestis, Jayel Huestis, Keturah Huestis, and Tyra Huestis (the grandma who shares my grandchildren), William Mosman (thanks for your enthusiasm to do it again), Jacob Wentworth (a student of mine who brought tears to my eyes when he came to school so excited after reading my first book), and Reece Smith (thank you that you couldn't stop after reading *Redemption at Dead Man's Hole*).

To my husband's and my youth pastors, Jim Newby and Bob Dexter, Jr. I combined their names for Rogan's new youth pastor, Dexter Newby, to honor their significant contributions to our lives. Thank you and God bless you both.

Chapter drawings 3,8,12,17, and 18 by Laura L. Morgan

Photo credits: cover photos by Laura L. Morgan

Author photo by Allise West

Advance Praise for
Forgiveness at Skeleton Cove

"This book has been a really amazing way to have deep conversations about so many topics: faith, prayer, life, respect, friends, our next adventures. I've noticed a change in (my son) since we read your two books. He takes accountability for himself, offers to help, verbalizes gratitude, and is willing to pray out loud more. I think he admires who Rogan is and it has inspired him."

~Michelle

Praise for *Redemption at Dead Man's Hole*

(Book one in *The Adventures of Rogan Chaffey Series*)

"As an avid adventurer, I love the story. As a self-improvement author and international speaker, I love the lessons built in! Not surprising considering the author- a teacher and outdoors person herself! Highly recommend this fun read!"

~Terry L. Fossum, author of #1 bestseller,
The Oxcart Technique- Blueprint for Success

"THIS BOOK WAS WRITTEN EXCEEDINGLY WELL. I COULD PICTURE EACH ADVENTURE…glad you are writing another book. You are truly gifted."

~Fran

"This is a great book for all ages, with humor, fun adventures, and a keep you on the edge of your seat climax. The Christian perspective makes for a clean book and an insightful look into loss and life. Read it!"

~Rylee

"When you start reading this book, you can't stop reading because you can't help yourself from being anxious about what will happen next. The book is so good! I have read thousands of books and *Redemption at Dead Man's Hole* is unbeatable. This is coming from a thirteen-year-old boy who is a big book worm and I have never found a book better than this book.

~Jacob

"Really, a wonderful example of a book with a grand range of emotion. Written cleverly, it doesn't fail in impress and satisfy those with a thirst for a good read."

~Amanda

"A great read. Had me engaged all the way through. Thoroughly descriptive and took me to Alaska in my mind without ever having been there. Made me cry and laugh and hold my breath at times. Anxious for the next adventure the author will take us on. Appropriate for teens and adults."

~Debbie

"I enjoyed reading about Rogan and his family and crew of friends as they navigate life in southeastern Alaska. The author skillfully weaves pulse-raising wilderness adventures and mishaps into the spiritual crisis that Rogan faces after losing his older brother to cancer. Why DOES God allow bad things to happen to good people? Exploring this issue through Rogan's thoughts and the insights he gains as he interacts with the other characters, including a climax involving two people he never would have expected to help provide the answer to that question, adds depth to the story's intricate detailing of modern-day Alaskan life.

Readers of Gary Paulsen's "Hatchet" and similar outdoor adventure books would find this book of interest."

~Maire

"This was an easy read. I learned some stuff about Alaska and God. I would recommend this book to teenagers and adults. I enjoyed reading this book while visiting Alaska."

~Steve

"This book was a great and entertaining read for my 11-year-old son and I. We were scared, thrilled, amused, nervous, and we even cried. It was hard to put down at night in order to get to bed. My son remarked that he, "Rogan, and his buddies would be great friends" because they have so much in common. The kids in the story have hearts like him and love the same kind of outdoor adventures. The only drawback is that now I have to take my son to Alaska, because it sounds so much better than our wilderness. We highly recommend this book and can't wait for the next."

~Michelle

Dear Reader,

I planted my heart
a dormant seed, packed with hope
and expectation
Long had it waited
Now was its time

My heart took root
sending shy octopus tendrils curling out
Anchors
to keep me growing
when the winds of
dry desolation dared across
the landscape of my mind,
scattered leaves of thought
swirling particles of ideas
into a roaming twister

I planted my heart
on a misty, rainy mountain
above the alpine
Where I can see
the melted, silver sea meander
between lonely islands
Where I can see
sharp-eyed eagles ride the
unseen sky waves
piercing through the mist
Where I can see
my characters
running free on the beaches
of adventure
reaching out to readers afar
Come join us

I planted my heart
and it grew
into living words
I breathe a prayer that they will
touch the hearts of others
and inspire them to
plant their own hearts

CONTENTS

CHAPTER 1

The Sniper

PATIENTLY LYING IN WAIT, HE SHIFTED SLIGHTLY, MINDFUL not to make a sound, carefully resting his finger on the trigger guard. The dampness of the fall-colored leaves strewn on the forest floor, like the aftermath of a confetti party, was slowly seeping into his camouflage jacket, bleeding its way to his army-green T-shirt. The thought that at least the leaves weren't dry, and therefore crackly-noisy, flitted through his mind, but his concentration was on the small clearing in front of him. This is where he expected his prey to emerge from the surrounding trees, although there was a slight possibility that what he sought would stay in the tree line. Even so, he had positioned himself for a clear shot.

The problem was that he was also prey. It was only a matter of who had superior skills: stealth, intelligence, an uncanny sixth sense.

His thudding heartbeat, the result of his recent flight through the forest, was finally slowing. A deep breath.

I have to be ready for the shot, he said to himself. Thanks to his awareness of the possibility of also being stalked at that moment, his blood still raced.

Moving only his eyes, he looked to his left. *Was that a whisper of a branch reaching out to caress passing fabric?*

His pulse ticked up another notch. His straining eyes, slightly squinted, flitted back and forth, looking for movement out of the corners of his eyes. He'd learned he could notice something better if he wasn't looking directly at it.

Nothing.

Maybe it was nothing. Don't take anything for granted.

Damp earth smells filled his nose. He could almost distinguish the soil from the ferns from the fallen leaves. Sunlight filtered through the dense canopy of alder trees.

Patience, he reminded himself. *It is better to be silent and still and patient. Wait for the prey to get antsy and move, giving away his position.*

He opened and closed his fingers so his hands wouldn't be frozen in position, instead ready to move when needed. They'd gripped the black stock of his weapon for a while now. He checked again that the safety was off and that it was ready to fire at a moment's notice. He may not have much time to squeeze off his shot. The red warning toggle was indeed showing.

Where are you? he whispered in his mind, not daring to voice anything out loud.

Presently he did hear the clues that someone was sneaking along, coming closer. Again, only his eyes moved. To the right. *There!* He could see a figure, bent over, moving slowly, stopping behind the trunk of a tree, hoping to stay hidden. The shooter could see enough to distinguish that it was indeed his intended target. The outline of a weapon was also visible. He'd have to wait for the perfect timing. So far, he felt confident that the target had no idea that he, the sniper, was lying in wait.

Two more steps, he thought. *Two more.*

The target snuck forward, and the sniper was ready. He squeezed off a shot and quickly triggered two more. He watched as his skill was confirmed. As the figure cried out in surprise, two bright red spots appeared, spraying out on his target's upper torso and then on a leg. Confirmed kill.

The zing of a projectile screaming through the silence, mere inches above his head, surprised the sniper. He could hear its *thunk* as it hit a nearby tree instead of him. Lucky this time. He took immediate, evasive action, rolling quickly to the side and at the same time realizing that with his very own shot, he'd given his position away to another hunter.

He'd chosen his spot well, mapping out an escape route, planning for this possibility. As he rolled, he was heading to a depression in the forest floor with a fallen tree along the lip on one side, an effective barrier or shooting rest, whichever was needed.

Silence descended in the forest again, like an audio dimmer switch was activated. He sucked in some deep but silent breaths, scanning from his hideout.

Where are you?

A seed of concern that the other hunter may be attempting to flank him took root. He suddenly ducked down and rolled onto his back, weapon shooting from the hip as a black-clad apparition rose from out of the ferns and ran at him, spraying cover fire.

This time he allowed himself to break the silence. "Ahh!" he yelled as he, too, was spraying bullets. Amidst the hail of fire, he was satisfied to again see the red spray of his ammunition finding its target. The black hunter hit the lip of the depression, and his gun went flying as he jerked with the impact, tumbling down to land by the feet of the one who had caused his demise.

The sniper inspected himself, incredulous that not one of the projectiles had found its mark on him.

CHAPTER 2

Home Sweet Home

"YES!" HE SHOUTED. "BOOM CHAIN. GAME OVER! COME ON out. I got them both. We won!" Rogan lifted his paintball gun over his head and nudged Runt with his foot. "You can get up now, loser," he chuckled.

Runt groaned, stood up, and pointed out three paintball splats that had found their marks. He lifted the edge of his shirt.

"That one's going to bruise. Ow!" he complained, fingering a welt on his stomach that was already beginning to swell. "Not forgiving you for that one, man."

"Hey, we're supposed to forgive our enemies, right? Isn't that what the Bible says?" laughed Rogan.

Runt threw his friend a disgusted look. "Nice try."

Fifteen-year-old Rogan Chaffey placed the orange barrel plug in his paintball marker, his friend Runt doing the same. Rogan's first casualty, Tuff McIntosh, and Rogan's teammate Boom Chain Ryan followed suit, adhering to safety protocols. Now they could take off their face protection. Rogan's was camo-ed paint on the hard plastic that covered his lower face and around the safety glass that was the goggle part. He had stuck a few sprigs of a spruce tree into the top and sides for further concealment. Pulling it off, he revealed thick brown hair standing straight up in front, courtesy of his annoying cowlick. His hair was slightly curly in the dampness of the southeast Alaskan forest where he and his friends lived in a small community on the island.

Runt, who had been Rogan's best friend since they were five years old, ran a hyper hand back and forth across his almost white, blond-haired head. His startling blue eyes were alight with the fun they'd just had. His real name was Timothy Petersen, but for years had been affectionately called Runt, since he was yet to hit a major growth spurt. He was wiry, athletic, and full of boundless energy, however, to make up for his lack of height. His hair thrashing stopped. He straightened up and pasted on a cheesy grin for his friends.

"How's the 'do?" He put his hand behind his ear like he was patting a fancy hairdo.

"Oh, man, you ain't gonna catch any girls that way," warned Boom Chain.

Boom Chain's sandy blond shock of hair fared no better. He was the stockiest of his group of friends. His father was a logger for Island Lumber and, much to the chagrin of his wife, had insisted on naming his son after a piece of logging equipment. No one who had been around the boy for a few months thought anything strange about his name. It just fit.

"Now, looking at you all, that is why I keep mine cut short," explained Tuff, running a smooth hand over his buzz cut. "So I am handsome *all* the time."

Tuff was tall and thin, part Tlingit native, and had the black hair and milk-chocolate-colored skin to prove it.

Rogan reached over and pulled a piece of slimy moss, the kind that draped from the branches of the cedar trees, from Runt's mask.

"What is this?" he teased, his slightly off-kilter smile appearing.

"My camouflage!" Runt was indignant.

There was a pause. His three friends burst out in laughter, Boom Chain slapping a knee.

"What?" Runt choked out before joining in the merriment.

"Ah!" Rogan's laughter was cut short as he slapped at the side of his sweaty neck. "I'll be glad when the cold weather finally moves in. The bugs are terrible this year."

"Oh, I know. I have three black fly…white sox…whatever you call them, bites right on my hairline. They itch so bad." Runt pushed his messy hair off his forehead.

"They don't bother me much, but mosquitos sure like the taste of my blood," mourned Tuff. "It *has* been a bad year for bugs."

"Well, we told our parents we'd be home before six, so we'd better head out. That was fun, guys," said Rogan. "What are we up to now, Boom Chain?" he asked, knowing full well the running score but not missing the opportunity to rub it in.

"Oh, let's see, Rogan." Boom Chain pretended to pull out a ledger and ran his finger down the imaginary page. "Looks like we're seven to five."

"Yeah, yeah. You just got lucky this time. I almost went the other way, and then I'd have been behind you and shot you for sure." Tuff tried to make an excuse.

"Whatever. You didn't even know Rogan was there. I was watching," cried Boom Chain. "In fact, I could've nailed you too."

"Then why didn't you?"

"I didn't want to give away my position quite yet."

The friendly banter continued as they headed to where they'd parked their four-wheelers on the old logging road.

The southeast Alaskan forests were filled with dense, lush vegetation in many places. Lacy ferns, spongy moss, medium-leafed salmon berry bushes, large-leafed and thorny Devil's Club, downed trees, and more populated the area. The spot where they played paintball was a piece of Tongass National Forest on the west side of town. They picked this spot because it wasn't as dense here, even providing a clearing of sorts. It was important to have some cover, but too much made it impossible to maneuver through or to spot any opponents.

Rogan loaded his gear in the storage compartment of his family's dark green Yamaha Grizzly. Soon the boys were racing down the gravel road that connected houses and small communities on their island.

Rogan gave a wave to each of his friends as they peeled off to their respective homes. Runt was last before Rogan continued to his house.

"See you, Chaffey."

"Later, Runt."

As Rogan crawled the quad up the semi-steep driveway, the family Siberian husky, Sitka, came bounding out to greet him with a "Woof." She then trotted alongside as he pulled under the lean-to, parking the machine. Dismounting, he affectionately scratched Sitka's white and black fur between her ears.

"Hey, girl. How are you?"

Her ice-blue eyes implored him.

"Oh, hungry, I see. I suppose I should feed you."

Sitka bounced on her front and then her hind legs in anticipation. Rogan fed her, fed the cat, and threw some scratch grains to the chickens. They were locked in the coop at night to avoid being a tasty meal for a wandering, hungry bear. Before retrieving his paintball paraphernalia, he paused to take in the view he never tired of seeing.

The Chaffey family lived on a hill that rose up from the bay below. Tall cedars with moss-draped branches stood alongside scrubby spruce and hemlock trees. The hill was dotted with green-leafed huckleberry bushes that had already been picked, delicate ferns of various varieties, and some scattered wildflowers.

A light rain began to fall. Rogan didn't mind since he was already wet, but it was time to head in for dinner with his family. He entered the mud room and sat on the wooden bench built into the wall to remove his wet, dirty boots.

His ten-year-old sister, Lainey, skipped over when she heard the door open and close.

"Hey, Rogue."

"Hey, Lane. What's up?"

"It's dinner time. We were wondering where you were. Did you do chores? How was paintball? Did you win again? I'll bet Runt and Tuff were mad they lost." Lainey prattled on with her hyper-talking, not stopping to take a breath long enough for her brother to answer. She bounced up and down on the balls of her feet, her dark blond braids bouncing against her back.

"Do you ever hold still?"

"No. Mom! Rogan's home." She skipped off to the kitchen.

The mud room was the entrance to the main part of the house. It opened up to the living room of their wood-crafted home. Beyond that was the kitchen, sporting a bay window with a seat on the ocean-view side of the house. The family dinner table, made of oak, sat in front of the window. Deeper in the kitchen, a utility island with pots and pans hung silent and still. Brown cupboards surrounded the utility island. His parents had their room on the other end of this floor, but his sisters' bedroom was upstairs. They shared the space, just as Rogan used to do with his older brother, Peter, who had died from a brain tumor five years ago.

Rogan had struggled quite a bit over the past few years with why God hadn't healed Peter, his hero, when they had all prayed so fervently. Through talking with his parents, wrestling through sermon ideas, and experiencing life, he had just recently come to a peace and understanding, and even a hope about the situation. The teenager realized that God hadn't given Peter the fatal illness, but that these things happened in a sinful, fallen world. He was mostly over his anger and confusion as to why God didn't choose to heal Peter on this earth but instead healed him by whisking him away to Heaven. Rogan tried to remind himself when he was feeling frustrated and sad that God sees the big picture. He also clung to the image of God keeping his tears in a bottle as the Bible said in Psalm 56:8. The hope he had sprang from the idea that God works together for good in everything that happens to His children.

Just last month, the Chaffeys saw a glimmer of that hope with their reclusive neighbor, who Rogan used to secretly call Crazy Hoffman. Ben Hoffman was beginning to ask questions about having a relationship with God. Rogan had elicited Mr. Hoffman's help, when no other adults were readily available. They needed to rescue a wayward teen, Nico Vega, who had attempted to jump Dead Man's Hole.

This was a seven-foot chasm over a deep sinkhole, and he'd done it to impress a girl. Nico had fallen short and ended up on a narrow ledge twenty feet down, badly injured.

Mr. Hoffman's ingenuity in previously constructing a Rescue Machine, Rogan's bravery in being lowered into the sinkhole, and with many heartfelt, desperate prayers, Nico had been saved. He only recently had returned to the island from the hospital in Ketchikan and was still recovering from his injuries.

Rogan humbly downplayed his heroic role in the entire situation, even though everyone said it was well-deserved, simply wishing life to go back to normal.

"Hey, everyone. Sorry if I made you wait."

Elise Chaffey, Rogan's mom, walked to the table with a platter of deep-fried, breaded halibut. Steam rose from the delectable-looking fish.

"You're just in time, actually." She paused before placing the platter on a trivet in the center of the table, giving her son a one-eyebrow-up look.

"Sorry, I'm a little dirty."

"Just wash the mud from your face and join us." Mrs. Chaffey smiled, her long, light brown hair was in her typical ponytail, and it rested over her shoulder as she turned back to her task. Rogan was proud that his mom was a tough Alaskan woman who wasn't afraid to use a shotgun to ward off an angry bear or who happily went on a caving adventure led by her husband.

Jim Chaffey worked for the U.S. Forest Service, mapping caves, among other duties. He had the dark brown hair he'd gifted Rogan but without the cowlick. His face was kind, and he had an infectious smile, which he beamed at Rogan.

"How was paintball?"

"Great. We had fun. Boom Chain and I annihilated them."

"What does annie lated mean?" asked Peg, his youngest sister. She was eight and had petite, delicate features. Her greatest fear in life was insects.

"It means," explained Rogan, "That we beat them playing paintball. We really beat them."

"Yay!" she said, clapping her hands. "Good job, Rogan."

"Tell us about it after we pray," said his dad.

The Chaffey family held hands and sincerely thanked God for His blessings.

CHAPTER 3

Hunting Camp

SLEEPING BAGS IN TIGHT STUFF SACKS, ROLLED UP FOAM sleeping pads, battery-powered lanterns, trusty Stihl chainsaw, white canvas wall tent, fire-blackened sheepherder stove, sharp hatchet and ax, sustaining food, and the necessary rifles and ammo were all loaded up.

"Everyone double check that you have your hunting licenses," Jim Chaffey reminded the crew waiting to leave for the much-anticipated fall hunting camp.

This had become a tradition of the past three years amongst the Chaffeys and the Petersens. In early September, when the leaves were bright and the winds warm, the kids were permitted to miss a few days of school. They all headed for their spot in the woods where they set up a hunting camp. Rogan had already gotten one deer this year, as had Runt. They all had the opportunity to harvest six deer with the subsistence hunting permit afforded to Alaska residents. The Sitka blacktail they hunted were smaller than many breeds of deer, so it took more to feed their families. The meat they procured during these hunting trips helped them survive the harsh winter. Many times, Rogan had heard his mother exclaim how expensive meat was at the grocery store. It was due to all the trouble it took to get it to the island. Rogan and his family preferred the taste of venison anyway and found the natural protein healthier.

Standing on the slate-gray rocks littering the Chaffey's driveway were Jim and Elise Chaffey, Rogan and his sisters, Monty and Carol Petersen, and Runt, who was an only child.

"I think we're ready." Elise smiled.

Rogan was proud of his mom for being adventurous. Many of his friends' mothers weren't interested in hunting or things like caving, but his mom was. Runt's mom, Carol, always came along, but hunting wasn't her thing. She enjoyed staying at camp, keeping the fire going, and cooking meals for the famished hunters.

I guess I'm glad she doesn't like to hunt, thought Rogan. *She's a good cook.*

"Okay. Let's load 'em up and move 'em out," Monty sang out. They all began climbing into their loaded-down rigs. The Chaffeys had an older model, gun-metal blue 4Runner, and the Petersens drove a four-door Jeep Wrangler. Both vehicles were towing trailers with four-wheelers on them.

Runt hadn't moved. He scrunched up his face and held up a finger.

"I think I'd better go to the bathroom before we leave."

Lainey and Peg giggled into their hands.

Monty sighed. "Hurry it up, Son."

"You'd better use the outhouse since the house is locked up," instructed Jim.

Every residence in their small community had an outhouse as a backup. Sometimes, winter's grip froze and broke pipes, so they came in handy even if the seat was uncomfortably cold. The Chaffey's was up the hill behind their house.

Rogan watched Runt disappear behind the far wall, and then he climbed into the back seat of the Jeep. Monty sighed. Minutes later, Monty turned the engine back off.

What is taking Runt so long? Rogan thought.

Monty must have been thinking the same thing, because he got out of his Jeep and wandered over to Jim's open window. Rogan trailed along behind him.

"Sorry, guys. I don't know what is taking him so long."

"It's all good," Jim replied.

"I'll go see if he fell in or something," Rogan teased and started up the hill. His eyes were down, watching his footing on the mud, slippery vegetation, and fallen logs, when he was startled by Runt's shout.

"Help! Bear. Big bear!"

Rogan halted, wondering if Runt was joking as usual, when he heard another panicked cry for help. Rogan turned back, intending to alert his dad and Mr. Petersen, but Jim and Monty were out of the vehicles, quickly following Rogan on the way up the hill. They were each "packing some heat," as their sons enjoyed saying. Rogan knew they would draw their .44 magnum pistols from their holsters if needed.

The three had reached the corner of the house. They cautiously peered around it. A large black bear was ambling off into the woods and up the hill, seemingly unconcerned about the yelling coming from inside the outhouse.

They hiked the rest of the way as Runt kept up his shouts.

"We're here, and you can come out now." Monty reached up and pounded on the door to get Runt's attention. The latch jangled as it was undone.

"It's gone?" Runt opened the outhouse door a couple of inches and peered out.

"It is. You're safe."

"Yikes! Look at that track." Rogan pointed.

There, in the moist earth, were two distinct bear tracks. The marks from the claws were evident.

"Wow. That is a nice sized one," Jim observed. "It sure looked like it was a big one. We saw it as we came up the hill."

"What happened?" Rogan asked.

"Okay, so I came up here, well, you know. When nature calls…" Runt let loose one of his signature snorts that often happened when he laughed.

For some reason, this struck Rogan's funny bone, and he joined in, chuckling softly at first but quickly laughing out loud with Runt as he looked at his friend's flushed face.

"Man, what an adrenaline rush." Runt held up a shaking hand.

"You two." Monty good-naturedly shook his head. "Tell us when we get down to the rigs. The ladies will all want to hear this, I'm sure."

Halfway back down the hill, the boys were still snickering when Runt's feet flew out from under him. Out of the corner of his eye, Rogan saw him fall onto his backside with a loud "Oof."

Runt looked at his dirty hands and tried to wipe them off, but in vain. Rogan's and Runt's gazes collided. There was a silent pause, then the laughter bubbled back over. Rogan bent over and hugged his stomach with one arm while the other pointed at his friend.

Suddenly, a clod of mud came flying toward Rogan. He lifted his hand to ward off the assault, but he was too slow and it thunked him on his shoulder.

"Monty, I think we'll be strapping these two dirt clods to the roof of the rigs," Mr. Chaffey joked.

"Not a bad idea there, Jim," Monty agreed. Mr. Petersen was shorter than Rogan's dad. He had light brown hair and a thin but wiry build. Runt's blond, almost-white hair came from his mother.

When they finally arrived back at the waiting vehicles, Lainey, always impatient, yelled out her window, "What's going on, you guys?"

Gathering everyone, Runt began his story again. "I went to the outhouse…"

Rogan had to look away, so he didn't laugh again. He cleared his throat, trying to control his mirth. Rogan watched Runt's lips twitch as if he was trying to rein in his smirk.

"I'm in there," Runt continued, animatedly using his hands as he spoke, "When all of a sudden, I hear a pounding. Honestly, it sounded like hoof beats, but I'm like, 'There aren't any horses around here.' Then I can see between the slats, something big and black, and I realize it's a bear. It was this high up the wall." He gestured as he explained. "Now it sounds like a bear because it's all kind of half huffing and half growling. I was worried it was going to stand up and put its paws on the outhouse and push it over with me in it."

Runt's hands came up, and he pantomimed a bear pushing against the structure, like on the Nature Channel when a bear leans against a tree. "I didn't know what to do, but then again, all I could do was sit there."

Rogan had an idea. "Hey, you could've been like on *Jurassic Park* when the T-Rex knocks over the outhouse with the guy in it." Rogan squatted down and pretended to hold up a newspaper while looking from side to side, a shocked expression on his face. That mental image caused the entire group to bust out in laughter.

"Brush off, Runt, and let's get going…again." Mr. Petersen smiled.

Runt punched his chest with both fists, then playfully gave Rogan a jab. "I am a bear attack survivor."

Rogan punched him back. "I'd hardly call that a bear attack."

Rogan rode with Runt and his family, and their excited chatter switched from the bear incident to looking forward to hunting camp, to who would have bragging rights for the biggest deer.

Camp set-up was efficient, with each family helping the other erect their canvas wall tents. Rogan liked camping in these because they were roomy, and the ground was the tent floor. The ridgepole and upright braces made the pitched roof eight feet tall. They laid down a large tarp for the sleeping area and had cots where they would put their bags. The old, partially rusted sheepherder stove had a stovepipe that peeked out of the roof, and it easily kept things warm and dry in the tent. It also added a nice smoky smell. A kettle of water always sat on the top, ready to be used in making a cozy cup of hot cocoa, tea, or coffee when they needed to be warmed from the inside.

As he was working, Rogan could smell the delicious pot of stew that his mom and Mrs. Petersen had premade and was already bubbling on the stove.

They all ate together in the Chaffey's tent, sitting in their camp chairs and making plans for the morning.

"Who's up for being ready as soon as it's barely getting light?" questioned Rogan's dad.

Everyone raised their hands.

"Rogan, we talked about you going with your mom, and I'll let Lainey go with me."

Lainey smiled and clapped her hands, bouncing up and down in her seat, almost spilling her bowl of stew balanced on her lap.

"You know you need to be quiet, and stay behind me, and listen to what I say, right?"

"Yes, Dad. I know. I will."

Rogan grinned and winked at his sister. She smiled back and gave him a thumbs up. This was the first year she was getting to be in on the actual hunt even though she wasn't going to be armed. Peg would stay in camp with Mrs. Petersen. She had brought her dolls, two stuffed animals, and some drawing material to occupy her time.

Runt and his dad would comprise the final hunting partners.

"Which direction do you and Timothy want to go?" Jim asked. Rogan's parents were basically the only holdouts who still called Runt by his real name.

"We'll head west on the skid road that leads to the upper ridge, if that's okay."

"Sure. Rogan?"

Rogan glanced at his mom. "Mom? Can we go on the Lower Road where we saw that big buck last year?"

"Definitely. If we're lucky, maybe Sayyid is still around."

Last year, they had literally almost run into a five-point buck that managed to disappear quickly before either of them could get off a shot. Rogan had named him Sayyid because he thought it sounded like a tough name for a wily deer.

"I'd say Sayyid is a Fig Newton of your imagination, Rogue, except that your mom saw him too," Runt teased.

"Fig Newton? Yeah, you're just jealous. Just wait until I bag him, and then you'll be a believer," Rogan responded. "Dad, where are you and Lainey headed?"

"I think we'll head back down the road we came in on and then walk some of the spur roads."

"Peg and I will hold down the fort," said Carol.

The evening had crept in softly, and it was going to be an early morning, so they all turned in for the night. Rogan usually had trouble falling asleep that first night of hunting camp because thoughts, plans, and fantasies filled his mind in a chaotic swirl. He also always felt a twinge of regret that his older brother, Peter, could not be there with him. As he lay there, however, the exquisite silence of the dark calmed the racing in his head, and he drifted off to sleep.

* * *

The familiar, metallic rattle of the door on the wood stove squeaking open brought Rogan instantly awake. He knew without seeing it that his dad was rekindling the fire. His eyes opened to semi-darkness, and as he got up to gather his gear he'd set out the night before, he could hear the others moving around quietly.

As Elise and Rogan wished everyone luck and headed out, Rogan breathed in the coolness of the early morning. He loved the damp freshness and the slightly biting chill that hinted winter was waiting in the wings, ready to burst onto center stage.

They did not speak, wanting to be stealthily silent, but Elise reached over and gave Rogan a quick hug which he returned with a smile. Strapping the sling of his Ruger Number One, single shot rifle over his shoulder, Rogan and his mom headed out to what they had named the Lower Road. It was a good spot to hunt, since it was preceded by a bend in the overgrown logging road and then opened up to a flat shelf with a small clearing. A clearing was rare anywhere below timberline in the thickly forested area. It was a good vantage point where they could sit and watch for deer moving about.

Even though they had at least a mile to hike before reaching their destination, both hunters moved slowly, stepping carefully and as quietly as possible.

Keep your eyes peeled, Rogan told himself. He had learned that just when he wasn't paying attention, feeling like he wasn't going to see anything, that was when a deer would suddenly appear—and likely disappear before he had a chance to even raise his rifle.

The clouds were spitting a light rain, so Rogan chose to keep his scope covers on for the time being. He also had a piece of black electrical tape over the barrel to keep the rain out. As they trudged on, his eyes scanned the ground in front of him for sign. He then swept his eyes to both sides, looking for movement or for the variation in color that could give away a deer standing amongst the green leaves.

He could hear an insistent woodpecker in the distance, hammering his beak into an unlucky tree. The echo of it sounded loud in the morning air. A crow cawed, seeming to answer whatever message the woodpecker was telegraphing. By now it had lightened enough that it was "shooting light," legally light enough to hunt.

Straight ahead of him and his mom, about fifty yards away, a deer stepped silently out of some ferns and onto the road. Rogan instantly froze and noted his mother had also stopped. It was a doe, and she was on the logging road, so he didn't ready his rifle. The doe took a few steps on delicate legs and then stopped and looked over her shoulder. A gangly-legged fawn was following her. It had been born in the spring and had lost the white spots lining its back.

Man, I wish I had my camera, he thought. *That would make an awesome close-up.* Rogan and his dad shared a love of photography.

Just as noiselessly as they had appeared, the doe and fawn disappeared into the brush on the opposite side of the logging road. Mother and son shared a smile.

Lord, please let one of us get a deer today, Rogan prayed. Sometimes he wondered if God thought it was silly to pray for something like that, but then Rogan mulled it over and decided that God cared about the little things in his life, too.

The bend in the road before the clearing was up ahead. It was time to hike up a gentle slope above the road. Rogan bent at the waist and swept his arm forward like a fancy butler welcoming an honored guest. Elise put her hand over her heart and mouthed, "Aw," before leading the way, her .243 rifle in hand. Rogan wanted her to have the first shot if the opportunity arose. Typically, she only got to hunt during their yearly hunting camp.

Rogan's rifle was unslung as well. He walked softly, behind and off to the right of his mother, careful that his gun wasn't aiming in her direction.

Elise froze. Rogan froze. Slightly below them, yards off the grassy flat, stood a basket-rack, three-point buck, looking straight at them. The deer was on high alert but not yet ready to bolt. With agonizing slow motion, Elise brought the scope up to her eye, the butt tucked into her shoulder. The buck looked antsy, sensing danger, but perhaps curious or uncertain as well. Its ears flicked back and forth.

Boom! The shot cracked loudly in the still air, causing Rogan to jump, even though he was ready for it. He hadn't made the move to plug his ears for fear of scaring off the deer, and the concussion from his mom's rifle made his ears ring, the sound like a far-off telephone buzzing inside his head.

The buck did a Scooby-Doo, running in place without going anywhere, before finding traction and plunging off the steep embankment on the downhill side. Rogan saw the top of a tree thrash wildly back and forth before settling.

Silence.

As much as they wanted to rush and look over the edge, Rogan and his mom squatted down near each other, staying above the road.

"You definitely got him, Mom. I think he pitched over the edge and went down." Rogan whispered congratulations.

"I sure hope so," she responded, a bit breathless. "I haven't heard anything for a while. Whew! That was exciting."

"Did you see how he Scooby-Doo-ed? I've never seen that before."

"I know. It was crazy, like he was running on air. I hope he went down fast. I never want them to suffer."

"I think he did go fast, Mom. What do you think? Ten minutes?"

Rogan was asking how long they should wait before looking for the deer. They didn't want to spook it and have it run off.

"Sounds good to me."

When the allotted time finally elapsed, they cautiously snuck to the edge of the road and peered down the steep bank.

"There he is. Nice job, Mom."

Rogan turned toward her, and they high-fived. Elise grinned like a schoolgirl getting an A on an assignment.

"Wow. That is really steep. How are we going to get him up onto the flat?" His mom grimaced. "Sorry, Rogan. This will be a lot of work."

"It's okay. We'll figure it out. At least we have all day if we need it."

They unloaded their rifles, took off their day packs, and put them in a pile.

"You stay here for a minute, and I'll go down and check it out," Rogan offered.

He slipped his way through thick brush to a spot right above where the deer lay, wrapped around the base of the tree Rogan had seen swaying back and forth. He stood on a fallen, mossy log.

"Mom. This is crazy. I'm standing on this log, and if I look down past my toes, I see the deer. That's how steep it is."

"Oh, boy."

"We're lucky he ran into that tree and didn't keep going."

Rogan realized it was going to be impossible to gut it down there to make it lighter for hauling up, so he set about figuring out how to best haul it up.

"I think if I tie some rope to his antlers, we can pull it up to this spot." Rogan pointed to where the brush wasn't quite as thick. "You stay and pull from up there, and I'll help out down here. Then, I think you'll have to come down, and we'll just have to muscle it up the rest of the way." Rogan flexed his arms in a muscle man pose.

Elise laughed and went to retrieve a length of cordage from her backpack, tossing the rope down to Rogan. With some finagling, they extracted the Sitka blacktail from the brush and, grunting with effort, wrangled it up to the previously determined spot.

"I'm coming down, Rogan. Whoa!" Elise caught herself as she slipped.

"Careful, Mom."

They now had only twenty yards left to get it up onto the grassy flat, but the distance felt a bit insurmountable to Rogan.

"When I prayed for one of us to get a deer, I should've been more specific, like it falls on the road." Rogan laughed.

Elise chuckled. "Oh, so this is your fault, Rogan? Thanks a lot," she teased. Then, more seriously, "Do we need to call for backup?"

"Naw. We can do it."

It became one of those trying times that wasn't pleasant while it was happening, but it sure made for a good story later when the muscle-straining, breath-stealing ordeal was finally over.

Elise lay on the damp ground, panting, her legs still dangling over the lip of the slope.

"We did it! Thanks, Rogue. I could never have done that by myself. What a good son you are," she said between sucking in gulps of air.

"Anytime, Mom," Rogan panted back.

After recovering some energy, Elise stood. She patted Rogan on the shoulder and said, "We've kind of been making a lot of noise, so maybe we scared off any other deer in the area, but you never know. Why don't you keep going and see if you can find anything. I'll stay here and get this one gutted. If I hear a shot, I'll have my radio, and you can let me know what's going on."

Rogan knew his mom was perfectly capable of gutting her own deer, so he readily agreed.

"I won't be gone long, although I may sit on that rocky point and just watch for a while. Maybe Sayyid is still around."

"Good luck." Elise unclipped her Buck knife from her belt.

Rogan gathered his gear, loaded his cartridge back in the chamber and made sure the safety was on. He wrapped his coat up and tied it to his backpack, since he was still sweating from their ordeal. Eyes quietly scanning for deer again, he headed further down across the slope.

He loved being in the stillness of the woods. He could hear birds trilling and the echo of a far-off creek rushing, but there was still a comforting quietude that made him feel settled and peaceful. Rogan made it to the rocky point jutting out over an old clear cut that was partially regrown. Stubby cedars and hemlocks dotted the slope. The rest was carpeted in swaying grasses and ferns.

I'll just sit here for a while, Rogan told himself. He was glad he had his hat on since a misty rain was still falling. It kept the water out of his eyes. His body cooled off while he sat and surveyed the landscape, so eventually he put his jacket back on. It was still early in the morning, but he was a little hungry after the deer workout, so he quietly pulled out his bag of Gold Rush Griddle cookies. These had become a staple of hunting, hiking, and camping trips. As he munched on the pancake/biscuit cookie dotted with plump raisins, he mused.

I'll bet Mom is about done gutting her deer, and I'm not seeing anything. Guess I'll head back.

Just as he started to get up, a movement through the trees caught his eye.

Is that a deer?

It wasn't quite the right color. Rogan brought his binoculars out from under his jacket.

There it is again. Oh, no. That's a wolf!

The grayish-colored predator was loping along, singularly focused on going somewhere, it seemed.

Keep moving on, said Rogan's thundering heartbeat. He stayed statue-still, hoping the wolf would not notice his presence. The animal disappeared into the tree line far below, allowing Rogan to release his pent-up breath.

I really don't want to have an encounter with a wolf. I'll just sit here a few more minutes to be sure he's really gone and that there aren't anymore.

Listening to the soft patter of rain made Rogan sleepy. He ate the last of the Gold Rush Griddle cookie he had hurriedly set aside and took a few swigs of water to wash it and the leftover taste of fear away.

"Well, Sayyid," he said out loud. "If you're out there, I guess you get to live another day." Rogan threw a salute in the downhill direction and stood up.

He froze. *Is that a...?*

From this higher vantage point, he saw a deer bedded down by some huckleberry bushes. It was just lying there, head up and facing away from him, ears not even twitching. It was close enough that Rogan could see it was a forked horn. There was nothing to rest his gun on, and he couldn't see the deer while kneeling, so he would have to make an offhand shot. This wasn't as stable, especially after his heart had an instant infusion of adrenaline. He would have to control his shaking.

Rogan wrapped his left arm in and around the vinyl sling on his rifle and then grasped the wood under the barrel. He widened his stance for better support and took in a cleansing breath. Raising the scope to his eye, he tucked the butt in securely.

Steady. Breathe.

He took one more breath, and as he slowly released it, his finger steadily tightened on the trigger. Taking his time paid off. He had his second deer of the season.

Thank you, Lord. And, thank you, deer.

He turned on his walkie-talkie. It crackled. He keyed the radio.

"Mama Bear, do you copy?"

"Was that your shot, Rogue One?"

"Ten-four. It's just a forked horn, but I'll take it."

"Awesome. It's meat. Tell you what. I'll radio and make sure the four-wheeler is at camp, then I'll hike back and get it, since we have two deer now." The Motorola's transmission clicked off. The radio squawked back on. "Unless you need help hauling it out. Over."

"It's in a pretty good spot, and it didn't go anywhere. I shot it when it was bedded down. Go ahead and hike back for the quad but be on the lookout. Earlier, I saw a wolf."

"Ten-four. Thanks for the heads up. I'm heading back to camp."

Rogan cut the notches in his harvest ticket, one each for the day and month. He had his deer gutted and dragged to below the rocky point and even had time to rest before he heard the purr of the four-wheeler approaching.

Elise pulled up just short of his deer. "Lucky for us, it was still at camp."

"Nice."

Rogan and his mom hefted the inert animal onto the front rack, tying it down. They drove back to where his mom had left her deer. Thankfully, it was undisturbed.

"It makes me nervous just leaving it on the ground where critters can get to it," Elise said.

They quickly loaded her buck onto the back rack.

"You want to drive?" his mom offered.

"Sure."

They arrived back at camp just as Jim and Lainey walked down the road from the direction they'd gone when everyone had gone their separate ways.

"Wow! Two deer. Dad saw one, but it was hauling, so he couldn't shoot it. I did a good job being quiet, and it wasn't my fault it ran off. Who got the deer? Which one is yours, Mom, or are they both Rogan's?"

Lainey finally took a breath. Rogan took her by the shoulders and steered her near the quad.

"The big one is Mom's, and the little one is mine."

Lainey clapped her hands and then launched herself into a waist-wrapping hug for her mom.

"Good job, Mom."

The adults began to offload the deer. They had lashed a hanging pole the night before, so they just had to tie the deer on it, hanging it for skinning. Lainey headed for the wall tent and, she said, some hot cocoa.

Everyone flinched as a shriek pierced the air. Jim and Elise looked at each other, dropped the deer they had been offloading back onto the four-wheeler, and ran for the tent. Rogan followed close behind, wondering what could be wrong with Lainey. It didn't take long for them to find out.

"That's mine. Peg! You ate it. I bought that with my own money. How could you?" A loud *grr* followed her exclamations.

Rogan threw back the tent flap and entered to see his youngest sister, Peg, sitting cross-legged on a sleeping cot, surrounded by her dolls and stuffed animals. He glanced over at Lainey. She had started to cry. Her fists slammed the air at her sides, and she stomped her foot.

"No!" she wailed.

He looked back at Peg, who sat there holding a thick tube of lip moisturizer, a guilty look on her face, and something red smeared around her lips, spilling onto her cheeks.

Lainey's sobs amped up to bordering on uncontrollable.

"Hold on, girls. What is going on?" Jim inquired.

Elise walked over and plucked the tube of lip balm from Peg's waxy fingers. She inspected it.

"This," she explained as Lainey continued to cry, "Is the long-awaited Bonnie Bell Lip Smackers strawberry lip balm Lainey saved up her money to buy. She had to wait three weeks for it to come in the mail." Elise paused. "It appears that Peg has used at least half of it." She gave her youngest the "Mom look" that Rogan tried to avoid since it meant the recipient was in big trouble.

"I didn't eat it. I just used some." Peg's voice was barely a whisper.

"I'm never going to forgive her," exclaimed Lainey.

"Hold on right there, young lady," Jim told his wailing daughter. "You need to go outside and get yourself together. Then, we'll talk."

Lainey stormed past Rogan, flipped the tent flap angrily out of her way, and stomped out.

I guess all thoughts of a cozy mug of hot chocolate are out of her mind, Rogan thought. He looked back at Peg, who was sitting in the same position, shoulders slumped forward, huge tears rolling down her pale cheeks. Rogan decided it was a good time for him to get back to the deer.

Later that evening, when they were all gathered in the Petersen's tent for dinner, everyone had a chance to tell about their day's adventures. Monty had also gotten his deer. Runt told Rogan he was bummed that he never even saw one.

"Sorry, man. Better luck tomorrow," Rogan encouraged.

Jim asked Lainey to bring him his Bible. "I have a verse I would like you to read for us. This can be our quiet time for this evening."

She did. Jim turned a few pages, pointed his finger to a spot on the page, and asked Lainey to read it. "It's Colossians 3:13."

Lainey took the Bible onto her lap. "Bear with each other and forgive one another if any of you has a gr…What is this word, Dad?"

"Grievance. It means you're mad at someone for what he or she did to you," Jim explained.

"Oh. Grievance against someone. Forgive as the Lord forgave you." Lainey's voice got quieter as she finished.

Jim reminded everyone that God had forgiven them, so they were all expected to forgive their fellow humans. "Jesus even forgave the people who nailed Him to the cross, so I know it seems like a big thing when something upsetting happens, but we have to try and remember what God says to do. Even if it is hard."

Rogan thought back to when he was younger, and he and Peter had gotten into a tiff over something. He still remembered the feelings of injustice and how he thought he'd never forgive his brother.

Or, what about the time I dropped his brand-new Leatherman in the bay by accident? Sheesh. I remember how it feels to be on the other end and wanting someone's forgiveness.

He also remembered the feeling of light relief—a burden being lifted off—when the forgiveness came. He looked at Lainey and could see by the frown on her face and by the way she avoided looking at Peg as she handed the Bible back to her dad, that she was still too upset over the incident to forgive yet.

She'll get there, Rogan thought.

CHAPTER 4

El Cap

AS THE BELL RANG TO BEGIN CLASSES ON MONDAY, ROGAN stifled a yawn. Hunting camp had been productive and successful, but strenuous. His family had stayed up late last night after unloading their gear to hang their deer in a bear-proof shed. They would be cutting the meat up tonight, since the weather wasn't yet cold enough to hang the animals for very long, allowing the meat to tenderize. Rogan's favorite part was using the grinder to make burger and sausage.

In his second-hour class, science, he sat at the desk behind Boom Chain.

"Hey, man. You look rough. How was hunting?" his friend asked.

"I'm just tired," Rogan explained, rubbing his eyes. He proceeded to fill Boom Chain in with the exciting details of their hunt. The teacher, Mr. Spiker, was still out in the hall, so Rogan related the story of Runt's outhouse visit from the bear.

"Oh, my word. That's awesome. I wish I could've seen the look on his face."

"It was classic," Rogan whispered as all six-foot-two of Mr. Spiker came walking in. Rogan happened to glance to his right where his backpack lay, his eyes meeting the eyes of the girl sitting at the desk across from his. She gave him a timid smile. He answered back with his slightly crooked one before turning his attention to the front of the classroom.

"Today," Mr. Spiker began, stroking a hand down his black goatee, which was his signature move. "We are going to go over the information you will need to know for the upcoming campout this weekend. As you know, this will be a prep for learning some skills for Survival School, which will take place in early October."

An excited buzz arose from the ninth-grade students. This was *the* right of passage. Stories were passed down from siblings along with tips that had been tried and true over the years. Every ninth-grade student was required to attend, unless they had a legitimate doctor's note for something major, and most had been looking forward to it for years. During the last quarter of eighth-grade science, they had learned about local animals and which plants were edible.

"We will get to try out your camping gear and learn fire-starting skills," Mr. Spiker continued when it had quieted down. "The forecast calls for rain, so be prepared for that."

Mr. Spiker walked around the room, handing out information sheets stapled to a permission slip.

"Be sure to get these signed and returned no later than Wednesday."

Boom Chain swiveled in his seat. "Dude. This is going to be awesome."

In response, Rogan leaned forward and rubbed his hands together. "I can't wait."

"You will be able to pick your own partner. It can be any ninth-grader, even if you don't have the same hour of science," Mr. Spiker explained.

This was not news to Rogan and his friends. They had already decided Rogan and Runt would be paired, and Tuff would be partnered with Boom Chain.

New information followed, however, as their teacher continued, "You and your partner will be combined with one more pair, making a foursome. Of course, girls will be with girls and boys with boys. The four of you will be in one tent. For the activities, one group of four that is considered more experienced in the outdoors will be paired with a group of four that is less, shall we say, in the know."

Rogan leaned toward Boom Chain and whispered, "That might be interesting."

"For sure. It might be fun to mess with them. Heh, heh."

"A Squatch hunt?" Rogan agreed.

"Perfect."

"Mr. Ryan and Mr. Chaffey. Do you have something to share with the class?" Mr. Spiker asked and was answered by quiet giggles from their classmates.

"Sorry, Sir," Rogan apologized, sitting back in his chair.

"We were hoping we'd be camping somewhere that we might have a Sasquatch sighting," Boom Chain added.

The girl next to Rogan gasped, her hand flying to her mouth.

"It's okay, Natalia. He's just joking." Mr. Spiker tried to assuage her fears. His hand slicked down his goatee again. He gave Boom Chain what Rogan knew to be a mock, stern glare. In his experience, Mr. Spiker was kind and fair.

The class giggled again.

"Okay. Settle down. Make sure you pay close attention to all the items on the equipment list. If you don't have something, you can hopefully borrow it from someone. Come see me if you truly can't find something." The bell clanged as Mr. Spiker reminded them, "Get those permission slips signed."

At lunch, the four friends speculated on the preparation camping trip.

"I wish we could skip this one and just show up for the real Survival School. We already know how to start a fire and pitch a tent," Tuff complained.

"Yeah. How can you live in Alaska and not know these things?" Runt added.

Rogan agreed. "For sure."

"Rogue and I were talking about how it would be fun to mess with some of the kids and scare them with Sasquatch," Boom Chain told Tuff and Runt.

"Ooh, I like it." Runt drummed his fingers together and looked around at his friends. "Commence Operation Bogus Bigfoot."

Rogan chuckled along with his friends. "Ha, ha. Good one. Let's start thinking of ideas on what we could do."

The Survival School conversation kept up between bites of chicken nuggets and fries and swigs of school-carton milk. They discussed how they would be taken to one of the many islands in the area and dropped off, eight of them, with one chaperone. The boys would then have to survive from mid-day Thursday to Sunday evening when the boat would come back for them.

"They promise they'll give us more details about Survival School on the campout this weekend," Tuff pointed out.

"I kind of like how they're keeping some things under wraps," said Rogan. "It makes it more exciting. What are we going to do when we're not busy trying to survive?"

"We could build another raft with our awesome skills and go find the girls' island," Tuff offered.

Milk exploded. Right out of Runt's nose.

"Ew!" Rogan wiped the white splatter off the front of his shirt. He was the lucky one sitting across from his friend in the cafeteria.

"Here's a napkin." Boom Chain pretended to be helpful but stuffed it down the front of Rogan's shirt.

"Thanks a lot." Rogan dug it out and began wiping himself off.

The four friends had built a raft on their end-of-summer camping trip to Half Moon Beach that had sort of floated.

By now, Runt had finally stopped choking and snorting.

"Speaking of girls," Boom Chain said, "They're all looking at you right now, Runt."

Runt pinched the bridge of his nose. "Ow. That one burned." He blinked rapidly and then turned and did a parade wave to the students in the cafeteria. "I'm okay. Thanks for asking."

Rogan saw Tuff look past him, over his shoulder. "I wonder who will partner with Martin?"

Four pairs of eyes swiveled to lock in on the lone figure at the cafeteria table in the far corner. Martin Wolfe was always eating lunch alone. His long, stringy, greasy hair, held down by a red bandana headband, seemed to add to his filthy, tattered clothes that emitted an unpleasant body odor. This held most students at least a fathom away.

Besides wearing clothes that were out of date, ripped, and looking like they were gotten free from the Clothes Exchange, Martin was an easy target for bullies. He acted like a half-starved hound dog, slinking around, trying to avoid getting kicked, and never making eye contact with anyone.

"I do feel sorry for him, but I wouldn't want to sleep in a tent with him because of how he smells," said Rogan, his face twisting into a grimace.

"Ten-four on that," agreed Tuff.

"He kind of does it to himself," Boom Chain whispered. "Can't the dude take a bath?"

"He could go stand in the rain right now. It's a downpour that would…" Tuff trailed off, turned slightly away, and pretended to scratch his head as he saw Martin heading their way. The other boy had his head down and was hurrying along.

Apparently, he's on a mission to turn in his lunch tray without any human interaction, Rogan thought. He silently tracked Martin out of the corners of his eyes and noticed his friends doing the same as the outcast shuffled past, leaving an invisible contrail of body odor.

"Whew. That is pretty bad." Boom Chain turned toward his friends and fresher air.

The end-of-lunch bell rang, sending everyone traipsing to their next classes.

The rest of the week passed like a giant hourglass slowly releasing its sand as the anticipated practice campout approached. Students gathered gear, got permission slips signed, speculated, planned, and partnered up.

Thursday morning, the ninth-graders arrived in the misty rain, hoping they hadn't forgotten anything, and waved goodbye to their parents who had dropped them off. Their gear was loaded into two van-buses. One seated the girls, the other the boys.

Mr. Spiker boarded the boys' transport and raised his hand for attention. The excited chatter abated.

"Okay, everyone. We are heading to…" He let it hang in suspense.

"Tell us!" someone shouted from the back of the bus.

"We will be going to El Capitan to camp." He pronounced it, "El Cap-ee-tan."

"As you know, this is a dry run. Well, not exactly dry in this weather." He chuckled.

Rogan heard Runt snort at the joke as their teacher paused.

"But, it is practice for Survival School. You have let me know who your partners are, and when we arrive, I'll hand out the tents and let you know your groups of four and eight. These will be the same groups you will be with for Survival School, so figure out how to work together. Let's move 'em out."

Mr. Spiker plopped into the driver's seat and started the engine. The girls' van-bus was already headed out in the opposite direction.

"I wonder where they're camping?" mused Tuff.

His friends all shrugged their shoulders.

"Who knows?" said Boom Chain.

"Who cares?" added the boy in the seat behind them.

The van-bus bumped along for a solid half an hour before arriving at its destination. They pulled onto the spit of land that reached out to the sea. It was a grassy, circular area with one picnic table and an outhouse a small hike away.

The boys emerged from the bus like a swarm of bees from a hive. Mr. Spiker made good on his promise and announced the groups. Rogan and his friends would be a foursome. They all fist bumped.

"Yeah," said Rogan.

"Woohoo!" added Runt.

Mr. Spiker's next words threw cold water on their celebration.

"The group you will be working with is Damien West, Cory Boots, Thorin Knight, and Martin Wolfe."

Rogan looked at his buddies. Their smiles had done a flash freeze and then quickly melted.

"Seriously?" Tuff muttered under his breath.

"How'd we get so lucky?" Boom Chain mumbled between clenched teeth.

Runt turned to face them and whispered, "At least he won't be in our tent. Hopefully, we can breathe fresh air when we're around him."

Rogan found himself quickly agreeing with the disappointment of his friends and sighed a heavy lungful. Almost immediately, he felt a niggling of shame and regret. His chin dropped to his chest, and his hands went to his hips.

"Come on, Chaffey," hollered Runt.

His friends had moved on, heading to collect their gear as directed. Rogan followed, silently vowing to be at least a little nice to Martin.

The first order of business was to set up their four-man tents for the next two nights. Rogan's group had no problem quickly and efficiently assembling their geodesic dome tent as they were all experienced in the set-up process. They threw their sleeping pads and bags into the tent, laying them out in a neat row.

"Wow. So much for a four-person tent. We can barely fit all of our sleeping bags in here," observed Tuff.

"Yeah. I guess we need a six-person tent since you're taking up so much room," Runt mock-complained while hefting Boom Chain's oversized backpack and tossing it to him. "Ugh. What all have you got in here? Did you bring a chainsaw?"

Boom Chain countered, "Hey, don't knock it. I like to be prepared."

"You won't be able to bring all of that stuff to Survival School," Tuff reminded him.

Rogan wondered out loud. "That's crazy. We get one number five can is all. Well, besides our sleeping stuff and a tarp. How am I supposed to fit anything in that?"

"I think I'm just going to bring one from the store that has pork and beans in it, so at least I'll have something to eat. Then, I'll just rely on my friends to bring the rest."

Rogan laughed at Runt. "In your dreams. Besides, if you have pork and beans, you'd have to share them with us."

"Who says?" countered his friend.

"I'm going to figure out a way to bring Pop-Tarts." This was Tuff's favorite camping food. "In fact…" Tuff looked around to see if the coast was clear and dug into the side pocket of his backpack. Out came two shiny foil wrappers. He quickly opened them and passed one iced strawberry treat to each of them.

As one, they turned their backs toward their classmates who were busy figuring out tent poles and shoved the Pop-Tarts into their mouths.

"Thanks, man." Runt spewed a few crumbs as he talked.

Suddenly, Mr. Spiker was behind them. "Gentlemen, good job on your tent. Don't forget you have your buddy team. They look like they might need help. That's your next responsibility."

Without turning around, and their mouths still full, they gave Mr. Spiker a thumbs up and headed in the direction of the struggling team.

"Dude. I had to chew too fast to get that down. I didn't get to enjoy the flavor," Tuff grouched.

Rogan started coughing. "I just inhaled some crumbs."

Runt reached over and slapped him on the back.

"Ow. You trying to make me choke more?"

"I'm just trying to help," Runt snickered, still talking around a mouthful.

"You'd better wipe those red crumbs off your face," Tuff said and laughed.

Runt swiped a hand over his mouth and made a show of swallowing loudly. "Is the evidence gone?"

"Yep," said Boom Chain, peering intently at Runt. "All that's left is just an ugly face."

Rogan couldn't help but join in. "Ooh, roasted."

"Hey!" Runt feigned mock indignation and tried to push Boom Chain, but his friend had anticipated the play and stepped aside, sending Runt falling into the tent of their buddy team, which still lay in a heap on the ground.

"Watch it," came the sharp rebuke.

Rogan looked up to see Martin Wolfe's face contort into an angry scowl.

"Chill out, dude. We're actually here to help. Runt just likes to trip over his own feet." Rogan tried to smooth things over.

"What if we don't want your help?" Martin continued.

Anger issues much? Rogan thought to himself.

"Mr. Spiker told us to come help you guys," Boom Chain explained.

"Thanks. We'll take it." Cory reached over and slugged Boom Chain on the upper arm. His eyes widened as he looked at Rogan's team as if pleading for them to rescue him. "Seeing as how our stuff is getting wet while we flail."

Rogan and his teammates showed them how the tent poles went together and where to thread them through the fabric. They were able to set it up in short order.

"Thanks, man," offered Cory.

The rest of the boys chimed in with their thanks, even a grudging one from Martin.

"No problem. See you around," said Rogan as they headed back to their campsite.

"What is his problem?" asked Tuff when they were out of hearing range.

"Who knows? He's sure got a chip on his shoulder," agreed Boom Chain.

After tents were assembled and gear stowed, Mr. Spiker picked up the megaphone.

"Boys! It's time for fire starting practice. Everyone, please assemble at the fire rings."

When everyone was there, milling around with anticipatory energy, the teacher continued. "Today we have the privilege of having Bow Breeden, an expert in outdoor survival skills, here to teach us how to start a fire with flint and steel and a bow drill. Even if you know how to do that already, I know you can learn a few important tips, so pay close attention and be respectful listeners. We are also lucky that the rain has stopped for the time being. Let's welcome Bow." Mr. Spiker's arm swept toward the tall, granite-faced man. The ninth-graders politely clapped.

After instructions and demonstrations, the boys were off to practice in their groups of eight. Rogan and his friends had no trouble getting the spark to ignite a fire with flint and steel. In fact, they resorted to a competition, timing each other to see who could do it the fastest. Cory and Thorin got it down quickly, while Damien and Martin struggled. Eventually, all fires were blazing, and it was time to roast hot dogs for lunch.

The afternoon consisted of a nature walk. Edible plants and animals were identified and discussed. The boys all had an hour of free time before their dinner of spaghetti and French bread. They had fed the large, central fire all day, so it still burned. After dinner and clean-up, they all had fun sitting around the campfire's dancing, glowing flames, telling jokes and ghost stories.

Tucked into their respective tents that night, Rogan could hear the rustling of boys settling in and the soft waves breaking on the rocks of the shore.

"Tuff? Do you still have food in your backpack?" Rogan said into the darkness.

"Oh, phooey. I forgot about my Pop-Tarts."

A light clicked on, and Tuff squirmed in the confined space to reach his backpack and extract the treats. "I guess I'll run and put them in the bus. Does anyone else have food?"

"I've got some jerky," said Boom Chain.

The zipper made a *zzzt* sound, and Tuff scrambled out, ran to the van with the food, and returned swiftly. "I hid them under the third seat back on the driver's side."

"Ow! That's my leg," Runt complained as Tuff stepped on him on the way back to his sleeping bag.

"Sorry." Tuff's snickering betrayed his sincerity.

CHAPTER 5

Fishing Line and Flying Squirrels

ROGAN HAD JUST GOTTEN HIMSELF READJUSTED IN THE cramped space and relaxed into his pillow when startled and panicked cries shot through the darkness to electrify his heart. Each beat was a loud thump against his chest. He sat up.

What is going on?

He and his friends bumped into each other in their haste to get out of the tent and get their shoes on. A terrible ruckus came from the direction of their buddy group's tent. Flashlight and headlamp rays swept across the tent in crisis, spotlights in a circus ring, as adults and boys alike converged.

"Help! Get it out of here," someone yelled.

"Aah! I think it bit me," cried another.

"Open the zipper," shouted a third.

The tent was rocking back and forth like it was in hurricane-strength winds, but the storm was happening inside.

Mr. Spiker, hair askew and in his baggy shirt and sweatpants, commanded, "Stand back." He reached for the zipper on the tent's fabric door, quickly opening it. As the flap fell outward, he let out his own startled yell and fell backward. A brown furball missile fired straight out of the tent and into the unsuspecting teacher. Everyone watched in fascination as the terrified animal clawed its way over poor Mr. Spiker and raced off into the night. There was a stunned silence followed by a cacophony of excited chatter.

"What was that?" someone asked.

"A flying squirrel. That was epic," replied another.

"Mr. Spiker, are you okay?" asked a concerned student.

Eventually, it was all sorted out that Martin and Damien had left food in their tent, which was a good object lesson in why it is a bad idea when camping. They had learned something important for all the ninth-grade boys. Mr. Spiker had some minor scratches on his arm where the squirrel had scrambled over him in its flight to safety and mud on his backside, but otherwise everyone was okay. Damien had not been bitten, just scared.

Tucked back into their sleeping bags, Rogan was relieved.

"You guys know how lucky we are? That could've been us."

Nervous chuckles answered back.

"I won't forget next time," Tuff promised.

"Yeah. Me too," added Boom Chain.

"Is our midnight caper still on?" questioned Runt.

"Of course. Did you bring the fishing line?" Rogan asked into the darkness.

"I did."

"Okay, then. Tuff, set an alarm."

"Copy that, Rogue."

The couple of hours until Operation Fishing Line could commence stretched out like a long dark tunnel with no end in sight. Rogan finally felt himself drifting to sleep when the soft beep of Tuff's alarm roused him. He and his cohorts carefully unzipped their tent and crawled out.

"The coast is clear," whispered Boom Chain. "At least I think it is. I can't see anything."

"I think we're good if there aren't any lights," Runt said.

While it was still daylight, they had scoped out the tent site of some of their friends. This would be the target. Trying their best to tiptoe quietly and not trip over anything in the dark, they cautiously made their way across the grassy spit.

"I think my eyes are adjusting. I can kind of see," Rogan told his patrol.

They had arrived. Runt pulled the spool of clear monofilament out of his pocket and tied it to the tent stake closest to the zippered flap, low down by the ground. He handed it to Rogan, who threaded it around the next fiberglass pole and handed it to Tuff, who did the same and then passed it on to Boom Chain. Boom Chain stretched it across the door and back to Runt, who passed it around again. Halfway through their prank, they froze.

"I don't want your cookies," mumbled one of the boys in the tent.

Rogan's pulse stuttered in his chest. *Should we run?* Then he realized what was happening. "He's talking in his sleep," he whispered. He stuck his hand over his mouth to keep the laughter from escaping.

"No more cookies!" the boy continued.

It was impossible to not laugh, but Rogan and his friends tried valiantly to keep it quiet. The sleeping boy snorted and shifted and settled into quiet. Continuing the operation, they kept wrapping the line around the tent until it was a third of the way up from the ground. During their planning session, they had determined to go no higher so someone wouldn't get clotheslined, running into it with their face or neck. It was just high enough to trip them. They hoped. Rogan could just make out the fuzzy shapes of the others in the blackness. Rogan waved his arm, and they scurried back to their tent.

"Heh, heh. We did it," Tuff chuckled.

They quietly high-fived, congratulating each other.

"Uh. Uh oh. What now?" asked Boom Chain. "I want to see it. I hope it works."

"Oh, yeah. I guess we are lacking a critical component," began Runt.

"How do we get them to come out?" they asked in unison.

That gave everyone pause, and Rogan figured they were all wracking their brains for a solution, as he was.

"Duh. What got all of them to rush out of their tents earlier tonight?" Rogan spread his hands, questioning.

"Another flying squirrel. Excellent," agreed Runt, catching on to Rogan's line of thinking.

"How do we do it?" Rogan wanted a plan.

Minutes later, they had it worked out. Rogan took his station near the tent closest to the line-wrapped one. He waited for Runt to yell, "Another squirrel. Ahh!" and shook the tent fabric. He and the other two co-conspirators yelled indiscriminate words from different points around camp. As soon as everyone was once again scrambling for the show, they clicked their lights on and aimed at the ground a couple of feet in front of the target tent.

"Over here!" Rogan yelled above the melee.

The zipper was undone, and a boy named Brody rushed out, caught his foot on the invisible line, and did an ungraceful face plant. To add insult to injury, the boy behind Brody ended up falling on top of him and rolling off into the mud. Their tentmates hadn't clued in and did the same, stacking up like firewood. Half the ninth-graders were laughing at the spectacle, and half were calling out, "Where's the squirrel?" but not certain how they all ended up at this tent.

"What's going on now?" boomed Mr. Spiker's voice.

The laughter did not abate. He reached up and repeatedly smoothed down his goatee. Eventually, the fishing line was discovered. The teacher's usual mischief detector failed to ferret out the perpetrators since they all looked guilty, and by now, everyone was laughing, even Brody and his tentmates.

Mr. Spiker sighed and gave up, ordering everyone back to their tents. "And no more squirrel pranks." He sounded stern, but Rogan caught a hint of a smile as his teacher turned and walked past him, back to his tent.

Rogan smiled and headed back to his own tent as well. He heard a boy next to him say, "That was awesome. I wish I would've thought of it."

"Yeah. Me too," Runt piped up, with a laugh and a snort.

* * *

The next morning, Rogan looked around to see some groggy-looking boys. They congregated to grab their breakfast of cereal in single, plastic containers and a carton of school-sized milk. Donuts bolstered the meal.

Boom Chain observed, "I don't think we'll be eating like this on the real campout, guys."

"For sure. Hopefully we don't starve to death since we pretty much have to scavenge for all our food," Tuff lamented.

"Peter didn't get to do Survival School because he was sick with the tumor by then, but I remember he had gotten some inside intel," Rogan told his friends. "He was talking to my mom about it. You put your knife, fishing line and hook, and whatever else in your can, and then fill it up the rest of the way with rice. That way you have rice to eat, at least."

"Huh. That's a good idea," said Tuff.

"Yeah. I think I'll do that," Boom Chain concurred.

Runt nodded his head, agreeing, but his mouth was full.

After breakfast, Mr. Spiker told the campers that they would each receive two ten-by-twenty pieces of Visqueen per group.

"Take your tarps and practice making a shelter today. There is some paracord here that you may use. Two of you will share one piece of plastic for a shelter that you will sleep in tonight."

Excited chatter erupted.

"Please remember what we've learned in class about shelter building. You have all day to set it up, and you will be testing how well you did when you sleep in them tonight." He looked around with a mock scowl. "Absolutely no fishing line." He pointed to the nearby forest. "You may choose to set up here on the spit, or in the forest. There are pink boundary markers about one hundred yards out. Do not go any farther than that. The adults will come around to check on you. Good luck."

"I'll go get our tarp, Runt. You want to cut some cordage?" Rogan asked.

"Sounds good."

Rogan ambled over and got in line. Cory Boots ended up right behind him.

"Hey, Cory."

"Hey, Rogan. Man, you are so lucky to get good partners." He leaned in close. "We had to draw straws for who will be in the shelter with Martin, and I lost. Phew. It stunk so bad in our tent last night. We were all practically gagging."

"I'm sorry." Rogan didn't quite know how to respond. "Maybe you can make a plastic wall between you." Rogan felt guilty for being relieved that he wasn't the one who had to be with Martin.

"Good idea. I'm not even looking forward to the trip now, let alone tonight. I think the guys are laughing at me behind my back." Cory huffed his frustration.

Without really thinking, Rogan replied, "Naw. I think they just feel sorry for you." Once again, guilt stepped in and waved a dark hand at Rogan. He mentally kicked himself. *Lord, sorry. Help me to be nicer.* He shot out a prayer.

Once they had their materials, Rogan and Runt headed off into the forest in search of an ideal spot. They wanted some trees where they could tie the thick plastic sheeting to create a tent sort-of structure.

"This looks pretty good." Runt pointed to a flat spot at the base of some trees.

"I like it. Let's clear the ground off first." Rogan began grabbing water-rotted sticks, rocks, and miscellaneous debris. Runt joined in, and soon they had a spot cleared.

"So, we definitely want this on the dirt as a ground cloth," Rogan proposed.

"Yeah. I don't want to get soaked." Runt wiped his muddy hands on his jeans before grabbing the sheet of heavy-duty, clear plastic.

"I think this is the piece we have to use at the actual Survival School, so let's be careful to not poke a hole in it."

Runt agreed. "Yeah. That'd be bad."

The wan sun had moved to almost straight overhead when they stood back to observe their handiwork.

"What do you think?" Rogan cocked his head to the side.

"I think I like it. I also think we didn't use too much cordage. We can hopefully fit that in our cans."

"Okay. Let's go find Tuff and Boom Chain and see how they're doing."

"I think I saw them heading over that way." Runt pointed.

The two friends trudged across the forest. Soon they heard heated arguing.

"That's not going to work. What a dumb idea. How'd I get stuck with you in the first place?"

Rogan turned to Runt with a grimace. Cory and Martin had a lean-to of sorts strung up, but none of the plastic sheeting was used as a ground cloth.

"Fine!" Martin yelled back. "Since you're so smart, why don't you do it by yourself?" Rogan saw that Martin's angry face was almost as red as his headband.

"Why don't you go take a bath?" Cory screamed back. "And while you're at it, throw away that dumb bandana."

Martin clenched his fists at his sides. Rogan thought he was getting ready to take a swing at Cory, but then he swiftly turned and ripped the corner of the Visqueen off the rope that tied it to the tree and stomped off.

"You jerk!" Cory yelled after him. "Now our tarp is ripped."

Martin just kept going.

"I guess he doesn't care," observed Runt.

One of the adult volunteers had heard the ruckus and arrived just as Rogan and Runt were offering to help Cory.

"Who's his partner?"

"Martin, but he just stomped off," Runt explained.

The adult reminded them that the partners had to figure out how to work together.

"Great." Cory pounded off to go find Martin.

Rogan gave a low whistle. "Runt, let's go see how Tuff and Boom Chain are doing."

Most of the boys were anxious to try out the shelters they'd constructed, and after dinner, everyone hauled their pads, bags, and day packs to their new sleeping arrangements. Rogan and Runt got settled in.

"Not bad if I do say so, myself." Runt patted his bag and sat down.

"I actually wish it was raining so we could know if it really works," Rogan said.

The pattering rain had ended earlier that day. Things were still wet, per usual, but not from above.

"I wonder if Cory and Martin got theirs figured out. Man, I'd hate to have Stinky Boy as my partner." He eyed Rogan. "Did you remember your B.O. juice today?"

"Yes, I put on deodorant." A pause. "I feel kind of bad for him."

Runt questioned, "Cory? Yeah, duh."

"No," Rogan corrected. "Martin. Everyone makes fun of him."

"Well, he kind of brings it on himself, don't you think?"

"I suppose you're right."

"Plus," Runt added, "He's not very nice to anyone. You heard him yelling at Cory."

"You're right. I don't know…" Rogan's voice trailed off.

"Well, I'm not going to worry about it. Good night, Rogue."

"'Night."

The plastic crinkled as they settled in.

"Improvement number one," Rogan began, "Is to put something down as a cushion under the tarp."

"I agree. A little uncomfortable."

"Do you think our roof is a little too high above us? It's a little chilly."

"Yep. Taking notes for next time."

"At least it's not raining."

CHAPTER 6

Sword Drills

EVERYONE SURVIVED THE PRACTICE CAMPOUT. THE
ninth-graders returned Saturday night. Rogan admitted to himself
that he was happy to sleep in his own bed after a chilly night on the
hard ground. His family enjoyed a conversation around the breakfast
table before heading to the small community church they attended.

"I think there may be a surprise in store for you today, Rogan."

Rogan looked at his dad. "What's that?"

"Something at church, but I'm not going to tell you, or it wouldn't
be a surprise."

"Come on, Dad," Rogan wheedled.

His father just gave him a cheesy grin.

"Mom. Do you know what he's talking about?" He thought maybe
he could soften up his mother enough to get her to spill the beans. Elise
Chaffey made the motion of zipping up her lips.

"Fine," Rogan huffed with mock indignation, rolling his eyes.

His sisters were giggling.

"Do you know what it is?" Rogan demanded.

"Nope," giggled Lainey.

"Nope," emulated Peg.

"Hmm. That sounds suspicious. Why are you two giggling?"

Lainey shrugged. "I don't know."

Peg shrugged. "I don't know."

The girls burst out in more giggles.

"I'm going to do chores before we head to church." Rogan threw his hands up in mock surrender.

The wood-sided, weathered-looking church, quaint and country-style, sat off the dirt road and at the edge of the woods. The Chaffeys entered, greeted friends, and sat in the second-from-the-front pew. Pastor Greg began with prayer and then announced he had some exciting news to share that pertained to the youth. Rogan swiveled in his seat to make eye contact with Runt, then Tuff and Boom Chain, but they looked as clueless as himself.

"I am happy to announce that we have hired a youth pastor."

The congregation's excited chatter interrupted his message. When conversation abated, he continued.

"As you all know, we've been praying about this for some time and interviewing possible candidates. The board decided to offer the position to Dexter Newby, and he has accepted. Dexter and his lovely wife, Sylvia, have a daughter Marie, age eight, and a son, Michael, who is one. They have lived in Petersburg for the past five years. Dexter, will you and your family please come up front?"

Applause welcomed their new youth pastor to the podium. Rogan watched as a brown-haired man who was tall and lithe with a friendly, open face, raised his hand.

FORGIVENESS AT SKELETON COVE

"Thank you all very much. My family and I are very excited to join your congregation. Beginning today, we will have a Sunday School class for junior high and high schoolers, and next Wednesday evening will be our first youth group activity. We are excited to get to know everyone and to be able to work with your youth."

Rogan smiled at his parents. *This is a good surprise,* he thought, as his mom wiggled her eyebrows up and down at him.

Soon, the junior high and high school youth filed outside, heading to the fellowship hall where they would be meeting.

"He looks like he's pretty cool," Runt observed.

"I hope he likes the outdoors," Tuff commented.

Boom Chain added, "I didn't even know they were hiring one."

"Where've you been?" Runt scoffed.

"I guess I wasn't paying much attention to that, either," admitted Rogan, "But I'm glad we have one now."

"Well, if you had my superior intellect and keen powers of observation..." Runt was saying.

"We'd be tripping over rocks." Rogan and his buddies laughed as Runt stumbled.

"That we didn't see," added Tuff. "With those keen powers of observation."

Runt's signature snort joined in, rather loudly, as they entered the room, causing Dexter's head to whip around at the sound.

"Whoa. You scared me there for a minute."

"It's just Runt," Rogan explained. "You'll get used to it."

"Runt, eh?" said Dexter. "There's got to be a story behind that name."

Runt looked to his right, then left, put his hands out at Rogan's and Tuff's head height and then lowered them to his own, giving Dexter what Rogan knew was a, "Do I need to say more?" look.

Dexter had a hearty, jovial laugh. "Okay. I get it."

"He's a quick learner," said Boom Chain.

Introductions were made with a handshake. Boom Chain also had to explain his name. There were going to be seven kids in their first official youth gathering: Rogan and his three friends, one other boy, and two girls. They sat in folding chairs that had been arranged in a circle. After some introductory activities, Dexter got down to business.

"I've been praying about what topic to begin with for our Sunday School, and the Lord has impressed upon me to teach about forgiveness. Let's begin by looking up some verses to see what God has to say about forgiving others. We'll do it as sword drills. You guys know what that is?"

No one did, so Dexter went on to explain that the Bible is like a sword, figuratively cutting through confusion, deceit, and conflict.

"Therefore, just like a soldier has to train with his sword, so he can effectively ward off his enemies, we need to learn to use our sword. Here's how it works," Dexter explained. He went on to say that everyone had to begin with a closed Bible in their laps. "I'll say a verse, and it will be a competition…"

"Oh, yeah! And I'm going to beat you all," Runt enthusiastically interrupted.

Dexter chuckled.

"Oh, yeah? We'll see about that, stubby fingers," Tuff taunted.

"Stubby fingers? Where'd that come from?" Runt made a face, raised his hands, and wiggled his fingers. "More like magic fingers."

"Quit with the fingers and listen." Rogan was ready to give it a try. He knew where the books of the Bible were pretty well. "You're all going down, so don't cry when it happens."

Runt's snort filled the sudden silence and made one of the girls jump, as she startled at the noise.

"Okay, here's the first verse," Dexter interjected.

Rogan leaned forward, casting sideways glances at his competition. They were all poised for action.

"Do we get candy if we win?" Boom Chain was hopeful.

Many voices combined, "Shh!"

"Whoever finds it first, give a shout, raise your hand, and we'll have you read it out loud." Dexter paused and scanned the youth's faces. "The first verse is Hebrews 4:12-13. Again, Hebrews 4:12-13."

Rogan was vaguely aware of the rustling sound of the thin Bible pages being rapidly turned.

"Hebrews four," he muttered to himself. "Hebrews 4:12." He ran his finger down the page. "Got it!" Rogan's arm shot up. He gave a celebratory fist pump. "Told you, you're going down. Heh, heh," he directed toward his friends.

"Don't let it go to your head," said Boom Chain, good-naturedly slamming his Bible shut.

"Let's hear it. Rogan, is it?"

"Yep." Rogan cleared his throat. "'For the word of God is living and active. Sharper than any double-edged sword, it penetrates even to dividing soul and spirit, joints and marrow; it judges the thoughts and attitudes of the heart. Nothing in all creation is hidden from God's sight. Everything is uncovered and laid bare before the eyes of Him to whom we must give account.' Just to thirteen, right?"

"Yes. Thank you. What do you think all that means?"

No one spoke.

"Don't be shy."

"I like how it says the Bible is 'sharper than any double-edged sword.' It's like it really cuts into us and helps us know things." Boom Chain bravely offered his thoughts.

"Good. Anyone else?"

Rogan was thoughtful. "It says it divides soul and spirit. I guess they seem like the same thing to me. What's the difference?"

"That's a good question. I'm not completely sure, so you've stumped me on day one." He pulled out an iPad and began swiping the screen. He looked up when the students all snickered. "What?"

"There's no Internet," Tuff informed him.

"Oh. I didn't even think about that. I'm used to our church in Petersburg. Where is the Internet available around here? Do you all have it at your houses?"

Tuff explained, "There's Internet at the library and at the school, and most of us have it at home."

"Well, we all have homework for next week's Sunday School. Me included. Let's all research the difference between soul and spirit. Now that we see how the Bible is a sword, we're going to start learning what God's word says about forgiveness." He paused. "Bibles closed."

"Sheesh, Runt. You're trying to cheat, and it's only round two?" Boom Chain teased.

Runt stuck his tongue out at his friend.

"I'll give you a hint. This one's in the Old Testament. Who can find second Chronicles 7:14?"

Everyone again scrambled through pages to see who could find it first.

"Me! I've got it," yelled Tuff.

Rogan looked over to see Tuff still turning a page. "You're still looking, Tuff. No cheating."

Tuff stabbed his finger down on the page. "No, I've got it. Right here."

"Okay," said Dexter. "Please read it for us."

Tuff sat up straighter. "Listen, everyone." He paused. Rogan saw his friend making sure he had an audience. "The verse says, 'If my people, who are called by my name, will humble themselves and pray and seek my face and turn from their wicked ways, then I will hear from heaven, and I will forgive their sin and will heal their land.' Whew. That was a long one. And, Mrs. Drake wouldn't like all of those ands. She's our English teacher."

Dexter smiled and spoke again, "This verse is conditional. What do we have to do to be forgiven?"

"Pray," said Boom Chain.

"Humble ourselves," added Tuff.

"It says we need to seek God's face," one of the girls piped up.

"Turn from our wicked ways," Runt said in a Count Dracula voice.

"Basically," Rogan summed up, "I think it's saying that God wants us to be honestly sorry."

"Exactly." Dexter smiled. "Have any of you ever said you were sorry to someone and wanted forgiveness, but you weren't really sorry?"

"Well, not too long ago, we were playing paintball…" Rogan began.

Runt whipped his head around to stare Rogan down.

"And…" Runt punched Rogan in the arm, but Rogan continued. "And, Runt here wouldn't forgive me for my superior sniper skills, but I reminded him that the Bible says to forgive your enemies. I don't think Runt was sincere."

"But I actually didn't forgive you, Rogue, or wait…I didn't ask for forgiveness, or…I'm lost. I think we got off track." Runt threw his hands up.

"I think we did, too. Let's go to the next verse. Luke 6:37." Dexter repeated the verse.

"Got it," Runt yelled, right as Rogan was about to do the same.

"Oh, man. I just found it. I think that should count as a tie," Rogan complained.

Runt threw back at him, "Too slow, Joe. Too bad, so sad."

Dexter had to break in again to focus the conversation. "Read it, please, Runt."

"'Do not judge, and you will not be judged. Do not condemn, and you will not be condemned. Forgive, and you will be forgiven.'"

"Great. What do you notice about this verse?" the youth leader asked.

One of the girls raised her hand.

"Yes? What do you think?"

"I noticed that it's conditional again. Is it saying that if I don't forgive other people then God won't forgive me? That's kind of scary."

"It *is* a sobering thought," agreed Dexter. "In order to answer that, let's find the next verse. Close those Bibles. Okay, let's find Matthew 6:14."

Rogan was determined to win this one. He opened his Bible to where he thought the New Testament began and hit the book of Mark, so he backed up a few pages. "I have it," Rogan hollered.

Runt was right behind him. "I have it."

Rogan grinned at him. "What was it you said, Runt? Too bad, so sad. Too slow, Joe."

"Yeah, yeah."

Rogan read his verse. "Matthew 6:14 says, 'For if you forgive other people when they sin against you, your heavenly Father will also forgive you.'"

"We're almost out of time, so we'll end with this verse. Again, we're seeing a condition. If you do this, God will do that. How do you guys feel about that?"

"It does make me think," Rogan began. "I should make sure I'm forgiving people, so I can be forgiven, because I definitely want God to forgive my sins."

"True, that," agreed Runt.

The other youth murmured their agreements.

Dexter nodded. "It's a great reminder for us. This week, try to pray about it and see if there's anyone you feel like you haven't forgiven. I hope to see you all on Wednesday evening. I also hope you like to sing. I'm playing my guitar, and we'll start with some praise and worship. Let's close in prayer. Lord, I thank You for bringing me to this church and for the youth who are here today. I'm looking forward to getting to know them and pray that as we learn about forgiveness, that You would speak to our hearts. Help us to become more like You."

That's cool, thought Rogan. His head was still bowed. *That's what I want with my life, to be the best I can be and to be who God wants me to be. I want to have all the adventures and experiences I can and to live life to the fullest. I want to avoid big mistakes if I can, and I want to help others.* "Help me, Lord," he whispered.

Rogan felt a smack on his arm. He opened his eyes and saw Runt standing there.

"You comin', man?"

CHAPTER 7

Survival School

THE TIDE WAS GOING OUT, BUT WAVES STILL CRASHED against the barnacle-covered rocks, sending salty spray into the air where a soft ocean breeze carried it inland. Rogan and Runt stood watching the skiff that had deposited them, their tentmates, their buddy team, and their gear onto the shore of an unknown island. The wake splashed a goodbye up the tideline.

Rogan felt a slight trepidation. He was used to being outdoors on his own, but usually only with his close group of friends or with his family. He felt a burden of responsibility for his classmates even though a chaperone was assigned to each group and was here on the island. They had been told that the adult was there basically for any emergencies. Some of the boys in the other group weren't as outdoor savvy as he would've liked, so that worried him. He remembered how they'd struggled to assemble their tent at the practice campout. Runt was uncharacteristically somber.

Maybe he is feeling the weight of it too, Rogan thought.

"All right, guys. I'm going to show you where your fresh water source can be found and then where my camp will be. After that, you're on your own," Mr. Miller, their chaperone, announced.

Rogan and Runt turned and walked back up the beach. Their gear was all thrown into a pile. They were allowed to bring a sleeping bag, two changes of clothes, a raincoat, a jacket, and their number five tin can. Rogan had managed to fit quite a bit into his twenty-eight ounce can that was previously full of baked beans: a Leatherman tool, his flint and steel for fire starting, a headlamp, some fishing line and hooks, a small packet of lemon and pepper seasoning, a Milky Way bar, and the rice that filled the spaces in-between.

The eight boys hiked behind Mr. Miller across the tidal grass and up into the woods where they followed an indistinct trail through the hemlock and cedar woods that inclined up a hill. Rogan periodically turned around to see what the path looked like going the other way, hoping to recognize it on the return trip.

"What are you lookin' at?" Martin snarled when Rogan turned around for the third time.

Taken aback, Rogan turned back around and muttered, "Not at you. What's your problem?"

The spring was a good fifteen-minute hike. When they arrived, Rogan realized his mistake.

"We should have emptied out a couple of cans, so we could collect some water. Now we'll have to come back to do that."

"Oh, yeah. We should've," agreed Tuff.

"Why? Let's just take a drink while we're here," Martin said.

"Well, for one thing, genius, the water needs to be filtered or boiled, so it doesn't make you sick," Cory scoffed. "And for the second thing, we don't want your germs contaminating our drinking water."

Martin ignored him, dropped to his knees, and slurped loudly as he drank from the spring. The rest of the boys looked at Mr. Miller who just shrugged. Rogan assumed that indicated it wasn't his problem.

Great, thought Rogan. *It begins.*

To add insult, Martin loudly proclaimed how hot he was feeling from the hike and removed his dirty bandana that always held down his greasy hair. He dipped it in the water, wrung it out, and replaced it on his head.

"Nasty!" Damien protested.

The rest of the ninth-graders looked at each other with wide eyes.

He's definitely going to be a problem, thought Rogan. *At least by the time we get back, the water will have cleared up since it runs out in a small stream.* A stream that unfortunately ran toward the other side of the island.

Mr. Miller swept his hand sideways. Rogan took the hint and led the way back down the hill to the beach.

Once they arrived back at their pile of gear, Mr. Miller announced, "I will be camped out on the south end of the island, right up inside the trees off the beach. I will be checking in on you periodically, even though you may not see me. Otherwise, that's where you can find me if there's an emergency." He shouldered his fully-stuffed frame backpack and headed down the beach. Rogan could imagine all the food that was packed in there.

The boys all watched him go and then turned to their gear.

"I don't know what your group wants to do, but mine decided the first order of business is to make our shelters and stow our gear. After that, we're going to get water and make a fire," Rogan explained.

"I think that sounds like a game plan for our group, too," Cory offered.

"Why hurry? I want to explore. It's sunny out right now, and the shelter can wait," Martin protested.

Rogan and his friends began grabbing their gear, leaving the sound of arguing amongst their buddy team behind.

"Where do you think we should set up?" Rogan asked Runt.

"I think far away from Martin. Man, what a jerk."

Rogan nodded, scanning the island. He noted the tall spires of rock that marched out from a cliff jutting into the sea on the north end. They were of various heights and thicknesses, but all sported a scrubby branch of a tree whose seed had been deposited on top. The trees grew crookedly due to the wind that constantly buffeted the island. The beach consisted of a grassy section next to an area of small pebbles with the usual driftwood littering the area.

Runt had come alongside his friend. "It kind of looks like Stonehenge. We definitely need to explore once we get the basics out of the way."

"For sure. I think if we go a few feet into the woods, it will shelter us, and we can use the trees to tie our tarp like we did before. Over there," he pointed by one of the monoliths, "Would be a great place for a group campfire. It's sheltered by the rock and has that nice piece of driftwood we can sit on. The fire pit can be sunk down in the rocks."

"I like it."

By the time Rogan and Runt had set up their shelter to their satisfaction, they were beginning to feel the hunger pains of not having eaten since breakfast. This time they gathered some hemlock branches to lay down as bedding, hopefully making it more comfortable. They had both agreed to eat a large breakfast that morning to tide them over until they could scrounge something to eat. Rogan knew from experience that just meeting one's basic needs when in the wilderness took a lot of work and time. They'd gotten to the island around ten that Thursday morning. *It must be around two o'clock,* Rogan reasoned, calculating.

Runt put the finishing touches on the last corner of the tarp to be tied to a tree and stood back. His stomach growled loudly enough that Rogan heard it.

"Ha! I'm hungry too."

"I'm already tempted to eat my candy bar I brought, but I know I should save it." Runt wrapped his arms around his midsection. "I'm wasting away already. Why is it worse when you know you don't have food?"

"I know, right? Let's go find Tuff and Boom Chain and see if they're ready to go get water and hunt for some limpets. I'm sure there are plenty around here."

"Do we have to include our buddy group?"

"Probably should. That's why we were paired with them. To help them."

"I suppose," Runt grudgingly agreed. "Did you see where Tuff and Boom Chain set up camp?"

The campers had been instructed to set up their shelters at least fifty yards from any other team of partners.

"I think I hear them farther down the tree line," Rogan said, and they headed in that direction.

They found the two boys just finishing their shelter, which looked similar to Rogan's and Runt's. They agreed they were ready to get water, make a fire, and hunt for some food. Quickly dividing up the chores, Runt ran back to camp to dump out the contents of his can, so he could use it for water collection. Tuff did the same. Rogan began gathering firewood, and Boom Chain went to the shoreline to gather limpets and mussels.

Rogan didn't have far to walk to find some good fodder for the fire. He was happy to gather dry firewood, which was a luxury. He made a mental note: *Before it rains, we should gather a bunch more and figure out where to keep it, so it stays dry.* He set up the fire ring at the base of one of the stone pillars where there was a natural depression. It was also a spot protected from the ocean breezes that perpetually galloped inland.

"Okay, now for some tinder, and I guess I need to go dig my flint and steel out of my can," he said to himself.

There was a hemlock tree with some dead branches, the needles a rusty red color, and he broke a few of those off. *This will catch quickly.* After hiking back to camp, he realized he didn't have anything to dump his rice into to save it from being a tasty meal for a foraging rodent or bird. *Hmm. Where can I put it?* He put his hand on his chin. "Well, I guess I'll sacrifice one of my clean socks."

He dumped the rice into the sock and dug out his Leatherman, fishing line and hook, as well as his other necessities. Most of these he deposited into the cargo pockets of his dark green pants. He returned to the fire pit and began the process of making a tinder nest, then a tepee-type structure of smaller twigs over that. Next, he was ready with some larger pieces with which to feed the flames after they were an established resident. Using his flint and steel, with a small scrap of char cloth on top of the flint to catch the fragile ember, he began striking. His experience paid off, and he got an ember on the second strike. He gently blew on it and then placed it in the tinder, blowing again, helping it on its journey to mature into flame. The dry needles caught, and he carefully fed it until the small sticks of the tepee flamed with welcome fire. Soon he had a roaring blaze and could add larger pieces of wood.

Rogan stood up and looked around. There still wasn't any sign of their buddy team, but he could see Boom Chain bent over, picking limpets and mussels off the black rocks and putting them into the front of his shirt that he held out at the hem. Rogan grabbed his empty can and went down the beach to help.

"Find many?"

"Yeah. They're all over, which is good. It'll take a lot to feed all of us, but they're here."

"Nice."

Rogan took out his Leatherman, opened the blade of the knife, and began using it to pry the conical-shaped shell from the rocks where they had a tenacious grip. They looked similar to a Chinese paddy hat. Even though they were in a shell, they weren't considered shellfish and could be eaten any time. There were also blue mussels, elongated double shells that clinched tightly to protect the meat of the shellfish inside. Mr. Spiker had checked the online reporting site for red tides. The water surrounding the islands where the ninth-graders were all camped had not had a recent occurrence. If the marine biotoxin had been present, they would not have been able to eat any shellfish for fear of contracting paralytic shellfish poisoning.

Rogan plunked one after another into his can and then looked up. Boom Chain was still nearby.

"I'm going to take mine back up and check the fire. Tuff and Runt should be back with water soon."

"Okay. I'll be up shortly," Boom Chain responded.

The fire was still burning well. Rogan added a few pieces.

"We're back," Runt announced.

"That's a lot of work for two small cans of water. I wish we could figure out something bigger to put it in." Tuff looked hot, beads of sweat shining on his forehead.

"Thanks for doing that," Rogan acknowledged. "Let's get some boiling. "Oh, wait. We need to soak the mussels first to clean the sand out a little. Hmm. How are we going to do that?"

"I say we don't worry about a little grit," Runt proposed. "It's not worth it to make that hike for more fresh water just for that."

"I agree," said Tuff. "Me, too."

Boom Chain had come up the beach with his culinary loot. "Me, three."

"Okay. Let's put one can in the fire to boil, then we'll add the limpets first. They won't be as sandy." Rogan used a long stick to spread the fire out a bit and make a level place for the can of water.

"I hope it doesn't take forever. I'm sure hungry," said Boom Chain.

The boys all nodded in agreement.

Rogan sighed. "I suppose one of us should go see how our illustrious buddy team is doing." He looked around expectantly.

The boys all put their fingers to their noses.

"Fine. I'll go. Watch for it to boil, then it takes about five minutes. Time them."

His friends gave him a thumbs up. Rogan headed down the beach, his feet sinking into the rolling pebbles. He noticed the wind was beginning to pick up, but the day was still pleasant with just a few clouds in the sky. He took a little more time to look around. Across the water, a couple hundred yards away, was a small, tree-dotted island, a bushy hump in the gray-green water.

I wonder if anyone's ever set foot on that island? he contemplated.

The tide was out, leaving a line of debris behind, and Rogan had plenty of beach on which to walk. *It's so pretty out here and so quiet. I can't wait to explore,* he thought.

One hundred more steps and he began to hear the sounds of something striking like a hammer. He headed inland and found Thorin and Damien still working on their shelter, but almost finished.

"Hey, guys. How's it going?" Rogan inquired.

They were doing well, hungry, and ready to have something to eat. Rogan encouraged them to pick a can full of the limpets and mussels on their way to the fire.

"Have you gathered any water yet?"

"No. We haven't." Thorin cringed a little. "We should do that, Damien."

Rogan left them to their tasks after getting directions to Cory and Martin's campsite. He found it easily enough as it was on the beach.

Hmm. Not sure how well that's going to hold up, Rogan thought.

Cory was the only one there, trying to arrange his sleeping bag on his side of the plastic partition. Rogan saw Martin had left his gear still haphazardly tied with a frayed rope in a pile on his side of the Visqueen.

"Hey, Cory. Where's Martin?"

"I don't know, and I don't really care. He can get lost for all I care."

Rogan wasn't sure how to respond to the vehement comment, so instead, he explained what everyone was doing.

"Okay. I'll head up and get some water and then meet you at the fire."

"Sounds good, Cory."

Rogan turned back. Presently, he became aware of a chopping noise. He altered course and soon came upon Martin hacking away at a green sapling he had bent over. The hatchet he held bounced off the wood, not really cutting anything except the bark.

"Whoa, Martin!"

The boy stopped, straightened up, and glared at Rogan.

"What do you want?"

"Well, you're trying to cut green wood, and it looks a little dangerous how the hatchet is bouncing all over the place. Plus, that kind of live wood isn't good for fires. It doesn't want to burn. Try getting some dry wood." Rogan was concerned for Martin's safety.

"You're such a goody-two-shoes," Martin scoffed and returned to his hacking.

"Suit yourself," Rogan muttered.

A piercing cry of pain halted Rogan's steps. He flinched at the sound. Rogan quickly turned.

"Now look what you made me do." Martin was accusing Rogan. He stood there holding his hand up. Blood dripped. "I cut myself because you distracted me," he grumped.

Rogan stood, his feet planted, not sure if he should approach or not. "How bad is the cut? Do we need to go get Mr. Miller?"

Martin didn't respond. He just threw the hatchet down, cursed, grabbed his hand, and bent over, putting it between his knees. "Ow!"

"Can I look at it?" Rogan asked. Inside his head, he was saying, *Sheesh. Great way to start a campout. Thanks a lot, Martin.*

"I hit my finger." Martin straightened up and held it out. Rogan took this as an invitation and moved closer. It was a fairly deep slice that was still bleeding.

"I think you're going to need a bandage and some first aid cream, which means we'll need to find Mr. Miller." Rogan sighed. *What a waste of time and energy,* he thought to himself. For his outward appearance, however, he smiled reassuringly at Martin. "I'll go with you if you want."

Martin huffed a grudging, "Sure."

You're welcome, Rogan thought to himself as they headed to the south beach.

By the time Rogan returned with a bandaged-up Martin, the other boys had eaten one round of limpets and were boiling batch number two, exclaiming that they weren't too bad, and wondering where the two boys had been. Rogan explained. He then pointed to the can of limpets. "They turned out okay, then?"

"We put some lemon pepper seasoning in with them to jazz it up," Tuff explained.

"Nice," said Rogan. "I can't wait to try some."

"Me, too. I'm starved." All eyes turned to Martin.

"Maybe next time you could help gather some food," suggested Cory.

After digging out the limpets and slurping them down, the boys boiled a batch of mussels.

"I know these go for about the same amount of time, and they should open their shells," Runt offered. "I did pay attention in class."

His friends congratulated him with pats on his back, which turned into a friendly assault of harder thumps, which progressed into pushing him back and forth like he was in a pinball machine. His almost-white, blond hair flew from side to side.

"Okay, okay. Enough already," he laughed.

The sun was on its way to getting ready to trade places with the moon by the time they'd all had something to eat.

"That didn't fill me up, but it will hold me over." Boom Chain patted his stomach.

Heads nodded.

Cory spoke up. "Maybe before bed, we should go get more drinking water and have it boiled and ready to go for morning."

"That's a good idea," agreed Tuff. "We'll need to head up right away. I don't really want to be trying to find my way in the dark, even with a headlamp."

"Maybe half of us could go for water and half of us could gather a stockpile of firewood while it's still dry," Rogan proposed.

"Good idea," agreed Damien. "What can we use to put over it to keep it from getting wet if it rains?"

"Good question. Hmm." Rogan looked around at the other boys.

Everyone paused, thinking.

"Hey," Thorin broke the silence. "We could drape a couple of our raincoats over it."

"That'd work great until we needed our raingear, genius," retorted Martin.

Thorin frowned, then shot back, "Well, if you're so smart, then what should we do?"

"Use some tarp," Martin threw back.

"No one has extra tarp, is the problem." Rogan held up his hands. "How about this? Tonight, we can put a couple of raincoats over the wood, and in the morning, we can lash some branches together to create an awning. That should keep most of the moisture off it."

The other boys agreed, and Rogan was happy to have made some peace between them. The buddy team headed off to get water. Rogan and his group began gathering firewood, stacking it up next to the stone pillar on the leeward side. They had accrued a decent-sized pile by the time their buddy team arrived back at the fire with four cans of water that needed boiling. The boys gathered around the welcome warmth and comforting light as the sky painted gray, then brushed with pink and orange, and finally closed a curtain of black. The fire cracked and popped, flames mesmerizing in their heated dance.

Rogan held his hands out toward the heat. "Well, guys, congratulations. We all survived our first day."

"Yeah," agreed Thorin. "It wasn't as bad as I thought it would be. What should we do tomorrow?"

"I want to go exploring," said Runt.

There were many statements of agreement from the ninth-graders.

"I think we could have a killer game of capture the flag." Rogan had scoped it out and was excited about the prospect.

"Oh, yeah. Great idea." Tuff nodded.

"Hey," Cory interjected. "Did you guys hear the story of Prop Man?"

"No." Runt leaned forward. "Do tell."

Cory began the first of many scary stories told before they finally decided to head to their camps. Rogan's buddy group clicked on flashlights and headlamps and headed down the beach to offered goodnights.

"There's no fire hazard, so I'm just going to bank the fire." Rogan used a stick now tipped with charcoal to move the glowing embers into a pile. "When should we do our Sasquatch scare? Tomorrow night?"

"Operation Bogus Bigfoot," Runt gleefully whispered.

They stood by the campfire, planning the prank in soft voices for another few minutes before saying goodnight to each other and heading to bed. Readying themselves to turn in for the night, Runt pulled back the flap of his plaid-lined sleeping bag.

"Oh, snap."

"What's wrong?" asked Rogan, looking over at Runt.

Runt threw up a hand and closed his eyes. "For one thing, you are blinding me."

"Oh, sorry." Rogan took off his headlamp and aimed the light beam downward.

"When I ran over here to get my can for water," Runt continued, "I didn't know what to do with my rice and stuff. I was in a hurry, so I just emptied it out into my sleeping bag. I kind of forgot about it. What did you do with yours?" Runt looked over at Rogan.

It was Rogan's turn to claim blindness. "I put mine into a clean sock, so now I'm down one, but it's okay."

"Good idea. I think I'll do that too." Runt rummaged around to find a sock. "What a mess."

"I'll help you clean it up. Here, I'll hold the sock open for you."

It took a while, but they finally had the little white grains picked out of Runt's sleeping bag.

"Where should we put our socks, now?" Runt held his up, twisted the top, and made a loose knot.

"I think if we put them in a zippered pocket, they'll be okay?" Rogan made it a question.

"Good idea. 'Night, Rogue."

"'Night, Runt."

The Visqueen crackled as they settled in.

"I think the branches make it a little more comfortable." Rogan sounded more skeptical than sure.

"Yeah, maybe. I think I'm tired enough to not care."

Rogan chuckled softly, agreeing. *Day one down,* he thought as he rearranged his hoody he was using for a pillow. He sighed and closed his eyes.

CHAPTER 8

Skeleton Cove

ROGAN AWOKE WITH A START. HIS EYES WERE OPEN, BUT he couldn't see anything, so it was still deep in the night. What had awakened him? Overhead, the tarp crinkled in a wave from one side to the other as a slight breeze rippled it. He heard Runt roll over and sigh. He lay there listening to the wind shifting and slightly rising. He heard some soft plinks on their tarp roof and knew pine needles and small twigs were the cause of those familiar noises.

Sounds like the wind is picking up a little. I wonder if rain is moving in? The forecast had been for partly cloudy skies but no significant precipitation, so Rogan hoped the weatherman was right. He lay there and listened to the night noises until he felt the fuzzy swirl of sleep take over in his head.

The morning light wasn't bright and blinding. It snuck in gently, but it was enough to awaken both boys.

"What's for breakfast?" Runt yawned. "Oh, wait. We have to find it and cook it first."

Rogan answered by giving his best impression of a caveman grunt, causing Runt to laugh.

"What? That one didn't deserve a snort?"

"Apparently not." Runt yawned again. "Can we cook some of our rice today?"

"Hmm. Today's Friday, so we still have two and a half more days out here. Maybe we should hold out until tomorrow if we can."

Runt sighed. "I suppose. I wonder if the girls get as hungry as us guys?"

"Not as hungry as you. You're always hungry."

"True that."

"I'm excited because we are going exploring." Rogan sat up in his sleeping bag and grabbed his clothes for the day from the bottom, near his feet, where they'd been kept warm and dry.

"Me, too." Runt sat up. Rogan looked over at him and burst out laughing.

"What?"

"You have rice stuck on your face." Rogan pointed.

Runt felt around for the grain stuck on the side of his mouth. He pulled it off and popped it in his mouth. "I must've drooled last night."

"There's one on your forehead, too." Rogan couldn't stop laughing.

"I guess we missed some last night." Runt laughed along, snorting.

The early day was chilly but promised fair skies and mild temperatures. Rogan stepped onto the beach and looked back to the tree line. The morning mist was heavy, but the sun was able to shine through, creating beautiful rays flowing from the veiled sun all the way to the ground. The trees were backlit, so their unique shapes stood out in dark-colored definition. Around the golden orb was a pinkish ring backed by fluffy clouds dabbed around it.

So beautiful, Lord, Rogan breathed. *Thank you for creating this.*

Rogan heard Runt joining him. Runt stretched and let out a loud sigh of waking up.

"I think we've lucked out on the weather so far," Rogan observed. "I don't see anyone else up yet. I'll stoke the fire, and then maybe we can start on the awning for the firewood."

"Sounds good," Runt said as he stretched his arms up again. "What's for breakfast? Oh, limpets and mussels, Runt. You could add some salty seaweed to that if you wanted."

Rogan chuckled as his friend held a conversation with himself. He was feeling the hunger pangs as well. It took a few hours for the boys to gather more wood, make a lean-to to ward off rain, get more water, and gather, cook, and eat more limpets and mussels. They congregated on the beach and decided to head for the north end of the island, since Mr. Miller was camped on the south end. The tide was on its way in but still left them plenty of beach to traverse. They left the square-topped rock spires behind to guard their beach, as Rogan had come to think of it. Seagulls swooped and cried in their squawking voices as the boys disturbed their roosts on the rocks near the water's edge. Rogan was happy that everyone seemed to be getting along this morning, even Martin, who was trailing slightly behind the rest of the boys. The round pebbles of the beach called to them, "Throw me." Some threw them into the water and some into the woods.

"Let's have a throwing contest," challenged Boom Chain. He set up two larger rocks for the starting line. "You have to throw from behind here. We're aiming at that fat cedar tree." He pointed straight ahead. "Everyone grab five rocks. Keep your own score."

"Do we take turns throwing?" Thorin asked.

"Probably should," said Boom Chain. "I'll go first." He levered his arm back and chucked one. It smacked squarely on the thick trunk. "One!" he shouted and moved out of the way.

Runt was next in line. His rock fell a couple of feet short. "Oh… kay. That was farther than I thought."

"Quit making excuses and move out of the way," teased Tuff. "I'll show you how it's done." His rock flew off to the right of the tree.

"Oh, that's how it's done, is it? I think not." Rogan had fun ribbing his friend, but he hoped his rock held true to the mark. It did, although it barely hit the left edge of the tree. His arms flew up in victory as he moved out of the way for Cory.

When everyone had thrown all their rocks, Thorin had won and, even though no one said a word, Martin had lost. His throwing style had the other boys surreptitiously looking at each other with wide eyes behind his back. Rogan concluded that Martin didn't seem to notice or mind, and the boy continued trailing behind the group as they continued on their exploration adventure.

Once, Rogan thought Martin was talking to him, so he stopped and turned. Runt, at Rogan's side, did the same. Rogan paused. Martin was strolling along, kicking at stones and sticks and talking away.

Rogan turned back around, looking at Runt. "I guess he's just talking to himself. Okay. Weird."

"Yeah. Weird."

They both shrugged and continued on. The island was a decent size. Rogan figured they'd come at least a half a mile so far and were now at a rounded point. He clambered onto some large boulders that were stocky soldiers, a barrier guarding the beach against the encroaching sea. Wispy white clouds hung near the water off in the distance. Rogan could see another island a few miles off in the vastness of the archipelago of southeast Alaska. It looked larger than the island where they were. The mist had burned off around their island but was clinging to the branches of the far-away island's trees like a see-through serpent winding between the dark trunks. Some of the boys had climbed the rocks with Rogan.

"Let's keep going," someone yelled from the beach.

"Wait!" Rogan pointed to the northeast. "There's a whale." He'd seen the tell-tale spout rising out of the ocean. Everyone scrambled onto the rocks.

"Where?" asked Thorin.

"It was there, traveling that way," Rogan began.

Just then, the blow streamed into the air, closer this time.

Runt said, "Oh, cool. He's coming our way."

The boys all watched as the whale followed its ocean path that was unseen to humans, disappearing for a minute or so at a time before resurfacing. So far, all they'd seen was the tip of its dorsal fin.

"Awesome. It's coming in pretty close to us." Rogan never tired of watching whales and taking photographs of them. He had some amazing whale tail pictures and some with the blow showing, raining down on a sun-glittering sea, frozen in time.

"Oh, man. Where'd he go?" Runt worried. "We haven't seen him for a while."

"You never know. Sometimes you think you know where they'll resurface, and then they've gone in a completely different direction." Rogan knew from first-hand experience. He began to say, "Keep wa…" when fifty yards right in front of them, the water suddenly frothed and built like a giant bubble, quickly exploding with a barnacle-nosed missile shooting up into the air. The humpback came completely out of the water in a graceful arc, turned over so its flippers were pointing up, and crashed in a giant cascade of water that boiled, sprayed, and splashed.

A collective, "Wow!" came from the group of boys.

"It breached! I've never seen one before." Cory's voice rose in volume and pitch.

"That was so amazing. It was *right* there," added Tuff.

Their excited chatter continued as they scanned the now placid waters.

"So cool. I hope he does it again." Rogan was wishful.

They watched for the next five minutes but never saw another indication of where it went.

"Someday, I'm gonna get a picture of a whale breaching," Rogan declared. "I have to. That would be so awesome."

They all clambered off the rocks back onto the beach and continued their hike. Some of the boys complained of hunger.

"You could eat some seaweed," Boom Chain suggested.

"Not the kelp tubes." Rogan stuck out his tongue. "We've already tried that." On their summer campout, Rogan and his friends had dared each other to eat a piece, and they had quickly found out how nasty tasting it was.

"Mr. Spiker taught us that you can take this leafy-looking kind and dry it in the sun. It's supposed to be better eating. Remember learning that?" Tuff asked.

Cory grimaced. "I guess I'm not that hungry yet."

They rounded the northern end of their island and were navigating their way along the backside. This beach had larger rocks strewn about and wasn't as open as their side where they'd set up camp. Rogan was glad they were camped on the other side, as it seemed better suited for a campsite and more hospitable.

One by one, the ninth-graders came to a halt. They had come to an impasse. The island was broken by a band of water flowing out from a hidden place. They would not be able to cross it without getting wet. It wasn't far, only about twenty yards across, but Rogan knew they had no way of knowing how deep it was out in the middle. He couldn't see the bottom, except close to the bank.

"Well…I say let's follow it inland and see what's there," Rogan proposed.

The boys all readily agreed and headed inland along their side of the bank.

"It looks like it's seawater," Tuff commented. "I can see some starfish in there."

"And there's a sea urchin," Boom Chain pointed out.

"Can you eat starfish or sea urchins?" Damien asked. "I can't remember."

"Yes, you can, but there's hardly any meat, and the part you eat on an urchin is disgusting," Boom Chain pointed out.

"Oh, yeah. I remember now," said Damien. "No thanks."

There wasn't a lot of room along the bank, so the boys rearranged themselves into a single file line. Coarse grass grew along the side of the seawater creek for a couple of feet, and then it butted up against downed trees and slippery rocks. The further inland they got, the thicker the trees were.

Rogan stopped. The stream suddenly opened into a small bay that couldn't be seen from the beach due to the angle. The bay sat parked off to the side. If they would have come from the other direction, the stream and land would've taken a sharp, ninety-degree turn into the cove. Rogan thought it was magical. The cove was not only hidden away, exclusively accessible from a narrow opening, but it graced the water with a nice crescent of beach, part of which was covered in…

"Beach asparagus!" Rogan yelled and ran toward the low, bushy plants that dotted the shoreline. They were usually a nice green color, but these had turned yellow and stringy. He snapped off a handful of the branching, jointed plant stems, held it out to show the others, and popped it into his mouth.

"It's a little tough," he said as he chewed. "Supposed to pick it in the summer."

The other boys followed suit.

"I don't care. It's food," said Runt. "Tastes just like green beans."

"Super salty green beans," Rogan added as they all grazed on the plant that grew wild on the beaches of southeast Alaska.

"Good thing we brought a couple of cans of water. We'll need a drink after this," Cory declared.

They were still snacking on beach asparagus and taking sips of water. Rogan stood and gazed across the cove.

"What is that over there?" He pointed across the water. "Something big and white. Oh, my goodness. I think it's a whale skeleton!"

He began running, thoughts of satiating his hunger on beach asparagus forgotten. He heard the rattle of pebbles and knew the others were behind him. By the time they reached the bones, they were all out of breath and sweating.

"Wow," was all Rogan could say.

In front of them was a behemoth. White, sun-bleached bones grew patches of green moss. It was lying on its side, and Rogan could tell some pieces were missing, probably washed away by tide and storm, but what was left on this lonely beach was awe-inspiring. The head was detached from the long line of vertebrae and consisted of a wide skull with two deep depressions where he figured its eyes would have been. The bone then stretched from the head to a long set of bones, reminding Rogan of pictures he'd seen of the beaks of pterodactyl skeletons. One side fin was missing, but Rogan recognized the shoulder blade piece of the pectoral fin with an arm-looking bone attached.

"Who would've known that the flipper has one, two, three, four... four fingers inside it?" he wondered out loud.

"Yeah. That looks a little creepy," said Runt, coming over to examine it more closely.

A crashing, crunching sound startled everyone, and Rogan saw the rib cage shuddering. His head whipped around to look at the tail, and he saw Martin hacking away at the vertebrae with a rock.

Shouts of, "Hey!" "Stop!" "Quit ruining it," made Martin pause, rock in fist, poised for another strike.

"What are you doin', man?" Boom Chain growled. He could be intimidating when he wanted to be with his stocky frame heading toward the wayward Martin in an aggressive stance, fists clenched at his sides.

Rogan watched Martin look at Boom Chain through slitted eyes, then look around, taking in the looks from all the other boys. Rogan thought Martin made a wise decision when he threw the rock down and stood up.

Martin whined, "I just wanted a piece of it to take home."

Everyone just stared at Martin until he turned his back on the group. Rogan glanced at Runt and shook his head. He reached out and patted Boom Chain on the shoulder. "Thanks, man."

Boom Chain gave a curt nod.

The mood lightened again as the boys returned to examining and exclaiming over their find. It lay stretched out at what Rogan figured was a forty-five-foot length. The rib cage wasn't as large as Rogan thought it would be, but it was still impressive.

Runt carefully bent over and stepped into the hollow created by the ribs. "Help me. I'm in whale jail." He said it in a high-pitched voice that made everyone except Martin laugh.

"Why don't you get on him?" Martin grumbled at Boom Chain as Runt extricated himself.

"Because he wasn't hurting anything," Boom Chain retorted.

Rogan was glad Martin let it go with a disgruntled, "Humph."

Rogan ran his hand over a piece of the vertebrae. He marveled at its size. It was probably at least twenty inches across, with the protrusions coming out from the top and both sides. "Well, I was wondering how deep the channel was. I guess there's my answer," Rogan addressed the group.

Runt added, "It must've come in on high tide and gotten stranded in here on low tide or something."

"Śéet," Tuff said softly, using his native Tlingit word for humpback whale.

The boys stood, silent, in what Rogan felt was a somber tribute to this mighty animal. He ran a hand down the rough, cracking bone that was weather-worn and aging.

"Guys, I suppose we ought to be heading back. We've been gone almost all day," Damien suggested.

"I suppose so," agreed Thorin. "It'll take us a while to make it back."

"Should we pick some more beach asparagus to take with us?" Runt cocked his head to one side and raised his eyebrows.

"Sure," Boom Chain responded.

They walked back around to the fading patch of edible plants, picked a bunch, and wrapped it in Thorin's sweatshirt. He tied the arms together so the sprigs wouldn't fall out. They also retrieved the two number five tin cans they'd brought along, now emptied of drinking water.

The return hike was more of a leisurely jaunt, with the boys taking small asides to check out an interesting rock or shell.

"Hey, guys. Look at this," Cory yelled. Everyone ambled over. Rogan ended up next to Martin. *Man, he stinks,* he thought, squashing the instinct to plug his nose. Instead, he casually repositioned himself.

Cory held a lumpy burl from a piece of a cedar tree. It was thick and round, but most importantly, had a hollowed-out inside.

"Good find," Tuff congratulated him. "That will make a great water container. After we boil the water, we can store it in there."

"That's what I was thinking, Tuff. Sweet." Cory smiled. "I'm glad we're getting close to camp. It's kind of heavy."

"I'll take a turn when you get tired," Rogan offered.

Back at camp, everyone needed a drink. This pretty much wiped out their supply of drinking water. Rogan's group offered to make the trek to the spring. Rogan and his friends took all their cans plus two extras from the other boys, so they could load up on as much water as possible. It was late afternoon by now, and everyone was hungry and thirsty.

"I think I'm going to eat half of my Pop-Tart when I get back," Tuff announced.

"What? You managed to bring a Pop-Tart?" Runt was admiringly incredulous.

Rogan wanted to know, "How did you manage that?"

"I broke it into pieces and put it in a baggie in my can. It kind of got pulverized, but I think it will taste divine."

"Ingenious," said Runt. "I keep telling myself to wait a little longer to eat my Butterfingers. If I try to eat just a little, I know I'll want to eat the entire thing."

"Yeah. That's why I'm waiting one more day," said Rogan.

"Me, too. If I can," added Boom Chain.

They made it to the spring, scooped up the slightly amber-tinted water, due to the tannins present from biomatter, into the tins and headed back down the trail. They exited the darkened woods onto the light-kissed beach. Rogan could see three boys down along the shoreline collecting limpets and mussels. Since they were burdened with water, they headed straight for the fire pit, so they could begin boiling it.

When they arrived, Rogan was surprised the fourth boy from the buddy group wasn't there. The fire had been built up, but no one was near. He didn't think much of it and set about the task of getting the water boiled to make it potable. Once that was started, he and his friends headed down to the beach to help collect food.

Rogan looked around and asked, "Where's Martin?"

Cory stood up, a limpet in his hand. "He was supposed to take care of the fire. Is he shirking his duty again? We sent him up there, hoping the smoke would cover up some of his B.O. It's so bad after our hike. Well, it's always bad, but now it's worse."

"He built up the fire just fine, but I didn't see him up there." Rogan tried to give him the benefit of the doubt. "Maybe he went for more firewood or headed to the latrine."

The boys had a designated spot where they'd dug a hole in the woods, far from camp, where they could take care of business.

"Who knows?" Cory plopped his shellfish into a can and continued on.

When they felt they had a sufficient amount, they headed back up. Rogan had sandy hands and decided to rinse them off in the ocean. He stepped across a tide pool, looking down as he did so. There was a crab, caught in the water-filled hollow of a rock. It was blowing bubbles and slowly moving its big, brownish-red claws.

"Guys, a crab!" Rogan grabbed it from behind and picked it up. "Woohoo!" He held his prize aloft. The crab squirmed and managed to reach a clawed pincher around to grasp the edge of Rogan's finger. "Ow. Let go." He used his other hand to pry the strong vice-claw open. He managed to extricate his now wounded finger. The crab dropped onto the rocks and began to scurry its escape. "Oh, no, you don't." Rogan lunged after it and this time did the pre-cracking-the-shell-off grab with both his hands hanging on at the base of both front claws from behind. "Yes."

His friends congratulated him.

"We're eating good tonight," said Runt, rubbing his palms together. "Just crack it now. The water should be boiling in the fire soon. We'll have to break it up into sections of each of its legs."

"That's perfect," Rogan agreed. "We can each have a leg since there are eight of us, and we can divvy out the big claws equally."

Rogan quickly cracked and cleaned his Dungeness, and they all went up to the fire. There was still no sign of Martin. After adding a little seawater for some salt, Rogan plopped the pieces into three of the cans of boiling water.

"I hate to use up three cans, but the legs take up too much room. At least we can reuse the crab water for the limpets and mussels. The other three we can keep for drinking water in our burl bowl that Cory found."

The crab was cooked, and their mouths were watering. Martin still had not appeared. Rogan began to worry about where the boy was and what he was doing.

"Let's just eat anyway," Runt suggested. "Who knows when he'll be back."

Rogan agreed. "Yeah. We'll save his part. It may be cold by then, but oh, well."

Rogan enjoyed the small feast for their dinner. They threw some of the over-mature beach asparagus in with the mussels, hoping to soften it up.

"I'll take the shells down to the water," Rogan offered. He knew the importance of keeping a clean camp.

"I'll help." Runt stood up and brushed off.

"I'm a little worried about Martin," Rogan confided to Runt when they were away from the others.

"He's a doofus. He's going to get himself hurt or lost," Runt agreed.

They dumped the shells and headed back. Cory and Thorin were heading back down the beach to their camp to look for Martin, so

Rogan and Runt joined them. As they approached Cory's beach shelter, they saw Martin sitting on his sleeping bag, a can in hand, using a stick as a spoon to collect the remains of whatever food was in the can. The stick came out, and Rogan watched it head for Martin's mouth. Martin saw the group coming and froze, his mouth open. They could plainly see the cooked grains of pearly white rice sticking to the piece of wood he was using as a utensil.

Martin closed his mouth, threw down the can and stick, and tried to stand quickly but hit his head on the overhead Visqueen, ripping it from its anchor. It flapped around as Cory sprinted forward and tackled Martin, further ripping the tarp. He grabbed the front of Martin's shirt.

"What have you done?" he demanded.

Martin held up his hands, reverting to what Rogan thought of as his whipped hound dog look instead of fighting back.

"I was hungry. I couldn't take it anymore," he whined.

"So…you ate *your* rice, right?" Cory questioned.

"Yeah."

Cory let him go with a shove and crawled into his half of the tent. "No! You ate my rice, too? It's gone. All of it." Cory was back out, red in the face and tight-lipped, advancing on Martin.

Martin tried to backpedal, scooting on his backside to get away from the angry boy.

"Cory, wait." Rogan put a staying hand on the fuming boy. "Martin." He drilled him with a glare. "Did you eat Cory's rice?"

Martin's eyes filled and then overflowed. "I couldn't help it. I'm so hungry."

Cory stepped forward again. "I'm gonna kill him. We were out there gathering food and he was up here being a thief."

Rogan turned Cory by the shoulders and headed him in the opposite direction of the blubbering Martin. Runt stood there blinking, looking back and forth between the mess on the ground and the stick of dynamite whose fuse had almost burned down. He turned and ran to catch up with Cory and Rogan.

"You can have Martin's crab." Rogan hoped this would help soothe Cory. "And I'll share my rice with you."

"Me, too," offered Runt.

"What a weasel. Here we are, worrying if he got lost, and he's cooking and eating my rice. Oh, man. If he ate my candy bar, I am really going to kill him." Cory turned on his heel.

"Runt, you and Cory head back to the fire. I'll go check. Did you have any other food?"

"No. My candy bar is in my jacket pocket, so hopefully he didn't see it."

"Okay. See you at the fire."

When Rogan arrived back at the half-shredded shelter, Martin was, again, nowhere to be seen. Rogan searched around and found the Snickers bar. He toted it back to the campfire and gave it to a grateful Cory, who had told the story of Martin's betrayal to the others.

Cory ended with words spat out of his mouth like he'd just tasted something rotten. "What a rat."

"Bring your stuff over, and you can stay in our shelter," Thorin offered to Cory.

"I think I will. Thanks."

Campfire time broke up early so Cory could get situated in his new place.

"This kind of puts a damper on doing Operation Bogus Bigfoot tonight. Should we abort, men?" Runt looked each of them in the eye.

"Actually, it might be better," Boom Chain reasoned. "Three of them will all be together under one roof. Who cares about Martin. What a loser."

Everyone laughed.

Rogan felt guilty for laughing along with his friends at Martin's expense, even though the boy wasn't around to hear it. It had just instinctively popped out, but he tried to not make fun of other people unless it was all in jest, roasting his friends, who were giving it right back. That was a different story.

Sorry, Lord. Please forgive me, he prayed. *I know you love Martin. Help me to treat him like You want me to. It's just kind of hard when he acts like a jerk.*

Rogan turned back to the fire. He and his friends had to plan the execution of Operation Bogus Bigfoot.

CHAPTER 9

Operation Bogus Bigfoot

"I WANTED TO TELL SQUATCH STORIES AROUND THE campfire tonight to, you know, set the stage," whispered Runt.

Rogan whispered back, "It definitely would've helped, but here we are, without setting the atmosphere."

"Equipment check," interrupted Tuff. "Headlamps—but keep them in your pockets. Just for emergencies."

"Got it," said Boom Chain, and the other two echoed confirmation.

"I've got the sticks," Tuff continued. "Rogan. Do you have the rocks?"

"Ten-four."

"Boom Chain. You got your boomin' voice?"

"That I do," he answered in a deep voice, low and growly.

The boys waited until it was dark, hoping they had given the others time to get to sleep. They walked straight down to the beach and planned to sneak along the shoreline until they were close to Thorin and Damien's shelter. Trying to make as little noise as possible on the rolling pebbles and avoiding the obstacles that peppered the beach would be tricky. They all wore their darkest-colored clothes. Their eyes had the time to adjust, and a faint moonlight reflected off the water. The sea was also sleeping tonight, mostly calm and placid. While creeping along, Rogan realized they'd end up semi-close to Martin's now lonely shelter on the beach. As the group moved closer to the tree line, Rogan saw a faint light come on further down the beach.

It must be Martin. He's still up. I guess it's good he's back.

Rogan refocused his attention on the large, downed tree that would be their final destination. *Almost there.* The boys all hunkered behind it. From here, they couldn't see their friends' camp since it was about ten yards into the trees. The plan was to have Runt sneak closer, so he could watch and report their reactions.

"Runt," Boom Chain whispered. "Once we're done, and it is safe for you to escape, remember your exit plan is to head back along the edge of the forest. Don't twist an ankle."

"Yeah. If we have to come rescue you, the gig is up. They'll know it was us." Tuff was intent on not being caught.

Runt let out a soft snort. "Oh, you of little faith."

There wasn't much more to say, so Rogan touched Runt on the shoulder. "Good luck, buddy."

He could see Runt's smile in the moonlight as his friend gave a thumbs up and headed out to his post. On his way to be The Observer, Runt would also be in charge of creating a fake Sasquatch footprint in a spot they had scoped out earlier. There was a perfect place, not far from their buddy team's tent, where one little patch of soil was plopped between the usual mossy, grassy earth, and the rocks of the beach. Rogan knew Runt had practiced at home and had made a decent-looking replica by using rocks and sticks for tools in the muddy earth. If their friends were overly observant, they'd see through the ruse. Rogan hoped they were tricked for at least a little while.

They waited a good fifteen minutes, sitting with their backs propped up against the log and facing out to sea. Rogan was enjoying the peaceful beauty of the secluded beach.

Plop. Plop.

"Oh, man. Here comes the rain." Tuff held a palm up, catching a few of the first drops from the weeping night sky.

"That's okay. It will mask our movements," Rogan whispered.

"I think it's time," said Tuff.

"Dude. I almost forgot the Squatch hair." Rogan reached into the cargo pocket of his pants and pulled out a mixture of bear and dog hair he'd clipped. Some was from a bear hide and some from his dog, Sitka, at home. "I hope the rain doesn't wash it away."

"Tuck it in under this crack in the wood, but make sure it's still showing." Tuff pointed to the spot on the log.

Rogan secured his trace evidence. He grabbed his rocks. Tuff had the sticks. They both looked at Boom Chain.

Rogan smiled in anticipation. "You're up, Squatch."

Boom Chain threw back his head, arched his back, and released a blood-curdling, half scream, half roar.

Rogan flinched like an unexpected gunshot had discharged right next to him. Out of the corner of his eye, he saw Tuff duck down behind the log before popping back up. Both boys released a quiet, nervous laugh.

"You scared me with that," Rogan admitted.

"Me, too. That was awesome," breathed Tuff.

"Do it again. I'm ready this time." Rogan decided to cover his ears.

Boom Chain roared again. "Augh. That one hurt my throat."

Rogan began crashing his rocks together like cymbals. The rain was coming down harder, so he hoped it didn't muffle their Bigfoot orchestra too much. Tuff was banging the sticks on the fallen log.

Rogan ran his finger across his throat, indicating his friends should kill the noise for a moment. They peered into the hazy darkness and strained their ears, hoping to hear some indication that their noise had the intended effect. Silence. It was getting harder to see through the rain and darkness. Wet drops ran off the brim of Rogan's Grunt Style baseball cap.

"I think I see a light in their shelter?" Rogan guessed.

"Where?" asked Boom Chain.

Rogan pointed, and his friends all squinted into the night.

"I'd say let's head down the beach a little way and do it one more time. What do you guys think?"

"Sure. I think I have one more Squatch yell in me." Boom Chain quietly cleared his throat.

The three of them went back toward their own camps another fifty yards and let loose one more time. They dropped the sticks and rocks and hustled back down to the shore, retracing their journey from earlier. They arrived back at the fire pit to a sputtering flame. They were a bit out of breath. Rogan added some more wood, and they crowded around, trying to absorb some warmth back into their damp clothes.

"Do you think it worked?" Tuff asked.

"Hopefully Runt gets back soon, and he'll let us know," said Rogan.

"I hear something. Maybe that's him now." Boom Chain turned around, expecting to see Runt, but Thorin, Damien and Cory were the ones who came running between the stone pillars, straight for the fire. They were gasping for breath and looking over their shoulders.

"Oh, my gosh. Did you guys hear that?" Cory was wide-eyed and bare-headed. His brown hair was plastered to his forehead.

"Hear what?" asked Rogan, hoping he looked innocent. "You guys okay? You look like you've seen a ghost."

The other boys all began to talk at the same time.

"It was right near our tent."

"That was the scariest sound I've ever heard."

"I think it's gone."

"I didn't think I believed in Sasquatch, but what else could it be?"

"Whoa, whoa. You heard Sasquatch?" Rogan thought Tuff did an excellent job acting.

Words jumbling over each other in an avalanche, the adrenaline-laced teens explained the roars, sticks, and rocks they'd heard.

"We figured we'd be safer by the fire," Cory began, "And, make sure you guys were okay, of course," he finished lamely.

A loud crack in the direction of the woods sent Damien hiding behind Cory as everyone startled.

"Is it coming?" Damien whimpered.

Rogan found himself suddenly scared, and his heart took an extra heavy thud. He sucked in a tight breath.

"Hey, guys." Runt came bouncing around the pillar, a big grin on his face.

"Where were you? Don't go out there. It isn't safe." Thorin's voice rose in pitch.

"What are you talking about?" Runt scrunched up his face.

After retelling their story and Rogan and his friends asking more questions, they fell into a nervous silence, hovering near the fire.

Finally, Cory broke the silence. "What are we going to do? Whatever it was may still be out there. I don't want to go back to camp in the dark."

The others murmured agreement.

"We could all sleep by the fire tonight. The rain has stopped," Thorin suggested.

Damien folded his arms across his chest. "We'd still have to go back and get our stuff."

"What if we all walk back with you, and we all have our flashlights on? We make sure nothing's around and get you back in your shelter. You said whatever it was, it was gone, right?" Rogan suggested.

After deliberating, they decided that was the best plan, and that they'd leave a flashlight on for the rest of the night. Rogan's group escorted them back. Runt couldn't resist a false-alarm sighting that almost sent everyone scurrying back to the relative safety of the fire. Rogan sent him a stink eye. Runt grinned.

Finally, back in their own shelter, Rogan and Runt fist bumped.

"That was awesome," Runt laughed.

"We'll have to make sure they see the footprint and hair tomorrow," added Rogan.

"Successful execution of Operation Bogus Bigfoot." Runt sighed happily as he changed out of his damp clothes and burrowed into his mummy bag.

Rogan did the same. As he drifted off to sleep, he realized that no one had even thought about checking on Martin.

* * *

A warmer breeze and a full sun greeted the sleep-deprived ninth-graders the next morning. Rogan and his group had slept well after their charade, but the buddy group had definitely fared worse. They had agreed earlier that they'd cook half of their rice for breakfast this morning. When Cory and his group, minus Martin, came staggering up to the fire area, Rogan could see messed up hair, droopy eyes, and yawns.

"I need a good breakfast after last night," Thorin commented.

"It's going to taste amazing. Thanks for sharing with me, guys." Cory smiled at everyone.

The talk turned back to the previous night's excitement. Damien admitted he'd never been so scared in his entire life. Rogan suggested they go look for evidence that something had roamed around the beach last night on their way to collect more water.

Made bold by the security of daylight, the group sauntered down the beach. Cory said they'd heard something pretty close to their shelter and suggested they begin looking there. When they arrived in the vicinity, Rogan and his group purposely held back, so their friends would hopefully make the "discovery" on their own. It didn't take long. Thorin made a choking sound and began to sputter nonsense.

Cory turned toward him. "Are you okay?"

Thorin's eyes were wide and wild. He pointed a shaky finger at the patch of soft earth. Everyone gathered around. At first, there was a shocked silence. They looked at each other, Rogan thought, for confirmation of what they were seeing. He and his buddies played along.

Damien let out a reverent, "Whoa. Is that what it looks like it is?"

Heads nodded. Thorin bent and felt around the footprint with two fingers, patting the edges. Cory cocked his head to the side and put his hands on his hips. Rogan was worried he'd already figured out it was a prank.

"It's not very deep," Cory mused.

"It hasn't been raining much lately, so the ground is harder." Rogan thought Tuff was thinking fast.

Rogan surmised Cory looked skeptical, and with good reason, so he quickly added, "Where did the sounds come from? We didn't hear it at our camps. Maybe because of the direction the wind was blowing."

"That way," said Damien as he ran towards the downed tree.

The boys all milled around, searching the ground for a few minutes. Runt finally walked over and leaned a hand on the log right by the lock of hair still stuck in the bark. It was ruffling in the slight breeze. He drummed his fingers and began whistling while looking skyward. To the right, to the left.

No one took the hint, and they were ready to move on until Boom Chain helped them out. "Runt. What is that by your hand?"

Runt pulled his hand away like he'd touched a hot stove. The others quickly gathered near.

"Oh, snap. That's hair." Damien looked around. "Is it okay to touch it?"

Runt snorted. "Why not?"

"Well, if it's Squatch hair..."

Rogan saw Cory pull some out and finger it. "It looks like bear hair, but there's also this grayish fur mixed in. Weird."

Damien grabbed the sides of his head and paced in a circle. "Oh, man. Maybe they are real. What are we going to do, guys?"

Cory was the savvy one. "I think someone has been having fun with us, Damien. Spit it out. Who did it?"

Rogan felt the slightly crooked grin tugging one corner of his lips upward. He couldn't hold it back.

Boom Chain threw up his hands and turned his back to everyone, but not before Rogan saw him also cracking up.

"What? We've been snookered?" Damien's voice was incredulous.

Runt let loose an explosive snort and slapped his knees. It caused a domino effect of laughter until they were all cracking up with mirth.

"Seriously? It was you guys?" Damien wanted to be certain.

"You have to admit, you fell for it," Boom Chain teased.

"How'd you like Boom Chain's Squatch roar?" Rogan asked.

"That was legit," said Damien.

The boys proceeded to tell their story as they headed up the trail to collect water. It took most of the way for them to recount the planning and execution, their words tumbling over each other like a gelatinous blob of jellyfish washing up on shore and being pulled back out to sea with the crashing waves.

Rogan bent down to fill his can. "What does everyone want to do today? We could hike back to Skeleton Cove or play capture the flag."

"Skeleton Cove?" Runt paused. "That's a great name, Rogue. I like it."

"Thanks. I just came up with it."

"Let's play capture," said Thorin.

"Yeah, I vote for that," Tuff agreed.

"Our numbers will be uneven unless Martin plays, too," Rogan pointed out.

"Whatever," Cory scoffed. "I don't care if we're one man down."

Everyone's cans were filled, and they turned to go. "Hey, guys. Uh." Rogan looked up to see the other boys staring at him. "Look." He pointed to some soft earth by the side of the small stream that ran away from the spring. They looked down at an impression with the appearance of five large toes and the ball of a human-like foot.

"We're not falling for that again," Cory scoffed.

"We didn't make one up here, I swear," Runt protested.

"Sure, you didn't," Thorin added.

"We really didn't." Tuff shook his head.

An uneasy quiet descended.

"Maybe it's not what it looks like. We just have Sasquatch on the brain." Rogan was trying to calm his own nerves, which were buzzing.

Another silent pause.

"Let's go cook our rice." Runt headed off down the trail, and everyone followed.

Rogan felt he needed to watch his back and then felt silly for feeling that way. He came up alongside Runt. "You really didn't make it?"

"No, man. That is just bizarre."

The hair on the back of Rogan's neck stood up like it had static before a lightning storm. He recalled the feeling of being watched and the unexpected encounter he and his dad had experienced while wood cutting. He shivered.

They made it back to camp safely and didn't bother to gather shellfish this morning but cooked most of the rice they had. As Rogan dumped his white grains out of his sock into the can of heated water, Tuff commented, "Please tell me that's a clean sock." He scrunched his nose.

"No. It's the one I wore yesterday on our hike," Rogan deadpanned.

"Seriously?" Tuff pretended to gag.

"I'm messing with you, of course. It's clean," Rogan laughed.

They each found a stick and whittled some off to make themselves a spoon as the rice slowly cooked. It was finally time. Rogan's stomach had been yelling at him for the past fifteen minutes. He pulled the sleeves of his hoody down over his hands and carefully picked up his can of rice, transferring it to outside the fire ring. He and Cory contentedly munched on their feast.

"Who would've known that rice could taste so good?" Runt sighed.

"It tastes pretty good with Pop-Tarts crumbled into it," Tuff said.

"Ew. That sounds disgusting." Rogan stuck out his tongue. "I'll take mine plain, thank you very much."

The day was a promise of sunny skies and mild October weather. Rogan enjoyed the easy banter with his friends. They ate their rice, cleaned up, and divided into two teams for the game of capture the flag. They decided to use Rogan and Runt's socks, the partners of the ones used for rice receptacles, as flags. As they delineated the borders and placed flags, they saw Martin. In a burst of generosity, Rogan invited him to play, and he surprisingly accepted. The teams divided along camp lines, and each team went to the opposite ends of the playing area which was part beach and part woods.

"We've got five minutes 'til playtime." Rogan consulted his watch. "What's our team's name?"

"I think we've got to go with the Bogus Bigfoots," Runt suggested.

"Ha, ha. We could. Any other suggestions?"

"I like it," voted Tuff.

"Sounds good," Boom Chain agreed.

"Okay, Bogus Bigfoots it is. Or, would that be Bogus Bigfeet?" Rogan's mouth twisted.

Laughter ensued.

"Seriously, did any of you make that print up by the spring?" Rogan still felt the niggling of tension over that.

Everyone denied it, and Rogan believed them, especially since they would've had to hike all the way to the spring in the dark last night. *Highly unlikely.* He put it out of his mind and focused on a game plan.

The boys spent the next few hours trying to sneak over and steal the other team's flag without getting tagged and put into their jail. They could be rescued by another team member, but it was difficult eluding the jailer. Their attack strategies became more elaborate as the day progressed. It was mid-afternoon when they flopped onto their backs on the beach to rest. They let the slight breeze evaporate the sweat that was dampening their skin. A couple of the boys decided to take off their shirts to help with the cooling process.

"We're so lucky the weather's been good," observed Rogan. "I thought for sure we'd have pouring rain the whole time."

"I know. It's awesome," Runt agreed. "I think I could actually get a sunburn today."

"It doesn't take much with that ghost-white skin of yours," Rogan teased.

"Hey, watch it."

Rogan snickered.

"I'm too hot. I'm going for a swim," Martin announced.

Rogan sat up. "The water's a little cold, don't you think?"

"See that island over there?" Martin said, ignoring Rogan and pointing to the small, bushy island Rogan had noticed earlier. "I'm going to swim out there. Anyone else want to go?"

Rogan looked around and saw the rest of the boys were looking at Martin like he was growing horns out of his head.

"Are you crazy?" Boom Chain asked.

"You know the water is way too cold, and that's a long swim," Rogan added, trying to dissuade the stubborn boy from his foolish idea.

"You guys are wimps." Martin stood and walked to the shoreline. He took off his t-shirt, shoes, and jeans.

He's really going to do it? Rogan panicked.

The other boys were on their feet now, moving toward Martin, yelling at him to listen to reason. Before they could reach him and physically restrain him, Martin ran, splashing into the small waves. Rogan's breath hitched, and his heart seemed to stop completely. He yelled out in desperation, "Martin!"

Martin was now waist-deep and wobbling across the sea floor. He yelled, "Cowabunga," plunged forward into the frigid sea, and began swimming toward the island.

"You idiot," yelled Cory.

Rogan whipped around. "Runt. You're a fast runner. Go get Mr. Miller and tell him what's going on. Martin's going to get in trouble, and he'll need help."

Without a word, Runt took off sprinting.

The stress meter inside Rogan's chest bumped up into red as he stared at Martin splashing in the water, moving farther and farther from shore. He raised his arms and clasped his hands above his head.

"Seriously?" Tuff shook his head. "I am not swimming out to rescue him. None of us are. It's too dangerous."

"At least he's getting a bath." Cory tried for humor, but it fell flat. He sighed. "He's going to get himself killed."

That's what worried Rogan. *Lord, what do we do?* he prayed. All he could do at the moment was watch and pray. Martin got about a third of the way to the island before he began to flail. Rogan watched him stop and tread water. He seemed to be rethinking his quest. Rogan hoped he'd come to his senses and turn back. *I just hope he can swim himself back. Please help him, Lord.*

The boys on shore watched with bated breath as Martin did, indeed, turn and start swimming back.

"He's not going to make it," Boom Chain surmised, "The water's too cold. He's going into hypothermia."

Proving Boom Chain's point, Martin seemed to be riding lower in the water. His mouth was open and gasping, causing him to choke on the saltwater splashing him in the face. His arms were slapping the water instead of cutting a swimming stroke. Rogan thought he could detect a look of panic in Martin's eyes.

"Come on. Swim. Keep going," Rogan murmured. He tore his gaze from Martin and scanned the beach. "Guys! Help me. Maybe we can float that log out to him, and then he'll have something to hang onto."

The boys rushed to a four-foot piece of driftwood. It looked like it was dried out enough that it would float. It took all of them to lift it and hobble down to the water's edge.

"Drop it on three," Rogan instructed. "One. Two. Three. Okay. I'm at least taking off my shoes, so they don't get all wet."

The other boys followed suit, some of them also rolling up their pant legs. Rogan snuck a glance at Martin before reaching for the log again.

"Where is he?" Rogan yelled.

Martin's red bandana rose above the water, and the boy sputtered.

"Let's get this in the water, guys. Fast." Rogan knew Martin didn't have much energy left, and time was fleeing the scene.

The boys grunted as they again lifted the log, wading into the surf to deeper water. Once it was floating, Boom Chain lined it up on a trajectory that would hopefully shoot straight to Martin and shoved hard.

Rogan cupped his hands by his mouth. "Martin. Hang on to the log. It will keep you afloat."

The log was a well-guided torpedo, but it slowed and stopped four feet short.

"Swim, Martin. Grab the log." Rogan could hear the desperation in Tuff's voice.

Willing him to make it, Rogan watched and prayed. With a burst of energy, Martin reached out and draped his arms over the log. His head collapsed onto the wood. Rogan blew out a sigh of relief. For the moment, one crisis had been averted.

"He needs to keep going," said Thorin.

"Kick your legs, Martin," hollered Damien.

There wasn't a response, and the boys all began yelling instructions and encouragement. Martin's head lifted wearily and small splashes behind him indicated he was, indeed, making an effort.

Rogan was too busy shouting encouragement to Martin to hear Mr. Miller's approach. The chaperone raced past Rogan and into the water, shoes on and all. He waded out up to his armpits, reached out and grabbed the log, pulling it the rest of the way in. Everyone rushed forward to help pull Martin up onto the beach, where he flopped down, curled into a fetal position, and began moaning as his body shook.

Mr. Miller was breathing hard, but he took charge right away. Runt was back and also panting from his mad dash to bring help.

"Rogan, grab that emergency blanket out of my pack and get it opened. We need to get him warmed up right away."

Rogan scrambled to retrieve the thin, mylar-coated space blanket. His fingers shook with the dregs of adrenaline as he worked to open the plastic cover. He managed to rip it away, grabbed the edges, and shook out the blanket. "Here, Mr. Miller."

The adult wrapped Martin up tightly, mylar side facing in to capture and retain any body heat. The boy lay twitching on the pebbles, eyes closed, wet dark hair strung across his forehead.

Is he having a seizure? Rogan thought.

"We'll keep him here until he has enough energy to walk to your campfire, and then I'll have him sit there to get dried off and warmed up." He handed Rogan a water bottle. "Get some water boiling for broth. I'll have him drink that, too. Are you boys all okay? Some of you got a little wet."

Heads nodded.

"Good. Go get some dry britches. Great job knowing what to do. Whose idea was the log, anyway?"

"Rogan's," said Cory.

Deflecting the praise, Rogan turned to Runt. "Good job running for help." His friend had been slowly pacing, hands on his head and elbows akimbo, taking gasping breaths, trying to suck in enough oxygen after his emergency sprint. Runt gave a thumbs up.

The rescuers headed back to their respective camps to don dry clothes and hang their pants on a branch, hoping they would dry in the weaker-than-summer-sun of October. Rogan and Runt built the fire back up. It took about half an hour before Mr. Miller was able to walk Martin to the fire. He sat him down and opened up the emergency blanket, so the heat waves were caught by the reflective surface and bounced back onto the still-shivering Martin.

"After Martin warms up, he's going to go back to my camp with me, so I can make sure he's okay. He'll be spending the night there. You all know, of course, how foolish this was?"

The rest of the group affirmed that, and relayed how they'd tried to stop Martin. Mr. Miller nodded.

"I think the water has boiled long enough, Mr. Miller." Rogan carefully removed the hot can from the fire, so the chaperone could make some broth for the trembling boy. The rest of the boys decided to head out for a water collection mission since they were almost out again.

When they returned, Martin and Mr. Miller were gone. They set about boiling more water and pouring it into their burl container.

"Well, it's late afternoon now. What do we want to do?" Tuff surveyed the group.

Rogan turned and looked up past the rock pillars to the cliff from where they were birthed. "I'd kind of like to climb up there."

"Let's go," Cory confirmed.

Rogan wasn't sure about the best way to ascend the cliff, so he just picked a promising-looking route. The climb was a bit steep in places, and the boys were careful, because of the climbers below them, to not send falling rocks in their wake. Once on top, they headed for the edge leading out above the stone pillars. A lone tree, gnarled fingers reaching out to the sea, peeked over the cliff toward their campfire. Rogan stood under it, careful to not get too close to the edge. Scanning the horizon, he could make out several islands in the distance, some small and others stretching their beaches for miles. The sun glinted off the rolling seawater like tiny lights, a sea of refracting diamonds. Rogan never tired of the beauty crafted by Creator God.

"That's amazing," Thorin breathed.

Rogan felt an urging to say something to give God the credit, but he let the opportunity pass by. *I don't really know what some of the guys think about God,* he reasoned, but he knew he should've shared his thoughts.

As they headed back to camp, Rogan looked down and saw a piece of hermit crab shell that had been broken off and worn in the tide to a polished swirl in the shape of a heart. He picked it up and pocketed it. *I think I'll make a necklace out of it and give it to Mom for Christmas,* he thought.

Later that evening, after more limpets and mussels and stories around the campfire, he and Runt settled in for the night. They talked about Martin and his poor decision, and then the conversation turned to how much fun they had with their Bigfoot prank and playing capture the flag.

The night was restless. Rogan kept waking up, uncomfortable on the pine boughs. The sky had stayed clear, so the temperature dropped. He pulled out his Buff and put it on, then raised his sleeping bag up around his head to help capture the heat. He knew some of a person's body heat escaped from one's head. *I think we learned it was from seven to ten percent,* he mused. Still not able to fall back asleep, he looked out past the Visqueen at the star-sprinkled sky, so vast and spectacular.

The next conscious thought was when he opened his eyes to another sunny day. He heard Runt stirring. Like the pop of a cork, Runt was suddenly sitting straight up.

"I get to eat my candy bar today," Runt sang.

"Oh, yeah. Awesome," Rogan replied. "I think I want to wake up a bit first," he added as he saw Runt grab his long-awaited treat and crinkle open the wrapper.

"I'm not waiting. I've been waiting three days." Runt took a slow bite, closed his eyes, and chewed deliberately. "Mmm."

Rogan laughed. "You're making my mouth water."

Talking around the chocolate and peanut butter crunchies, Runt said, "A candy bar has never tasted so amazing." He slurped some drool that had escaped as he was talking, simultaneously catching stray crumbs attempting to get away.

"That was impressive multi-tasking," Rogan laughed.

Runt smiled a chocolate-toothed grin. "I'm talented when it comes to food."

Since the day was sunny, the boys went ahead and tore down their camp, piling their gear onto the now-folded Visqueen, nearer the beach where a boat would come pick them up later, but not so close that high tide would reach it. Rogan relished his Milky Way, while the campers gathered to cook the rest of the rice.

"I made my mom promise me to make crockpot venison with mashed potatoes for dinner tonight when I get home. And a cherry pie." Runt was rubbing a hand around over his stomach.

"Ha! I asked mine to make steak and baked potatoes," laughed Boom Chain.

"Indian tacos," added Tuff.

"Barbecued venison over spaghetti," said Rogan.

Mr. Miller and Martin soon arrived, and they spent the rest of the morning cleaning up the island. "Leave no trace," Rogan recited.

After they loaded the transport boat and settled in, Rogan turned to Runt. "I wish we would've gone back to Skeleton Cove. That was so cool."

"Yeah. We should've," agreed Runt.

They hitched their jackets and zipped them up, faced into the biting wind, and let the craft carry them homeward.

CHAPTER 10

First Snow

THE SQUARES ON THE CALENDAR CLICKED OFF A FAST three days until it was Wednesday evening and youth group night at church. Rogan arrived a little early, so he helped Dexter set up some chairs for a game they would play. While they worked, Dexter wanted to hear about Rogan's experience at Survival School. He told the youth pastor the main details, including Operation Bogus Bigfoot, which elicited a hearty laugh from the man, and about Martin's disastrous swim. Dexter opened a folding chair and set it in the circle they were creating.

"He did what? That's nuts."

Rogan agreed and went on to explain Martin's social standing at school.

"It sounds like he needs a friend," Dexter observed.

"Yeah," was all Rogan wanted to say. He felt guilty for not doing the Christian thing and befriending the boy.

Dexter glanced at Rogan but didn't say anything.

Rogan heard a thump and turned to see Nico Vega enter the youth room, still on crutches. The previous month, Nico had made a poor choice to try and jump Dead Man's Hole. He was still recovering from not only a broken femur but a past filled with selfish actions and bullying other people. Rogan knew Nico was trying to amend his ways after the terror of his fall and rescue changed him for the better. Rogan was, however, surprised to see Nico at church because he had never been interested in attending and, in fact, had mocked those who did. Rogan still struggled with how to react to the older boy.

"Hey, Nico. I'm surprised to see you here," Rogan began, and then immediately felt it was a lame statement.

Dexter moved over to stand by Rogan.

"Welcome," he said, extending a hand for a shake. "I'm Dexter, the new youth pastor."

"Hey. I'm Nico." Nico leaned on his crutches and reached out to shake Dexter's offered one. "Hey, Rogan. Thought I'd come check it out. I heard there was free food," he finished with a laugh.

Dexter also chuckled. "That there is. It's nice to meet you, and I'm happy you've joined us tonight."

The others arrived shortly after, saving Rogan from feeling awkward by trying to make small talk with Nico. His friends were polite but a bit more subdued than normal around the notorious troublemaker.

They first sat on the circled-up chairs and tentatively sang some worship songs as Dexter Newby led them, playing his twelve-string acoustic guitar.

"I know this may be a new experience for some of you, but over time, I pray you'll see how powerful worship can be. You'll get used to the singing."

"We sing in church, but that's with everybody," Runt observed. "It's a little different here."

"That's okay," Dexter responded. "Now, it's time for our first game." He put his guitar away in its case, then carried a five-gallon bucket into the center of the circle. He placed it upside down on the floor. "This game is called sock-it-to-'em." He held up a long, white tube sock with another sock stuffed into its toe and a knot on the other end, tying it closed. He went on to explain that one person held the sock by the knotted end and cruised around the inside of the circle of chairs. They then chose a person to "sock" with the soft end.

"No hitting someone in the face," he warned. The center player then had to run to the bucket, place the sock on the top, so it didn't fall off, and run to sit in the victim's chair. This needed to be done before the person hit could spring forward, grab the sock, and whack the center player before he or she could get to the now-empty chair. "Sorry, Nico, but you're probably out for this game." Dexter pointed to Nico's cast.

"It's okay," Nico conceded.

After the game, they had snacks.

"You can tell which ones of us are competitive," laughed Rogan.

"Yeah. I still say Tuff cheated," Runt complained. "I didn't feel it hit me. I think you were making that up."

"Oh, whatever, Petersen," countered Tuff. "Don't be a sore loser," he teased.

"That was fun that Dexter played too. I whacked him a good one. Heh, heh." Boom Chain had tagged the youth pastor on the back.

"I like him," said Rogan. "He seems cool."

His friends agreed, stuffed the crumbs from their snack-sized packet of chips into their mouths, and threw the crumpled bags away in the garbage. They all wished each other a good night.

Runt was riding home with Rogan's family. As they stepped out into the night air, Rogan could feel a change. He shivered with the sharper cold, even as the vapor of his breath floated out in front of him.

"Brr," said Runt as he rubbed up and down his arms. "I guess I need to start wearing more than a hoody."

"Yeah. The weather seems to be changing," Rogan agreed. "Winter is coming."

Mr. Chaffey and Rogan dropped Runt off at his house and continued on to theirs. They walked into the living room and saw Mrs. Chaffey and the two girls on the couch. Rogan paused next to his father, thinking it looked like a serious discussion was taking place that he didn't need to interrupt.

His mother turned and saw them. "Hi, you two. Come on over. Lainey has something to share with you."

Rogan could see tears on both his sisters' faces, but a smile dawned beneath the salty drops.

"Mom and I talked," Lainey began. She sniffed loudly. "I decided God wanted me to forgive Peg for using up all of my Chapstick, so I told her I'm forgiving her."

"And I'm going to buy her a new one, with my own money," Peg added. Her small, delicate hands were in her lap, clasped about a tissue.

Mr. Chaffey smiled. "That is great to hear, girls. I know it makes God happy when you forgive each other. It makes Mom and me happy, too."

Rogan grinned, remembering the same speech directed at him and Peter. He told everyone goodnight before he headed to his room to finish his homework. The next speech he had to present was a demonstration speech. He was excited because his teacher had agreed to let him do "How to Clean a Rifle." He needed to make his notecards and begin practicing.

* * *

Thursday turned into Friday, which ushered in Saturday, which in turn greeted Sunday. Rogan and his family arrived for church service and sat in one of the pews toward the back, after the usual hellos to friends. The church was full this morning. Rogan had just opened the blue hymnal in preparation for singing "Blessed Assurance," when he heard the door open and close again. He automatically turned his head to see who had arrived and did a double take.

Mr. Hoffman?

Ben Hoffman was one of the last people Rogan expected to see in church. Their sort-of neighbor was on his way to becoming a friend, after all he and the Chaffeys had been through together the past few months. Rogan and his family had also been praying for him and his salvation. He still held the town stigma of "Crazy Hoffman," who scared people off his property with a shotgun and had evil-looking masks as sentries, but Rogan knew he was changing, softening. Ben had asked some questions about God. After he and Rogan had saved Nico from Dead Man's Hole, they had been getting to know each other better, but Rogan was still surprised by his presence. The older man had trimmed his scraggly beard and put on a clean, plaid shirt. He looked very timid and uncertain, his eyes scanning, then staring at the floor.

Rogan was still gawking, along with the rest of the congregation who happened to notice the old man's entrance, when his father pushed past him to greet Ben with genuine warmth.

"Please, come sit with us," Jim invited.

Rogan smiled and moved over. "Good morning, Mr. Hoffman."

"Mornin', kid."

Rogan handed him the hymnal as the piano began to sing out the chords. "We're singing that one," he said as he pointed.

"Oh, okay."

Rogan thought Mr. Hoffman looked like a rabbit about to bolt for cover. *I wonder if he's ever been to church in his life?* Rogan noticed some parishioners were flinging accusing looks at Mr. Hoffman. Some whispered behind raised hands. Rogan felt his face heat up. *Why are they acting like that? You'd think they'd be happy he's here,* Rogan thought to himself.

Throughout the whole sermon, Rogan was distracted by the unfriendly vibes he perceived from some of the people. At the end of service, Pastor Greg said a blessing and dismissal. Mr. Hoffman turned abruptly, pulled his cap on low, down near his eyes, and hurried out the wooden double doors.

Rogan broached the subject on the way home. "Why would people be mean about Mr. Hoffman coming to church? I saw them whispering about him. They're supposed to be Christians, so they shouldn't act like that."

"No, they shouldn't," his father agreed. "They are human and might feel like Ben doesn't deserve to be there after being a mean grouch all these years, but they need to realize that all of us have sinned."

"'And fall short of the glory of God.'" Lainey finished the Bible verse. "We learned that in Sunday School. It's in Romans."

"Yes, it is, Lainey. That's a good verse to know. Everyone has done wrong things and needs God's forgiveness."

Peg piped up, "Does God forgive everyone who asks?"

"Yes, He does," said Elise, smiling back at her children.

"There's another verse that talks about that," continued their father. "I John 1:9 says, 'If we confess our sins, He is faithful and just and will forgive us our sins and purify us from all unrighteousness.'"

"Pastor Newby is talking about forgiveness in youth group, too," Rogan added.

"It's an important subject. It's the whole reason Jesus came to earth, to save us from our sins," Mr. Chaffey said.

"So…" asked Lainey, "If Mr. Hoffman asks God to forgive him, God will? Just like that? He doesn't have to be a nice person first?"

"Just like that, Lainey. He will. He loves all of us that much."

Lainey looked thoughtful. "So, no matter how bad we've been, God will forgive us?"

"He sure will," Jim promised.

"Even when someone eats someone else's lip balm?"

"Lainey Mae!"

Rogan looked at Lainey with eyebrows raised. Fortunately, she knew when to quit because she clamped her mouth shut.

"Dad!" Peg wailed.

"Part of forgiving is not holding it against that person," explained their mom. "God forgets about it after we are forgiven, so we should too, young lady."

"Sorry," Lainey said softly, but Rogan could see a slight smirk on his sister's face and a twinkle in her eye.

* * *

Life continued on in a routine for Rogan and his family. The sun rose, fog settled in and then crept out, winds sighed or heaved, and the temperature slowly slid down the thermometer.

It was the week before Halloween and Rogan came downstairs for breakfast before heading to school. He decided to do chores before he ate. First, he fed Sitka, who inhaled her dry dog food and then trotted along beside him. He was halfway to the chicken coop when he realized a few tentative snowflakes were falling, twirling about and trying to stay unnoticed. He held out his hand, palm up, and watched as one of the delicate lacy crystals melted into his skin. Rogan tilted his face skyward, enjoying the happiness of a first snowfall. He remembered when he and Peter used to catch snowflakes in their mouths, running around and knocking into each other in their quest. *Fun times.*

Rogan finished his chores and then headed back in. His sisters were sitting at the table, eating bowls of Cheerios. He reached for some for himself.

"Hey, it's starting to snow out there."

Lainey's spoon clanked as she dropped it. "It's snowing?" She jumped up to run over to the bay window, hopped up on the bench seat, sat on her knees, and gazed out the window. "Yay! It's snowing." She clapped her hands.

Peg, who was still at the table, clapped hers too, which knocked over her glass of Tang. She froze. Rogan quickly rescued her from an orange soaking with a well-placed napkin. She gave a timid smile. "Thanks, Rogue."

"You're welcome, Peg."

"Okay, kiddos. Ten minutes until we leave for school. Finish getting ready. Your dad's working in the den, so make sure you say goodbye to him before we head out." Elise was the chauffeur today.

"Hey, Mom. Can I drive?" Rogan had his learner's permit and needed practice time.

"Yes, you may," she responded, taking her coat off the peg in the mudroom.

Rogan negotiated the steep driveway in their older model Toyota 4Runner, the tires bouncing over boulders and into dips, rocking the vehicle back and forth. The short drive to William H. Seward Community School on the town's dirt road took about seven minutes. By the time Rogan parked and everyone unloaded and headed into school, only one or two stray snowflakes were floating around.

Rats, thought Rogan. He enjoyed having snow and always looked forward to the time when enough had accumulated, so they could take the snow machines out for a spin.

The school day trotted right along. Rogan worked as quickly as he could, so he wouldn't have any homework that evening. During his last-hour class, he gazed out the windows and saw it was beginning to snow again. The cloud cover brought an early night, gray and fuzzy. By the time Rogan maneuvered the 4Runner up their driveway, the flakes were large, wet, and crowding the sky.

As Rogan parked the 4Runner and everyone piled out, his mother commented, "We'll have to check NOAA weather and see how much we're supposed to get. If it's going to snow all night, I'll have you drive the rig down and park it on the pull-out."

When the snow got too deep, it became impossible to get up their steep driveway, so the vehicle would stay where they could get out onto the road more easily. They still usually had to do some shoveling.

"Sounds good, Mom. Just let me know."

The Chaffey family ate dinner and was cleaning up when there was a *Wroo* sound, and all the lights flickered off. This happened often enough that everyone knew to freeze until whoever was closest to a flashlight or candle could create some light. The town's electricity came from a generator housed in a structure on the other side of the bay. Every so often, it broke down and no one had electricity until it was fixed. That is, until the backup generator kicked on, or until they fired up their own personal generators. It was important to have a backup, portable generator, especially if the power stayed off for more than a few hours. Meat in freezers would thaw, and food in refrigerators would spoil. Occasionally, there wasn't power for days.

The Chaffeys already had a fire burning in their Franklin stove, so Rogan wasn't completely blind. He stood in front of the soft, warm flames, flickering and dancing, and grabbed another log to add to it. His mother, meanwhile, had gotten out the battery-powered LED lantern and set it on the table.

"It's a perfect night for a read-aloud," Lainey chirped. Even though she had trouble sitting still, she loved when her parents and Rogan took turns reading a story to the family. They also liked to read when they road-tripped to town since that was a two-hour drive. Currently, they were reading *Snow Treasure* by Marie McSwigan.

"Can we?" Peg looked hopeful.

"I don't see why not, if everyone has their schoolwork finished," Mrs. Chaffey agreed.

Lainey skipped off to get the paperback, and Rogan helped bring chairs and pillows over in front of the fireplace.

The Chaffey family gathered around, cozy and snug in their log-sided home in the midst of a silently falling snowstorm and a forced outage of glaring, artificial lights. Rogan felt a sigh of contentedness inflate his lungs, then slip out past his lips. He listened to his mother's musical voice as she read the exciting tale, her face animated with emotions. He looked over at his father's enraptured face as he gazed at his wife. He observed his sisters, their eyes twinkling in the firelight.

Thank you for my family, Lord, he silently prayed.

CHAPTER 11

Danger on Salty Shallows Trail

THE ELECTRICITY CAME BACK ON SOMETIME DURING THE night. It snuck in like a thief and was suddenly just there. Rogan peeked out his window to see how much snow had accumulated. He was slightly disappointed to see it was only two or three inches.

But, he reminded himself, *Today is Friday, and tomorrow is Halloween.*

His sisters were eagerly awaiting the fun of dressing up and trick-or-treating for candy on their way to the harvest party at church. Rogan hadn't dressed up for years, but he enjoyed playing games and eating delicious sugary goodies with his friends.

When he went out to do chores, he felt a frigid snap in the air. "Brr. It's sure gotten colder out here, girl," he said to Sitka. "Good thing you have a nice fur coat." He reached down and scratched between her ears. Sitka's tail swung back and forth, and she gazed at Rogan with her ice-blue eyes. The snow crunched as he made his way back to the house.

The school day passed the baton to the weekend, and Lainey and Peg were in their pirate and princess outfits, respectively, ready to go. The fellowship hall of their small community church was full. Jostling bodies, smells of cinnamon and pumpkin spice, and the thrum of conversations filled the space. Rogan migrated to the back of the room where he could see Runt and Boom Chain talking with Nico.

"Hey, guys," he greeted them. "How's the leg coming along, Nico?"

"Slow." Nico flipped the lock of dark hair out of his eyes with a quick shake of his head. "I have the cast on at least another month. It stinks."

"I'll bet." Rogan wasn't quite sure what else to say.

"So, where's the candy?" Nico asked, leaning on his crutches.

"They're putting the food out now," Runt explained. "I'm sure there'll be some candy, too."

"This year I can't steal from little kids after I scare them, since I can't run away, you know." Nico chuckled and thumped a forefinger on his green, full-length cast.

An awkward silence ensued amongst the boys. Nico must have gotten the hint, because his laugh petered out, and he mumbled, "Well, I guess you guys wouldn't be doing that. Sorry."

The announcement of prayer before food saved them from further conversation. Nico hobbled into the line behind Rogan.

"Be sure to try some of Mrs. Tate's crab casserole. It's amazing. I'll show you which one it is when we get there."

Rogan was curious about Nico's motivation in coming to church when he never had before. He also appeared to be on his own, without his parents attending.

Three plates filled and emptied, games played and bobbing for apples later, everyone said their goodbyes and headed to their respective homes. The snow was again falling, and harder this time. Rogan liked watching the optical illusion of a vanishing point that presented in the 4Runner's headlights.

"I'll let you guys out, and then should I take it down to the pull-out?" Rogan asked.

"Probably should," replied his dad from the front passenger seat. "The weatherman says it's going to dump quite a bit on us. That way it will be easier to get out for church tomorrow morning."

After letting his family get out near the house, Rogan carefully drove back down the drive and parked it in the wide spot off the side of the road. He stood still for a moment before hiking back up. The sky was a bluish-black with a tint of purple. He blinked as a few snowflakes landed on his eyelashes. The world, at this moment, was so peaceful and quiet. He could feel the tranquility in his soul.

If only life could be so nice all the time, he thought.

He was still gazing at the falling snow when something cold and wet hit his hand. He jerked. "Oh, hey, girl. You scared me." He reached down to pet the husky. Sitka nuzzled him again. He crouched down and put his arm around her neck. "Isn't it beautiful out here?" He laughed as she gave him a lick on the chin. "I'll take that as a yes." They stayed like that for another minute before boy and dog trudged up the hill toward home.

Rogan estimated they had about six inches of snow the next morning. The world seemed to be only white, green, and blue. After he had warmed up the quad, he had fun ferrying his sisters and mom to the 4Runner at the bottom of the hill.

After another Sunday School lesson on forgiveness, Rogan was outside, heading back to the sanctuary, when he overheard two ladies talking. He paused behind a pickup that shielded him from their view.

"It just makes me so uncomfortable that Ben Hoffman is in church. He's just creepy."

"At least he's cleaned himself up, Mabel."

"I just think it's wrong. Why is he even here? I think he wants to see who goes to church so he can target us."

"Whatever for?"

"I don't know. You hear about people's pets going missing…"

The ladies' voices faded. Rogan shook his head and continued walking, taking his place in a pew for the main service. Ben Hoffman was again attending, sat by the Chaffeys, and attempted a quick getaway, but Elise had strategically cut off his exit until he agreed to come over for lunch.

Mr. Hoffman seemed shy during lunch, not joining in on the family's conversation much. Afterward, however, he went into the living room with Rogan's parents while Rogan and his sisters cleaned up.

Once that task was finished, Rogan called Runt. "Hey, it's still snowing. Want to go snowshoeing?"

"Sounds great. Hang on a sec." Rogan could hear a muffled, "Mom!" Runt came back on the phone. "I can. Where do you want to go?"

Rogan thought for a moment. "How about we hike the Salty Shallows River Trail?"

"I like it," Runt agreed.

"I'll be over on the quad in a few."

Rogan hung up after Runt's, "See ya soon."

Rogan already had permission from his parents, so he didn't need to disturb their coffee and conversation with Mr. Hoffman.

In short order, he had on his layers of winter clothing, his boots, hat and mittens, and had grabbed his snowshoes. The four-wheeler was kept parked in a shed, so he didn't have to clear off any snow. Rogan motored to Runt's house. Runt was waiting on his quad. The boys waved hello and goodbye to Mrs. Petersen, and then he and Runt took off down the road. They jockeyed for first, being careful to only do their horsing around on the straightaways when they could see if any other vehicles were coming.

Globs of slushy snow spit out by the four-wheeler tires flew up and hit them on their goggles. The crisp air reddened any exposed skin. Soon, they veered off onto a Forest Service road that climbed slightly in elevation. Branches heavy with new snow hung low on both sides of the track, reaching for the boys as they raced along, sometimes punching, throwing a cold slap on their arms.

Two miles up the road, the boys pulled off by a gravel pit, parking the quads next to a large rock.

"Agh. I have a brain freeze but from the outside." Rogan put a gloved hand on his forehead.

"Me, too. That was cold on the face," agreed Runt.

Snowshoes strapped on, they set out on a trail through the woods that would take them to the Salty Shallows River. The world was white except for a few ribbons of faded-out, pink marking tape tied to branches in places where they weren't hidden by snow. The boys had to hike single file, since the trail corridor was narrow. Rogan enjoyed the soft *pfoofing* sound followed by a small crunch of his snowshoes on top of the new snow when his weight pushed them down with each step. The vapor puff of his breath was a cloud in front of his face. He felt the coldness of the air hurry down his throat with each breath. Lightweight, tiny flakes played chase with each other until eventually making a gentle landing and adding to the creaminess of the snowdrifts.

They hiked quietly until the trail opened up enough for Runt to come alongside his friend. Rogan stopped and took off his gloves. He dug around in his coat pocket for a tissue.

"Man, this cold makes my nose run." He held up a crumpled tissue. "It's not used, so it'll work."

"That's what sleeves are for," joked Runt.

"Is that why your jacket's green?" Rogan pointed to the sleeve of Runt's down coat.

"You know it." Runt barked a snorting laugh.

Rogan grinned. Both boys looked around at the snow-laden trees and hillocks. "It's so quiet. I haven't even seen a bird," Rogan observed.

"I know. It's crazy. I did see some deer droppings back near the trailhead, but no other signs of life."

"I don't think it would be too fun being a critter in the winter." Rogan could only imagine the hardship of finding sufficient food. He looked over at Runt, who was pulling out his water bottle for a swig. His friend put it away and pulled out a granola bar.

"Case in point," Rogan said, smiling. "You'd starve to death."

Runt's reply was garbled, the words dodging pieces of granola bar on their way out.

"What?" Rogan laughed.

Runt made a show of swallowing. "I *said*, I'm sure twigs and leaves are very tasty."

They continued on, Runt leading when the trail again narrowed. The friends talked about being a mountain man or a prospector back in the day and what a difficult but adventurous life that must've been. They both decided they were far enough down on the wimpy scale to want a warm house with running water to come home to every night.

Runt came upon an obstacle under the snow in front of him that rose to about hip height.

"We've got something blocking the trail." He paused and brushed some snow away with a gloved hand. "Looks like a downed tree. Up and over."

Runt grunted as he swung a leg up while holding on to the snow-covered branches. With one snowshoed foot on top, he heaved himself up until he was standing on top. Rogan watched as he hopped down the other side. Rogan watched as Runt's snowshoe caught a piece of tree branch in the web of his snowshoe's crisscross weave. Rogan watched as Runt couldn't get both feet in front of himself and pitched face forward into another mound of snow, his foot still in the air, caught on the branch.

One of those, "I hope you're okay, but that sure looked funny" laughs bubbled up. "Are you okay?" Rogan snickered.

Runt put both hands down, trying to raise his chest off the ground, but they sank into the snow. He looked back at Rogan. "Ow."

Rogan let loose a full-on hearty laugh. He pointed at Runt but was unable to say anything through his laughter. Runt has snow stuck to his eyebrows, nose, and chin.

"Ahem. A little help, here? My snowshoe is still stuck."

Rogan obliged, still chuckling. Runt stood up and brushed the wet snow off as best he could. He tugged his beanie back down over his ears and hmphed. "Let's see you do it better. The judges give mine an eight."

Rogan looked over the scene. He turned left, walked five feet, then easily stepped over the fallen tree, and returned to the trail. He raised his hands.

"Well, that was way too easy. The judges give you a two," Runt scoffed.

Rogan countered, "Maybe for my form, but I get a nine for using my brains."

"Fine. If you're so smart, you lead the way." Runt threw his hand out in a sweeping gesture.

Rogan grinned a cheesy grin and dramatically made a show of moving on. He had taken two steps when a loud, metallic snap shouted into the still air. Rogan felt something grab his left snowshoe, and he went flying forward, unable to recover his step as something still held him in its grip. He crashed to the ground, catching himself with outstretched arms. The shock of it tingled from his wrists to his shoulders.

It was Runt's turn to enjoy the misery of his friend's fall. He doubled over and smacked his hand on his knee. "What are the chances?" When he could catch a breath, he guffawed, "Dude. Did you break your snowshoe? It sounded like it snapped."

Rogan rolled onto his side. "I don't know. It's stuck on something. Return the favor, will you? See if you can get it free." Rogan tugged with his leg.

"Well, hold still," Runt chastised. He reached down and brushed away some snow. "What in the world?"

"Quit messing with me, funny guy."

Runt raised his eyes to stare at his friend. "I'm not messing. You are caught in a trap." He pointed. "You are so lucky it just got your snowshoe and not your foot."

Rogan scooched back, bending both knees until he could look down at his foot. A gritty black set of fanged metal teeth were clamped around the now-mangled toe of his snowshoe like a pit bull that clamped onto its prey and doggedly wouldn't let go.

An injection of adrenaline took Rogan's breath away for a long second. "Whoa. That was a close call." He reached down and carefully unlatched the straps which held his boot in place. He saw that his hands were shaking. "I feel like I'm trying to diffuse a bomb or something."

"Yeah. I'm like holding my breath just watching you. Be careful." Runt's eyes were wide and staring.

Rogan successfully extricated himself from the snowshoe and stood, wiping the snow from his jacket and GORE-TEX pants. "I'd like to have my snowshoe back, but I'm not sure I want to try and pry that open, or if I even could."

"We could just take the trap and all," Runt suggested. "Why would anyone set a trap on a trail? That's totally stupid."

"I'll bet they were trying to trap a wolf, but yeah—bad place to put it. I wonder how long it's been here? At least long enough that it was covered with snow." He looked at Runt. "You're right, if I'd stepped on that with just my boot…" He let out a low whistle.

Runt nodded. "It could break your leg. And I almost landed in it face first." He visibly shivered with the realization.

They set about carefully following the chain attached to the trap, knowing that on the other end, there was typically a stake stabbed into the ground or the chain was tied to a tree.

"I think we should take the whole thing. My dad's going to want to see this. That's got to be illegal to set it here." Rogan reached the end of the chain attached to the death jaws. It was welded securely to a metal stake buried deep into the frozen earth.

"Oh, man. How are we going to get that beast out?"

Runt whipped out his Kershaw pocketknife. "This is all I've got."

Rogan shrugged out of the straps of his backpack. "I think I have a little folding shovel in here." He proceeded to dig through the various compartments. "Aha."

They took turns alternately chipping away at the dirt with the shovel and leaning their weight against the stake, trying to rock it back and forth to loosen it. Five minutes into the extrication attempt, they both sat back on their heels. Their breath was rapid from exertion.

Rogan wiped some sweat from his forehead. "I don't know if we're going to get this out or not." He reached for his water bottle.

"It's a bugger for sure. Whew. I need to take off my jacket." Runt peeled it off and placed it on top of his daypack. He intertwined his fingers and cracked his knuckles. "Okay, we can do this."

Much pushing, digging, wrestling, and kicking later, Runt grunted, "I think maybe we've got it."

They grabbed it near the top and pulled straight up as hard as they could. The winter soil finally released its grip.

Rogan held it up, the jaws still clenched about its prize. "I guess I get to walk out lopsided. I really don't think we should continue, do you?" Rogan asked as he strapped the trap and his snowshoe onto the outside of his daypack.

"I'm a little paranoid now that there might be more traps along the trail." Runt was jittery-bouncing.

"That's exactly what I was thinking. I guess we're not making it to Salty Shallows today. Bummer." Rogan smiled at Runt. "Your turn to go first?"

Runt reached up and grabbed the bough hanging above Rogan and shook it. Mounds of snow plopped onto Rogan's head and shoulders. Runt snorted.

"I was just kidding, but now…" Rogan smirked. He shook his head and shoulders like a wet dog. "Seriously, I guess if we step in our tracks, we should be okay, right?"

Runt reached up and brushed some snow off Rogan's shoulder. "You missed some." He looked thoughtful. "Yeah. That'd be my guess."

Rogan inhaled the crisp air. "Okay. Here goes nothing."

He lifted his snowshoe-less foot to take a step, paused, and then put it back down in the same spot. "Should I follow my footsteps around the tree or yours over it?" He looked to his friend for advice.

"I vote your tracks, so we don't fall on our faces again."

"Okay. Good plan."

Rogan gingerly stepped into the footprint he'd previously made. He sank up to his knee and stiffened, waiting for the snap he felt was sure to come. It didn't. His next step was with his remaining snowshoe, and he wobbled a little, feeling unbalanced with his handicap of only one snowshoe.

Another unmolested step. And another. One more step with his boot and he jumped as he felt something crack under his weight.

"What?" Runt yelled from behind. "Are you okay?"

Rogan felt perspiration bubble on his forehead. He looked down. "It's just a stick." He exhaled a grateful breath.

"This is freaking me out." Runt clapped the sides of his head with gloved hands.

"Me, too. I'm so paranoid about where to step, but we were okay on the way in, so we should be okay on the way out, right?" Rogan wanted assurance.

"Theoretically, yes." Runt grimaced, and Rogan could tell he was unconvinced.

"I'm really irritated at the numbskull who did this." Rogan advanced another cautious step. The frozen precipitation crawled over the lip of his snow boot and slid down his calf to his toes, where it melted. The wet intrusion registered in Rogan's consciousness, but his growing irritation at the situation took up most of his thought space. His brown eyes, however, ignored his bubbling brain and kept a vigilant watch on the trail.

The trip back is taking forever, his disgruntled mind thought-complained. The relief finally came when they made it back to their four-wheelers. "Whew, we made it back in one piece."

"I'm just glad I still have all my toes," said Runt.

Once they were on their way home and gunning the throttles, Rogan's bad mood flew out behind him, landing in a frozen pile of tire-chewed snow.

By the time they reached Runt's house, the light was fading, and the snow was falling harder.

"See you tomorrow at school," Rogan yelled as he continued to his house. As he crested the hill of the driveway and was going to head for the parking shed, Rogan saw his father, in his winter gear, running down the front steps of their deck and waving his arms. Rogan cut left instead of right and pulled up in front of his dad. He left the engine running.

"I'm glad you're back. I need to take the four-wheeler. A call came over the radio that Ben Hoffman's roof is on fire. I'm heading over to help. Why don't you come, too?" He turned and waved to Elise, who was watching through the window.

"Sure." Rogan put the quad in neutral, set the brake, and moved back onto the passenger seat. His dad climbed on, and they headed back down the drive. Jim Chaffey was about to veer onto the main road when another four-wheeler came zooming around the corner, following the beam of its headlights. Rogan saw Runt sitting behind his dad, Monty. He waved in recognition as they sped by.

"Catch them, Dad," Rogan urged.

When they arrived at Mr. Hoffman's, Rogan thought that the place looked better with a covering of snow. The grotesque masks were mushroom bumps of snow instead of sneering mouths and lolling tongues. The dilapidated house with a sagging porch looked almost quaint in the winter scenery. Rogan had been here a few times, but Runt never had. *I'll bet he's excited to finally come,* thought Rogan.

Crazy Hoffman, as the town's youth called him, had earned his reputation. Rogan now knew that the loss of Ben's son had shattered the man's life into so many pieces that only God could put it back together.

Quickly dismounting from the Yamaha Grizzly, Rogan could see that they and the Petersens were the only neighbors to answer the call for help. Runt ran over, and Rogan could see the excitement alight in his friend's eyes even in the evening gloom.

"This is so cool. I finally get to see his place. It's a bummer the snow covered the masks, though. I really wanted to see them," Runt chattered.

His revelry was cut short.

"Over here, boys. Help with this ladder," Mr. Chaffey called out.

They hop-ran through the foot-deep snow to help Runt's dad with a rusty metal ladder. It was hanging sideways on two hooks on the side of the shed where Rogan had first seen the Death Machine that, to his surprise, had really been the Rescue Machine.

All three of them helped set it up against the shabby house. It reached the roof where some flames were now visible, rising into the gloom of evening. The fire licked hungry tongues around the chimney as Jim Chaffey scurried up the ladder, shovel in hand. Rogan's hands were already aching from clamping his fingers onto the frigid ladder. He'd taken off his gloves to get a better grip.

Rogan yelled at his dad to be careful. The roof looked about as strong as the saggy porch. Its pitch wasn't super steep, and it was of wooden construction with shingles, rather than the typical metal roofing. Rogan felt trepidation that the roof would give way and his dad would fall in. Between the snow piled up and the possible weak spot where the fire burned, it was a dangerous proposition.

Rogan and Runt stood back and watched as Jim shoveled snow onto the burning part of the roof to douse the flames. Monty ran to help from the inside of the house. Due to the heat from the fireplace, there hadn't been snow around the chimney pipe that poked out.

"I think I should go help my dad," Runt said with a wink.

Rogan knew Runt had a burning curiosity about Crazy Hoffman's place.

"Go for it. I'll stay out here in case my dad needs help."

In the end, the fire was out before it could cause irreparable damage, and they all congregated in Mr. Hoffman's kitchen. The only furniture was a folding table and chairs. Mr. Chaffey and Mr. Petersen were concerned that something still may be smoldering in the roof.

They surmised that creosote, black tar-like soot, had built up in the stove pipe, restricting air movement and catching fire.

"You'll need a new stove pipe, Ben. This one has too much build-up. It's not safe anymore." Rogan's dad sounded concerned.

"I have a new one in the shop. Been meanin' to change it out, but kinda put it off after my accident."

"Do you have another way to keep warm tonight?" asked Monty. "We can come back tomorrow and help you install the new one, but there'll be some repair to the roof needed, too. Best done in the daylight."

"Yeah. I got a propane-run wall heater I can crank up," Hoffman explained. "I'll be okay."

A moment of silence.

"Alrighty, then. Monty and I will be back tomorrow," said Jim.

Rogan could see Runt trying to look around at everything, but from the corners of his eyes, probably so he didn't seem so obvious about it.

Rogan suddenly realized how tired he felt. It had been a day of physical exertion and stress reactions. He was ready to go home, have something to eat, and go to bed.

He heard Mr. Hoffman thank his helpers and looked up to see him shake hands with his dad and Monty. Rogan lifted a hand. "'Night, Mr. Hoffman."

"Good night." Runt threw his in.

The boys received a grunt as Mr. Hoffman went over and began fiddling with the wall heater, mumbling to himself, and scratching his gray beard.

Runt looked at Rogan with a shrug and a smile that seemed to say he didn't care about the apparent slight because he had seen the inner sanctum of the town's monster.

Rogan sighed as he followed everyone out into the smoky night. He regretted that he used to think of Ben Hoffman that way, too, but he had been getting to know his reclusive neighbor on a different level, after what they'd been through together, rescuing Nico from near death at Dead Man's Hole.

I'm seeing him as a person, not as a crazy monster, he thought. *He's definitely an interesting person, but I know God loves him, and I'm starting to really like the guy. He's just a hurting human being.*

Back home, they discarded wet clothes stained with smoke smell in the mud room, put on warm and comfortable ones after showers, and met in the kitchen. Mrs. Chaffey and the girls had already eaten, not knowing when Rogan and his dad would return. Two plates were waiting for them on the oak dining table.

Rogan hungrily dug in, while listening to his dad recount the night's activities and answer his family's questions. His brain felt foggy with fatigue.

"Goodnight, everyone. I'm heading to bed."

He lay down and was almost asleep already, experiencing that floaty feeling, when his dad knocked lightly on his door. "Did you do your chores, Rogan?"

Rogan groaned and slapped his hands on the bed. "No. I forgot. Can't Lainey do them tonight?"

"Sorry, Son, but it's your responsibility. I appreciate you coming to Mr. Hoffman's to help, but you were also off playing all afternoon."

A big sigh squeezed out. "Okay. I'm getting up."

"Thank you."

Rogan sat up and rubbed his face. Irritation bubbled up like carbonation. *Now I have to get dressed and go out in the cold.*

Stepping outside revived him a bit in the crisp, biting air. His headlamp barely cut through the heavily falling snow. When he had finished and re-entered the mud room, he realized he had left his daypack strapped to the rear rack of the four-wheeler. He went back outside to retrieve it. The trap crunching his snowshoe was still strapped on. He'd forgotten about it in the excitement of the chimney fire. Once inside again, he stood there, indecision and fatigue making his processing skills slow.

I'll tell Dad in the morning, he finally decided, and headed upstairs to hit the hay for the second time.

CHAPTER 12

By No Means!

SNOW FELL. ROGAN SLEPT. HIS ALARM SCREAMED. ROGAN turned it off, intending to get out of bed momentarily. Rogan slept some more.

Lainey's voice came floating at him from the end of a tunnel. "Rogan. It's time to get up. Rogan! Mom says get up."

"Huh?"

"Mom says get up, or you'll be late for school."

His brain finally clicked on.

Entering the mud room to get his boots and coat on for chores, Rogan saw his dad standing there, holding the chain from which dangled the mangled snowshoe, still caught in the trap's clenched jaw. It rotated slowly. Jim looked at Rogan, eyebrows raised.

Rogan apologized for forgetting about it last night, then hurried to tell his father the story. His dad's forehead creased to the middle as he listened to his son recount the near misadventure.

"How far up Salty Shallows Trail would you estimate you were?"

145

"I'll bet we'd gone a mile and a half or so," Rogan guessed.

"Okay. I'll call this in. They may want me to go check it out, or maybe they'll send a Fish and Game officer to help. That makes me angry. You boys could've really been hurt. And, maybe there are more traps up there."

Rogan nodded.

"On another note, I was going to tell you to take the snow machine today. The seat fits you and your sisters on it, and it's still dumping snow, with no end in sight. I'll take the other one and head up to the trail, check things out, and post a warning sign."

That brightened Rogan's morning, the prospect of driving the snow machine to school.

"Make sure you're not hot-doggin' it with your sisters on there."

"Don't worry, Dad. I'll be careful." Rogan headed out to do chores.

At school, Rogan saw a variety of four-wheelers, snow machines, and four-wheel drive vehicles used for dropping students off for school. Some students drove themselves in. Many arrived bundled up in snow gear. Throughout the school day, Rogan gazed out the windows to see the snow was still coming down and piling up. By the time he drove the sled home from school, he figured the snow was up another foot from yesterday.

He had just come inside when Mr. Chaffey opened the door to his den/office and came out.

"Hey, Dad."

"How was school today, Son?"

"It was fine. Did you go up to Salty Shallows Trail today?"

"I did. I posted a sign about possible danger, but it was snowing too hard for me to effectively check for more traps. That, unfortunately, will have to wait."

"I'll bet it was. Well, at least people will know now. What kind of a rotten person would do that?" Rogan still felt the chilly fingers of a too-close call reaching for him.

"Some people don't think, and some people don't care."

Lainey came skipping in. "Dinner's ready."

Rogan went to bed that night contentedly full of lemon-pepper seared salmon, garlic and butter sautéed spotted shrimp, this summer's crab, and homemade sourdough bread.

The week passed with spurts or hours of snowfall, seemingly endless shoveling of the deck and stairs, and making a path to the dog kennel, chicken coop, and parking shed. Temperatures began a steady decline.

Friday morning before school, Rogan's mother asked him to get four of the "blue jugs," as they called them, from the shop. They were five-gallon water containers used for camping, boating, and times like these in the winter.

"It's supposed to get down below zero tonight, and the high will be only ten degrees. I'm worried the water might freeze, even with the heat tape on the lines," she told Rogan.

This was a regular occurrence during this season, but winter usually gripped its hardest in late January or February. The Chaffey family prepared by filling the jugs with water and psyching themselves up to use a frigid outhouse.

"It's hitting us early this year, isn't it," Rogan observed.

His mother nodded. "It appears so."

The day passed quickly for a Friday. At lunch, Rogan and his friends threw out estimates as to when Buckbrush Lake would freeze over enough so it would be safe to play broom hockey on its icy surface. They were in the midst of an animated discussion concerning this when someone stopped at the end of the table where they were sitting. Rogan looked up as the boys' conversation petered out. Martin stood there with his empty lunch tray.

There was an awkward silence.

"Hi." Rogan spoke up first.

"Hi." Martin returned the greeting and then just stood there, staring.

"Uh, how was it spending the last night of Survival School at Mr. Miller's camp?" Rogan was sincerely attempting a cordial conversation, but it apparently struck Martin the wrong way. The other boy's stare morphed into a glare, and he wordlessly turned and walked away.

Rogan looked around at his friends. "Did I say something wrong?"

They all shrugged, and the chatter quickly returned to broom hockey. Rogan gave a slight shake of his head and put the strange boy out of his mind.

The trip home on the snow machine wasn't so pleasant. Rogan's sisters gripped each other and ducked their heads from the driving snow. They both hunched behind Rogan, using him as a windbreak.

"I'm cold," Peg complained.

"Hang in there. We're almost home," Rogan encouraged.

Lainey was silent for once, grabbing Rogan around the waist and holding on tight. It was a welcome comfort to get home and sit in front of a roaring fire to thaw out.

There was still a little light smearing the sky. Rogan walked over and sat on the bench seat of the bay window. *I could be in a snow globe right now,* he mused.

Big fat flakes blew around in swirls. He couldn't see but five feet due to the storm. The wind had picked up and behind the individual flakes was a wash of white. Rogan liked watching the blizzard. From inside the house, it felt peaceful and beautiful. It was mesmerizing.

The storm raged on for most of Saturday. The Chaffeys used the inside time for homework and cleaning. Rogan and his dad did some reloading for his .270. After dinner, he and his dad set about snow shoveling once again. There was an icicle hanging near the corner of the roof, and Rogan left that one attached. He wanted to see how large it might grow. He did break off two smaller ones, and then knocked on the window. His sisters came running, and he held up the icicles. The girls smiled, looked at each other, and ran for the front door. Rogan was waiting to hand them each a frozen water drip art. They took them and bit off the ends, happily munching.

"You two crack me up," he said.

"Thanks, Rogue."

"Yeah. Thanks, Rogue."

They both took another bite and then threw the remaining icicles over the deck rail and scurried back inside.

The door opened again, but this time Mrs. Chaffey stood backlit by the warmth of their home. She was carrying the cordless telephone.

"Jim. Monty needs some help. They had a big branch break off. Here." She thrust the phone at her husband.

When Mr. Chaffey hung up, he handed the phone back to his wife. "Rogan and I are heading over to help. Son, grab your chainsaw. I'll get mine, too. It sounds like it caused some damage to their roof."

Rogan gritted his teeth. That was not good news, especially in this weather. The snowfall had tapered off but was still drifting down lightly.

They took the four-wheeler so they could strap the saws onto the front rack. Rogan wore ski-type gloves and a balaclava. The fleece headgear covered all his face except a slit for his eyes. It reached down his neck, tucking into his zipped-up, down jacket. He'd also donned his snow pants, wool socks, and Sorel boots. Even with all this, the frigid cold seeped into his protective clothing to prickle his skin.

By the time they arrived, Rogan was stiff with cold. Monty came around the side of the house.

"Thanks for coming. Boy, first Ben's place and now ours. The Swansons are here, too. Nice to know we have good neighbors."

"You know we're here to help any time, just like you are there for us," Jim responded while unlatching the chainsaws. "Where is this branch?"

"Around back. Follow me."

Rounding the corner, Rogan gasped as he came into view of the destruction. A large cedar branch, apparently overburdened with snow, had snapped off and crashed into the back corner of the roof. It was long enough that it speared into the ground on one end and also lay its feathery branches across the top of the roof. It hit hard enough that it gouged a huge crease into the ridged metal roofing. The metal now cradled the branch like a taco shell. The outer edge had curled up after being yanked out of its anchors.

Rogan realized this was right over Runt's bedroom. His heartbeat ticked up, and he swiveled his head, trying to spot his friend.

"Aah!" The yell came from behind him, and before he could turn around, Rogan was hit. One hand grabbed his shoulder; another arm went over his other shoulder to grab his chest, and a weight barreled onto his back. Rogan staggered, unable to counter the surprise. He pitched forward into a deep drift, the ice crystals slapping his face through the slit in the balaclava.

Rogan rolled over, throwing Runt off his back. He got his feet under himself and grabbed a handful of snow, shoving it down Runt's collar. "Oh, yeah?"

"Ooh, that's cold." Runt grabbed the lower edge of his jacket and shook it, arching his back and trying to dislodge the snow before it all melted. Rogan was wiping the snow from his face.

"Okay, you two. Enough goofing around," Monty chastised.

He then laid out the plan of attack. Runt and Rogan were to delimb and cut lengths in the log after the adults had carefully extracted it from the roof.

"Were you in your room when it hit?" Rogan wanted to know. They'd moved back out of the way.

"Yes! It scared the livin' daylights out of me. It was so loud, and I thought the entire roof was caving in." Runt's voice was dramatic as he recounted the incident.

"Did it go all the way through and put a hole in the ceiling?"

"Yep. There's this branch about this big around." Runt paused to hold up his hands, indicating a circle with a four-inch diameter. "And it's sticking out of the ceiling where it cracked through the sheetrock. It's all broken off and sharp on the end."

The saws had started up, so they had to shout to hear each other. Runt pulled out a digital camera from his coat pocket. "Here, I took a picture of it."

The screen lit up, and Rogan studied it. "Wow. That's crazy. I'm glad it wasn't worse."

"I know, man. I could've died."

Rogan smiled, knowing Runt was overexaggerating. "I would've cried for you at your funeral." He reached up and patted his friend on the shoulder.

"Aw, thanks. You're such a good friend." Runt snorted.

Monty had set up a pair of work lights to illuminate the area. Rogan watched as his dad and Monty climbed ladders and revved their saws in preparation for the teeth to bite into the tree branch like ravenous woodchucks. Wood chips flew in all directions. The cold seeped in as Rogan stood watching. The saws stopped biting.

"I think we should tie a rope to this lower part and have the boys pull to make sure it falls that way and not come crashing back into the house." Monty was still yelling as he had on his earmuffs for hearing protection.

"Yes," said Runt. He clapped his gloved hands together. "We finally get to do something."

Rogan followed his friend to a spot up the hill from the affected corner of the house. Monty tied a rope onto the leaning branch and handed the end of it to the boys.

"Keep steady pressure on it, and when we cut all the way through, keep pulling, and it should land over here. Be careful not to get yourself under it."

Rogan grabbed the rope behind Runt. It felt like he couldn't get a good grip with his gloved hands, so he wrapped the rope around his arm in a spiral. They dug their feet into the snow and exerted some steady pressure.

Mr. Petersen climbed back up his ladder, carrying his saw. "You boys ready?"

"Yes," they chorused while leaning back.

The Stihl chewed more wood, and Rogan could feel the branch begin to break away.

Runt must've felt it also because he yelled, "Pull! Here it comes."

The branch disconnected from the top section. Rogan backed up as he held the rope as taut as possible, Runt doing the same in front of him. The branch stalled, pointing straight up, and Rogan could feel it wanting to fall back toward the house.

"Oh, no," said Runt.

"Pull, boys," Monty shouted.

Rogan pulled as hard as he could, backpedaling at the same time. Time seemed suspended as the heavy branch decided which way to fall. Rogan gave another hard pull. Runt was straining, arms stretched out and gripping the rope.

"Here it comes," Rogan hollered as he felt the weight shift. He stepped backward and his feet hit something solid, then slipped. He sat down hard, still holding on to the rope. Runt had been walking backward as well and apparently didn't know Rogan had fallen, because he tripped on Rogan's snow boot, bounced off his friend, and ended up in the snow next to Rogan. The large branch fell safely into the snow with a muffled thud.

Mr. Chaffey looked over. "Monty, we must not have raised these boys right. They're laying down on the job."

"Ha, ha. Very funny, Dad," Rogan joked back. He was glad he had on his snow bibs, otherwise he would've gotten snow up his back. Rogan awkwardly stood, still slipping on something under the snow, and brushed himself off.

"I think I will lay down on the job for a little while. It's comfortable. I have a nice chair of snow." Runt folded his arms across his chest and reclined into the snowbank.

"That's too bad," said Monty. "It's time to run your saw."

"Just kidding." Runt sprang up and dusted off.

The boys set to work delimbing and cutting the log into firewood-sized pieces. Their dads went back up the ladder to extract the top portion of the intruder. Rogan found out that Mr. Swanson was inside, removing debris and repairing Runt's ceiling, while Mrs. Swanson kept Mrs. Petersen company.

When they finished, Monty instructed them to leave the wood where it lay and that he and Runt would take care of it later.

"It's getting late, and tomorrow is church. I surely do appreciate the help," Monty told his neighbors.

The four-wheeler ride back was cold, but Rogan had warmed with the physical exertion of their task, so it didn't feel as icy as the ride over. Jim parked the quad, they put the saws away, and both headed toward the house.

It is a picture-perfect scene, thought Rogan. He appreciated the honey-colored logs glowing with warm light from frosty windows that also spilled rays out onto drifted snow. Trees laden with pristine snow bordered the house.

"Hopefully, none of our trees will break a branch," Rogan said to his dad.

"I hope not, too. We're getting a lot of snow, so you never know, I guess."

* * *

Sunday morning dawned with another gray haze and swirling flakes. The Chaffey family carefully made their way to church. They noticed that a plow had come through the night before and removed the latest pile-up of snow, but it was definitely four-wheel drive conditions. Rogan's dad drove, but he told his son he'd take him out later so Rogan could get some instruction and practice driving in these snowy conditions. Rogan thought that sounded like a lot of fun and had visions of spinning cookies.

Sunday School attendance was down two youth, but Dexter Newby greeted those who were there warmly and enthusiastically. They opened their time together with Dexter's guitar strumming out praise and worship songs. Rogan wasn't much of a singer, but he was beginning to enjoy the worship time spent in song.

Dexter set his guitar aside and opened in prayer. Everyone bowed their heads.

"Dear Lord, I pray that You will bless our time together today as we continue to look into the topic of forgiveness from You and then to remember to live like we're forgiven. Help us also to forgive others as You have forgiven us. Thank You for the youth who are here today and be with those who aren't. In Your name, amen."

Rogan murmured an "Amen."

Dexter's eyes scanned his students. "Today's lesson is a really important message. We're going to talk about the fact that forgiveness is crucial to salvation. I hope you will understand that Jesus forgives our sins, and that's what ushers us into His kingdom. The first verse we're going to look at is Acts 13:38."

"Can we do a sword drill?" Boom Chain interrupted.

Dexter chuckled. "Sure. Close your Bibles. Everybody ready? Okay. That verse was Acts 13:38. Go."

Rogan found it quickly. "Got it," he sang out. "It says, 'Therefore, my friends, I want you to know that through Jesus the forgiveness of sins is proclaimed to you.'"

Everyone closed their Bibles.

"And one more that is similar," said Dexter. "Acts 10:43."

Tuff narrowly beat out Runt. "It says, 'All the prophets testify about Him that everyone who believes in Him receives forgiveness of sins through His name,'" he read.

"Thanks, Tuff."

Mr. Newby lead a discussion about more verses that established Jesus is the forgiver of sins. Rogan found Ephesians 1:7 first, and as he read the verse out loud for the group, he couldn't help but think of Mr. Hoffman.

"The verse says, 'In Him we have redemption through His blood, the forgiveness of sins, in accordance with the riches of God's grace.' I like that one."

"That *is* a good one, Rogan. It shows that God has mercy on us when we don't deserve it. Does anyone know the definition of grace?" He paused, looking and listening for an answer. No one spoke.

"I've heard grace defined as an acronym, where each letter stands for something. It's **G**od's **R**iches **A**t **C**hrist's **E**xpense. I'd say that's a pretty good description."

Dexter went on to teach them that in the Old Testament, there had to be a blood sacrifice to cover the people's sins. They used oxen, bulls, calves, sheep, and goats. The animal had to be one considered 'clean,' which meant it had split, or cloven, hooves and chewed cud. The animals also had to be unblemished, the best of the herd. The Israelites had to do these grisly sacrifices, slitting the animals' necks to shed their blood, as a reminder of the consequences of the darkness of sin. He told them how that was why Jesus is called the Lamb of God.

"Because He gave Himself up on the cross, as a blood sacrifice for our sins," Dexter concluded.

"And He was perfect, without sin, so He was the one who was unblemished," added Rogan. He knew most of what Dexter was teaching, but it was always a good reminder.

"Exactly. Jesus was God's son, and therefore the *only* person who was worthy." Dexter flipped a few pages in his Bible. "Matthew 26:28 says, 'This is my blood of the covenant.' Jesus is speaking here. 'Which is poured out for many for the forgiveness of sins.' That's referring to Jesus dying on the cross, being crucified. And you know something amazing? He is so all about forgiveness that He took the time and effort to forgive the thief on the cross next to Him. He must've been in excruciating physical pain, not to mention being crushed by the horrible weight of all the sin of the world, but He had compassion and forgave a man who actually deserved to die. Runt, will you read Luke 23:34?"

Runt found the verse. "'Father forgive them, for they do not know what they are doing.'"

"Who is He forgiving now?" asked the youth leader.

"Dude. The people who killed Him." Runt's face was twisted in disgust.

"So, do you think that means Jesus will forgive you…and you…and you…for whatever sin you've done, even if you think it's something too bad for Jesus to forgive?" Dexter had posed an important question.

Everyone was silent. Rogan was lost in his own thoughts, pondering. Dexter let the stillness stretch on.

I know I'm forgiven for things when I ask You, Lord, but sometimes I still feel guilty and think I need to ask again. I sure hope I never do anything really bad that I feel like it can't be forgiven, Rogan thought-prayed. He reflected on how he tried to live his life according to what God wanted and to avoid mistakes by learning from others.

Some of the youth began shifting in their chairs.

"I'll leave you with this verse." Dexter put a pin in the balloon of silence. "Jeremiah 31:34 says, 'For I will forgive their wickedness and will remember their sins no more.' That is an awesome promise, don't you think?"

"Do you mean," asked Boom Chain, "That God doesn't remember any of our sins once they're forgiven?"

"That's right," Dexter confirmed.

"So, can I do some fun sin, and then just ask to be forgiven?"

Rogan's head whipped around to stare at his friend.

"Not that I'd want to do that, you know. Just asking…for a friend."

Rogan chuckled along with Boom Chain. Runt let out a snorting laugh.

Dexter cracked a grin. "You guys are keeping me on my toes. I actually have the perfect answer for you. It's from Paul the apostle, way back in the day. Romans 6:15 says, 'What then? Shall we sin because we are not under the law but under grace? By no means!'"

"Ha, ha. You got told, Boom Chain." Runt stomped his feet in glee and pointed at his stocky, sandy-haired friend. "By no means! I'm gonna use that from now on."

"Whatever, you weirdo," was Boom Chain's comeback.

On the slippery drive home from church, Rogan commented to his parents, "It's cool that Mr. Hoffman has been coming to church."

Elise smiled, and Jim answered, "We think so, too."

"He seems like he's kinder every time he comes."

"I think we're seeing God work in his life, Rogan. He's been asking some really important questions lately. I pray he's close to accepting Jesus."

"Really?" Lainey piped up. "I asked Jesus into my heart when I was five. Is he too old for that now?"

Elise half turned in her seat. "It's never too late, Lainey. God will accept you anytime."

"Yeah. We actually just talked about that in Sunday School today," said Rogan. "Lainey, Jesus even forgave the thief on the cross when He, Himself, was dying. The bad guy got saved at the last minute."

"That's cool," was her response.

Rogan was thoughtful. "I'm going to keep praying that Mr. Hoffman gets saved."

"We are, too," his dad replied.

They had arrived at the foot of the driveway.

"Okay," said Jim. "Who's walking, and who needs a four-wheeler ride?"

"Ride!" shouted Lainey and Peg at the same time.

"I'll walk," said Rogan.

"Me, too," said his mom.

The snow was deeper than they expected, but they were able to walk in the compressed tracks from the Grizzly going up and down the drive.

"What do you think we're up to, Mom?" Rogan was trying to gauge the depth.

"Hmm. Probably around three feet. We should measure it up by the house."

"We should. I can't remember having this much snow, this early, for a long time. And, it's really cold."

"You're right," his mother said. "We may be in for a long winter."

"It'll be fun to play in. I think I'll see if Lainey and Peg want to go sledding down the driveway after we eat lunch and Dad takes me out to spin cookies."

"I'm sure they'd like that, Rogan. You're a good big brother." Elise smiled at her son.

Rogan's slightly crooked grin spread across his face. "Thanks, Mom. I try to be a good brother like Peter was to me." A pause. "And by the way, what's for lunch? I'm starving."

"You helping me cook?" his mom teased.

Rogan smiled. "Absolutely, Mom."

CHAPTER 13

Song of the Whistling Wind

LATE IN THE AFTERNOON, THE CHAFFEYS WERE NOTIFIED that the water pipes at the school had frozen, so classes were canceled until further notice. Rogan was not sad about that. He knew it was quite cold out when he went to do chores that evening. He breathed in the night air and could feel the hairs in his nostrils stiffen and temporarily freeze.

"I wonder how long until our water lines freeze?" he mused. "Hey, Sitka. You like the snow and cold, don't you?" He enjoyed the husky's company while he did the rest of the chores. "Good thing your kennel is covered, or I'd be shoveling that too."

Sitka woofed two sharp barks and bounced up and down.

"You want to play? Well, let's make sure your water dish is still plugged in. We don't want it to freeze."

Sitka barked again.

"You're welcome," Rogan chuckled.

He entered the house after stomping snow from his boots. His family was in the living room.

"The thermometer says it's negative five out there," he told them.

"Brr," giggled Peg as she grabbed a cozy blanket and rolled herself up in it on the couch, a snug bug in a rug.

"I could take a day off since you all have one tomorrow. Is it too cold to go have some fun on the snow machines?" Jim was met by a chorus of "Noes."

"Dad, can we take the pull-behind sled for Peg and me? I love riding in that thing. Even if it's cold. Can we go up The Hill? That is so fun. It's scary but fun. Do you want to go, Peg?" Lainey finally paused for a breath. She was known for her hyper-talking.

"In answer to your first question, yes, we can take the sled."

"Yay!"

"And yes, I was planning on going up The Hill, Lainey. *If...*" He leaned over, putting his hands out like claws ready to attack and wiggled his fingers. "*If* you girls are brave enough."

Squeals of delight echoed in the living room.

"Mom, you can drive if you want," Rogan offered. They had two snow machines, so they had to share.

"Thanks, but I think I'll ride behind Dad, so I can watch their faces." Elise wiggled her eyebrows at her daughters.

"All right. Let's make the most of it. Shall we pack a lunch and some hot cocoa?" Jim asked his family.

The girls squealed again, and Rogan punched out a double thumbs up. The rest of the evening was spent reading more pages of *Snow Treasure*.

A bright sun that gave off light, but no heat, winked in and out of clouds Monday morning. The Chaffey family was eager and ready to go play in the snow by ten o'clock. Everyone was dressed in layers with their warmest clothes.

"Let's get outside before I sweat to death," Rogan commented.

His mom handed him the lunch and the thermos of cocoa. "Go ahead and store this in your daypack. Try to not squish it. I think we're all ready."

Outside, two Ski-Doo snow machines purred to life. Rogan had one to himself, and he loved to drive. Jim and Elise were seated together on the other one. They had rigged a fiberglass sled to tow behind. It was about five feet in length and had enough room for the two girls to sit crisscross, one in front of the other. Jim had, years ago when Peter and Rogan were younger, run a rope around the inside lip so they could cling to it while riding. Rogan could still recall the smell of the two-stroke exhaust swirling around in the winter air in front of his face while he hung on for dear life. His dad wasn't reckless but made sure and gave his sons a thrilling ride.

Sometimes, when the corner was sharp, or the sled hit a berm, he and his brother would topple off into the snow. They would roll, arms and legs flailing, or just stick into a snowbank. Often when they laughingly recovered, they would realize their hands were bare and getting colder by the second. They had separated from their gloves, which would be frozen in an icy grip, still clutching the rope that ran around the inside of the pull-behind sled. The gloves would be sticking straight up, empty of hands. That called for Operation Catch Up with Dad, then jumping back onto the toboggan and peeling the gloves off, so they could put them on again. It was all part of the fun.

Rogan had a moment of wistful melancholy. *We would have had so much fun together, now that I'm older, Peter,* he thought, sending it heavenward. *Wish you were here.*

His reverie was interrupted by the squeal his sisters let out as Jim thumbed the throttle.

"We'll lead the way," Jim yelled.

Rogan saw the big grin on his dad's face. *He's just a kid at heart,* he told himself. *I'm glad. I have such a cool Dad.*

Elise waved a mittened hand as they pulled past Rogan. He reached up and pulled his goggles over his eyes and then followed them off into a snowy playground.

They headed south. The first leg of the trip was down the road through town. The plow and subsequent snowfall had left enough of a snow cover on the road that the snow machine's tracks were not chewing into any dirt. Rogan had on his balaclava again, and with the goggles, his face felt warm enough. The cold always seemed to seep into his hands and feet first, but he didn't mind a little discomfort for the exchange of fun and adventure.

His dad was moving along at a good clip. Rogan could see the chunks of snow flying up and a blue haze spitting out behind them, but he kept his distance for safety reasons since his sisters were on the pull-behind sled. Snowy trees sped by on both sides as the Ski-Doos hummed the bright song of a world turned white. His warm breath, colliding with barely above zero temperatures, was building up a frost on the outside of his balaclava. He reached up and brushed it off. The yellow tint of his goggles made the world bright.

Eventually, Rogan saw his dad turn off onto one of the many Forest Service roads that crisscrossed the island. Rogan enjoyed the advantage of his dad knowing about obscure trails and caves, a perk of being a Forest Service employee.

This trail was a great run for the snow machines. The snowy path wound between fir, spruce, and cedar trees as it meandered its slow way up a knobby hill. There were patches of open terrain where the tips of young trees, mostly buried under winter's burden, peeked out like gangly porcupines. As he sped along, Rogan listened to the song of the whistling wind.

Shortly before the summit of The Hill was a steep incline. Rogan held back as the rest of his family went first. He'd been taught the importance of giving it enough throttle to keep up his momentum. He watched as his father expertly climbed it, even with pulling his sisters on the towed sled. Rogan heard the revving engine calm to an idle, knowing that signaled they had made the summit. Now it was his turn.

Rogan repositioned from sitting to kneeling with one knee on the seat and the other foot standing on the running board. He gripped the handlebars. Thumbing the throttle, he sent a wake of powder flying. Concentrating, he wrestled the handlebars over bumps and through tree trunks. The snow machine gave a final burst of energy, and he crested the summit, letting off the throttle with his right hand and braking with his left. He pulled up alongside the others amidst cheers from his sisters.

"Good job," his dad praised.

Everyone knew what was next. The drop. On the backside of The Hill, the land dropped steeply away through the forest, but it offered a fairly wide swath with no trees. Until the bottom. Here, one had to not only dodge some trees but first cross a small creek and then make a nail-biting sharp left. Rogan had solo-driven it twice, but his blood always ran faster with the anticipation. But first: the kids' favorite part. It was a tradition that hailed back to when Peter and Rogan were young.

Jim Chaffey eased the machine to the edge, then paused. He turned his head to look at his wife and daughters. "Everyone ready?" he shouted.

"Dad, can we really make it?" Lainey yelled back.

"No sweat," was always his flippant answer.

Rogan gleefully joined in the patented and expected response, "Just a lot of blood!"

That was the starting gun. Jim plunged the Ski-Doo down the hill. Rogan watched and remembered the drop stealing the oxygen right out of his lungs as he would hold on with a death grip, deliciously frightened. He looked on as his dad expertly made the turn and disappeared into the forest. There was a clearing in a few yards which opened up on a meadow, and Rogan knew they would wait for him there.

He inhaled sharply and let it out in a huff. *Okay, you can do this,* he pep-talked himself. *Here goes nothing.*

Rogan felt the sled tip over the lip and point down the hill. It was like the first drop on a screaming rollercoaster. Scenery rushed at him like a pack of wolves. He felt like he'd left his breath back on top. His arms strained to hold the snow machine on its trajectory. The creek glittered icily as he rushed over it. Seemingly at the last minute, he muscled the corner and leaned. The Ski-Doo responded. He had made it. "Oh, yeah! Woo!"

The meadow was the playground. Rogan's sisters unloaded and plopped into the snow on their backs, lying there swishing their arms back and forth to create snow angels. Rogan figured the next creation would be snowmen rolled up in three lumpy sections piled on top of each other. Elise took the daypack with their lunch while Rogan helped his dad unhitch the fiberglass sled.

The meadow was long and narrow, a perfect runway for a race-track. Rogan looked over the pristine whiteness. No one had been here since the last snowfall. It was perfect.

"Same finish line, Dad?" Rogan was grinning. His dad couldn't see the smile because of Rogan's balaclava, but his voice held the lilt of happiness.

"Sounds good. You ready?"

The flat meadow was a place where they could race, full-throttle, and Rogan loved the speed. He and his dad each climbed onto their respective sleds, which were parked side by side, and pushed the electric start button.

"Your call," his dad shouted over the noise of competition.

Rogan gave a bob of his head, faced forward, hunched over the handlebars, and yelled, "Ready, set, go!"

Both snow machines bolted off the line, a couple of racehorses intent on thundering down the track and carrying their riders to victory. Snow flew up and out behind them, the flakes flying spectators for a brief moment before cartwheeling away to the crowd of those left behind in a pile.

Rogan enjoyed the wind rushing past him, ruffling his jacket like a flag crackling and snapping in a gale. He kept an intense gaze locked straight ahead. Blobs of snow spit out by his dad's sled hit his goggles like a bug on a windshield and then dripped across, vibrating with the force of air until they flipped off the edge. So far, he had never been able to beat his dad but kept trying every year. The older he got, the closer he came.

There were maybe twenty yards left and, in his peripheral vision, he could see his dad pulling slightly ahead.

Go, go, go, he urged himself.

He let off the throttle and skied to a stop. He had lost again but just by the length of his dad's sled.

"One of these days, Dad, I'll beat you," Rogan called out good-naturedly.

"I was pretty worried there. That was close. I guess I'll start feeling old when you can beat me."

They both laughed.

Father and son decided to head to the west side of the meadow where there was a natural half-pipe, dipped in the middle with ten-foot snowbanks on either side. The snow on the top of the drifts was a fluffy swipe of frosting that had dripped over the lip, delicious-looking to the two adrenaline seekers.

They started at one end. Rogan went first and gunned it, going at a slight diagonal but heading for the top. Right as he perceived the front of his sled biting into the lip, he turned sharply. The snow machine was suspended in the air for a heavy but graceful second, sending out a spray of powder, before taking gravity's hand and letting it lead him back. Immediately, he ran up the opposite side in the same manner. Rogan could hear his dad coming behind him.

They rode the half-pipe again and again until the snow was well trodden. After satisfying that itch, they decided to ride past the half-pipe into more unspoiled snow. Rogan was scooting along on top of what may have been a ridge when the ground suddenly felt like it dropped out from underneath his Ski-Doo. Before he could do much to react, he hit bottom in a heavy poof of powder, went forward a foot, and stopped. The sudden drop and stop jarred him, but he was able to keep his grip on the handlebars. He was stuck, cocooned in a prison of snow. He hit the kill switch and in the sudden silence could hear his dad's machine approaching.

Rogan scrambled up onto the seat and waved his arms back and forth. He hoped his dad would see him before he came flying over the edge to the same fate. *Or land right on top of me,* Rogan thought with an inward grimace.

His dad stopped his sled on top and peered over the edge. His engine wound down, and he climbed off.

"A little stuck there, are you?" he teased.

Rogan's arms flopped down and slapped his sides. "You could say that," he sheepishly admitted as his dad slipped his way down the hill, sinking up to his hips in the white powder.

"We don't have our shovel, so maybe we could trample a path by tamping down the snow in front of it," his dad suggested.

"Sounds like a plan."

Rogan knew his dad wasn't upset. In fact, it added to the fun. A challenge. Rogan's gloved hands sliced into the snow like a dozer blade in front of the Ski-Doo and pulled it back, out to the side. Meanwhile, his father was stomping his feet, trying to pack down some snow. When he finished his part, Rogan moved over by his dad. They tramped, their body heat rising from the exertion. Rogan peeled off his hat and coat.

"Hey, what if I roll on it? That may pack it down more evenly. Right now, it looks like the Whac-A-Mole game."

"Sure. Go for it."

Rogan launched himself forward, arms extended, did a half turn and landed on his back. He wiggled in the snow until he could roll sideways like a log. His elbows dug into the snow, and he couldn't keep his body straight, leaving an indentation where he was more sitting than rolling. He gave up, crawling himself to a standing position.

He laughed as he brushed off and faced his dad. "Well, I felt like a beached whale, and it didn't really work."

His dad grinned. "It was fun to watch you try. Back to stomping?"

Rogan's pulse was beating hard against his collar when they decided they finally had enough of a path. They rocked the Ski-Doo back and forth to free it from any sticky snow, and Rogan climbed aboard.

"Keep going once you start. I think you'll be okay if you head that way." Jim pointed. "I'll meet you back on top."

There was a moment when Rogan thought he'd be stuck again, but he managed to throttle through it. Once on top, they sped back to Mrs. Chaffey and the girls. Sure enough, Lainey and Peg were busy constructing a snowman with the help of their mom. Rogan offered to take her place so she and his dad could go ride.

Rogan provided the muscle his sisters needed to roll bigger snowballs and then lift and stack them.

"What are we doing for a face and arms?" He looked at them both, hands on his hips.

"I'll find branches for arms," offered Peg.

"I'll work on the face," said Lainey as she went in search of materials.

They had a handsome snowman by the time their parents returned. He had cedar branches for arms, the flat, almost braided-looking needles serving as hands. Lainey had found some small stones near a still-running creek for his mouth, and some scrunched-up moss was shoved in his snow face to make his eyes.

Everyone was hungry now, so they doled out lunch and cups of hot cocoa, which might help warm them a bit on the ride home. They would return by another route since it was too dangerous to attempt going up The Hill, especially with the girls in tow.

Once home, Rogan helped his dad park the sleds and refuel them both. He then went to do the evening chores. He headed back inside to get some water to fill Sitka's dish, thinking a hot shower was in order after being out in the cold all day.

Lainey and Peg were standing by the wood-burning stove, hands reaching out to immature flames that weren't yet sharing any heat.

"Our water's frozen," Lainey announced.

"Frozen solid," added Peg.

"O…kay." He turned around and headed back outside, grabbing a tin bucket on his way. He packed it with snow and brought it back inside. He set it on the top of the Franklin stove to melt.

"Water rations and the outhouse. Yay," he grouched.

"At least we don't have to go to school," Lainey reminded him.

He chuckled. "You're right, Lainey. At least there's that."

That evening, Rogan stood by his bedroom window and gazed out at the skyline. The trees were a burnt black silhouette against the vibrant flames of the winter sky. Oranges, reds, and yellows were a painter's pallet that had spilled across each other, making streaks of burning colors. It glowed. The perfect end to a perfect day.

CHAPTER 14

Snowblind

THE COLD SNAP WAS HARASSED ENOUGH BY THE WINTER sun that it temporarily retreated, releasing its solid grip on their small Alaska town. Water trickled and then resumed flowing through frosty pipes. Rogan was delighted to get his hot shower but not as happy to resume classes at school. Church and youth group were going well. Mr. Hoffman continued to attend services. Some of the congregation had either warmed to his attendance or had decided to simply ignore his presence and what that might mean. Some still whispered behind their hands.

Pastor Newby continued with his lessons on forgiveness. So far, they had learned about forgiveness in general, and how God responds in love when people ask for forgiveness, so they can accept salvation. Now the lessons were on how people are called to forgive others.

"It only makes sense," Pastor Newby said, "That we pass on the forgiveness." He had some verses printed out on paper and wrapped around pieces of candy. "Who wants to read our first verse today?"

Everyone's hand shot up. "I think Tuff beat you all by a hair."

He threw the candy to Tuff, who caught it and unwrapped the verse. He smoothed it out on his leg and then unwrapped the Jolly Rancher and popped it in his mouth. He sat back in his chair, happily rolling the hard sugar around his mouth. There was silence until Runt snorted.

Tuff looked around to find everyone staring at him. "What?" His innocent-looking face melted into laughter.

"I think you're supposed to read the verse, genius," Boom Chain offered.

Tuff picked up the paper, snapping it straight, and sucked in a loud slurp. "It says, 'Bear with each other and forgive one another if anyone has a grievance against someone. Forgive as the Lord forgave you.' Colossians 3:13."

"Thanks. Is everyone familiar with the Parable of the Unmerciful Servant?" Dexter looked around and saw some heads nod, some shake no. "Basically, the story in Matthew chapter eighteen is about a man who owed the king a lot of money. He couldn't pay, so the king was going to sell not only him, but his wife and children, and all he owned until he could pay."

"Dude. That's rough," Runt interjected.

"It was a devastating sentence, but the man begged the king, and the king had mercy on him. He actually canceled the debt. What a huge gift. But, was this servant passing on the forgiveness? No. He went and found someone who owed him a small amount of money. This debtor couldn't pay him back, and just like he, himself, had done, this guy begged for mercy."

"Off with your head," Runt pronounced.

"Just about," Dexter agreed. "He choked him, and then got the guy sent to prison."

"What a rat." Boom Chain scrunched his face.

"What happened next?" a girl asked.

"Well, the king found out about it and called for the servant. He sent him to be tortured in jail until he could pay back what he had owed him in the first place."

Runt snorted again. "I'll bet he never got out. How could you earn money when you're in jail?"

"Exactly," Tuff agreed.

"This next one is similar." Dexter held up another verse-wrapped candy. He threw it at Boom Chain.

"'And forgive us our debts, as we also have forgiven our debtors,'" Boom Chain read. He turned to Tuff. "I get a green one, ha, ha." He held up his Jolly Rancher.

"Whatever. Purple is good, too." Tuff stuck out his now purple-stained tongue.

"So, what are our debts?" Dexter asked. "What do we owe?"

"Everything." The word just solemnly slid out of Rogan's mouth.

Silence descended as everyone appeared to be contemplating that statement.

"That does sum it up, Rogan. Jesus gave His life for us. We could never repay that. We don't deserve it, but He gave it freely." Dexter paused, rustled around in his candy stash, and threw another one, this time to one of the girls.

She read, "Mark 11:25. 'And when you stand praying, if you hold anything against anyone, forgive them, so that your Father in heaven may forgive your sins.'"

They discussed how if anyone holds unforgiveness in his or her heart that it will affect one's ability to pray effectively. It will also have a bearing on one's own forgiveness of sins.

Rogan was next with I Samuel 15:25. "'Now I beg you, forgive my sin and come back with me, so that I may worship the Lord.' So, is it saying that if you don't forgive, it can get in the way of you being able to worship?"

"I think so. It's a heart condition that needs healing," Dexter explained.

"So, what if someone keeps being mean to you all the time? Do you have to keep forgiving him?" one of the other boys asked.

Dexter opened his Bible as he spoke. "Good question. Remember the parable we just talked about? Well, a couple of verses before that, Simon Peter asked Jesus the same thing. He asked if he should forgive up to seven times. What do you think?"

"I'll bet that's not enough," said Boom Chain. Rogan knew the answer, but Boom Chain was the newest Christian in his group of friends, so he was learning some Bible stories and principles for the first time.

"And you would be right, Boom Chain. Jesus tells Peter to forgive seventy-seven times. Some versions say seventy times seven, which would be four hundred ninety, but what do you think He's really saying? Does Jesus want us to keep track on a piece of paper, and when we've forgiven someone four hundred and ninety times, then we don't have to anymore?"

Through the ensuing discussion, they concluded that Jesus was saying to forgive someone as many times as it takes. The youth thought that could be hard, especially with someone who was constantly doing them wrong.

Rogan left with things to think about. He mused over the situation with Nico Vega. The boy had been a mean bully until Rogan had helped save him from Dead Man's Hole. *Do I need to officially forgive him?* he wondered. Next, he thought again about how some of the church folks mistreated Mr. Hoffman. *I think they need some lessons on forgiveness.*

It was ironic that Rogan had been ruminating about Ben Hoffman, and then the elderly man was again a Sunday lunch guest after church. Their reclusive neighbor was finally feeling more comfortable around the Chaffey family and would contribute to the conversation. At the moment, he was in a discussion with Rogan's dad about some forest management issue. Rogan wasn't really listening, just as background noise. He was examining the man he used to call Crazy Hoffman, and for good reason, out of the corner of his eyes.

Rogan noted the changes in the grizzled old man. His gray hair was still a little stringy, but it was washed instead of greasy. His beard reached the front of his chest but was now neatly trimmed. He always made an effort to wear clean clothes to church and when he was a guest at their house.

His voice isn't so rough and gravelly anymore, Rogan thought. *He just seems like a nice man, in a grandpa sort of way.*

After their guest had left, the Chaffeys all migrated to the living room.

Mrs. Chaffey clapped her hands once. "I'm thinking about Thanksgiving, which is only two weeks away."

"Turkey!" yelled Lainey.

"Turkey!" Peg echoed. "And mashed potatoes."

"Everything we usually have," said Rogan. He'd just eaten but was somehow almost hungry again just talking about it.

"Pumpkin pie and Cool Whip." Jim had a dreamy look on his face.

"Okay, I'll put together a list and scoot to town during the lull we're having in the weather," Elise announced.

"Maybe you could take Carol with you. You know I worry a little when you drive that far all by yourself in the winter. Even though you are an excellent driver," he added.

Rogan's mom smiled and planted a kiss on her husband's cheek. "That's a good idea. I like visiting with her anyway, and she probably needs ingredients for the holidays as well."

* * *

Rogan came home from school the Wednesday before Thanksgiving to a house full of amazing smells. He stood in the mud room, lifted his nose to the warm, scent-laden air, and sniffed just like he'd seen Sitka do a thousand times. He threw his backpack onto a hook and strode to the kitchen.

"Mom, it smells so good in here."

Elise had a swipe of flour on her cheek and some strands of brown hair escaped from her ponytail.

"I'm glad. I've been cooking all day." She turned around toward the sink. She stopped. Quickly turned back. "And no snitching, young man." She pointed a finger at her son.

"Just one little bite? I've been slaving away at school all day, and I *am* a growing boy." Rogan tried for the puppy dog eyes.

Elise laughed. "On the table are some asparagus wraps for snacking, since I know it's hard for everyone to wait."

"Yes!" Rogan popped a couple of the tasty hors d'oeuvres into his mouth. "I'm glad we are on break now. Runt's family is still coming, right?"

"Yes, they are," his mother affirmed.

It was a Chaffey tradition to invite someone over for Thanksgiving dinner. Rogan was glad it was Runt's family this year. He and his friend had planned on spending the morning playing broom hockey on the ice that was now thick enough on Buckbrush Lake. Boom Chain and Tuff would comprise the opposing team. Dinner was always at three o'clock, so it would be plenty of time to build up a stuff-yourself-until-you-can't-eat-anymore appetite.

"Ben Hoffman is also coming."

Rogan stopped chewing for a brief second. "Oh, that's nice. Yeah. Cool."

"What's cool?" His father had just come out of his home office where he'd been working for the day.

"Hey, Dad. We were talking about Mr. Hoffman coming over for our Thanksgiving feast."

"I'm glad he is. I just have a feeling he is close to making a decision for Christ."

"That would be amazing," sighed Elise.

"Indeed," said Jim.

That evening, when they were seated at the table for dinner, Mr. Chaffey recounted what he'd said earlier about Mr. Hoffman. "Let's pray right now for his salvation."

Everyone grabbed the hand of the person next to him or her, and the ones on the end reached across.

"Rogan, would you pray?"

Rogan cleared his throat and opened his eyes back up, glancing at his dad. "Uh, sure." He always got a little nervous praying out loud, even when it was just in front of his family. He cleared his throat again.

"Dear Lord, thank you that Mr. Hoffman has been coming to church and asking questions about You. Please help him to want to become a Christian and accept You into his heart." A pause. "And thanks for the food. Amen." Rogan sighed. "I hope that was okay. I didn't really know what to say." He looked across the table at his parents.

"That was perfect," his dad replied.

His mom nodded. "God knows our hearts, and even if we don't have fancy words, He loves to hear from us."

Rogan smiled softly and dug into the enchiladas they were having for dinner.

The next morning, Rogan and his friends convened at the north end of Buckbrush Lake. The air was frosty enough to make the boys' breath look like puffs of smoke from a steam engine.

"I see everyone has their lucky broom," Rogan said, holding his out. Most of them were a little worse for wear, sporting strips of silver duct tape, cracks, and scuff marks.

Runt held his up. "I think I need to get a new one for next year. All of my…What are they called?" He ran his fingers across the remaining bristles, "Are almost gone."

Tuff laughed. "It's going bald."

Runt snorted. "So, it's called hair?"

Rogan laughed along. "Mine is a little short on…hair, too." His was a standard Rubbermaid broom with a red wooden handle and lines of blue stitching across the brush.

"Well, mine," Boom Chain began in a snobbish voice, "Is the top of the line for broom hockey. It cost me a fortune, but it has been well worth it."

"Yeah, we know the story behind your big purchase," Rogan scoffed good-naturedly.

"I seem to recall you found that in Old Man Tate's trash." Tuff gave Boom Chain a look that said, "You don't fool me."

"Enough yakkin'." Rogan ran a few steps and slid across the ice, arms out for balance.

The boys used two rocks to delineate the goals. For a puck, they had a small rubber playground ball, wrapped in duct tape. Rogan and Runt were teammates.

Runt bent at the waist and placed the end of his dilapidated broom next to the puck, facing off against Tuff. "Okay, big guy, you're going down. Team Terminator is ready to destroy you."

"In your dreams, small guy," Tuff laughed. "We're going to put you in your place. More like Team Loser."

Runt stuck out his chest and stabbed a finger at Tuff. "By no means!" He then added, "Ha! I knew I could use that again."

He was met with shouts of, "Weirdo!"

Boom Chain threw a branch into the air. When it hit the frozen lake, that signaled the start. Tuff managed to get the puck around Runt. He headed toward the goal, Rogan the only defender until Runt could dash back. Rogan held his broom in front of him, resting on the ice, ready to move left or right depending on which way Tuff went. His friend was heading straight for him. Rogan's muscles twitched with anticipation. Tuff batted the puck right and then tried to cut left in a fake out, but he met his match with the icy variable, and his feet ended up in the air. He crashed onto his side, the broom flying from his hands.

Rogan reached out with his broom and snagged the puck. He pushed it along, concentrating on avoiding Tuff's fate.

"Ha! One down already. Rogue, I'm open," yelled Runt as he gingerly sprinted toward the goal. The boys always dispensed with offsides, since it was two on two.

Rogan swung his broom backward and brought it back down to swat the puck, sending it flying to Runt, who skillfully received it.

"Watch out," was all Rogan had time to say.

Runt was looking down at the puck and didn't see Boom Chain's bulk slide in front of him. He turned his face just in time to watch himself plow into his friend, bounce off, and land on the ice on his back. Rogan could hear the air explode out of Runt's lungs. He cringed as his friend lay, trying to suck in some oxygen from lungs that had temporarily seized up.

"Ooh, that one hurt," said Boom Chain. He had no sympathy, however, and stole the puck from Runt, charging down the natural rink. He managed to pass it across to Tuff without Rogan being able to intercept it. Tuff scooted toward the goal. Rogan ran to try and beat Tuff, to get himself between the striker and the goal, but he wasn't sure it would happen. With a final burst of speed, he leaned over and lay on his right hip, sliding with his feet pointed toward the goal. The broom was extended over his head just as Tuff hit the puck with a flick of his broomstick.

Rogan was still sliding when he met the puck. It hit him in the stomach, traveled along with him for a brief moment, then broke free. Rogan's feet entered the goal, his body still extended. He saw the puck, reached out and flicked it from the goal with his hand, and finally came to a stop.

None of the other boys were moving or seemingly breathing. Suddenly, some unseen electric-like jolt shocked them all into action. They scrambled for purchase on the slippery surface. Rogan got his feet under him only to have them slip right back out. He landed on his stomach as the puck came barreling at his head. All he had time to do was duck. It hit him on the top of the head and careened off.

"Ow," he complained, pushing himself up again.

Runt had secured the puck and was slipping his way to their goal. Rogan followed. Tuff was on one side and Boom Chain on the other. Runt would soon be in trouble.

"Back!" Rogan yelled, coming up the middle.

Runt shoved his broom, pushing the puck to Rogan. Rogan touched it once and then slapped it, sending it between the rocks. He slid to a stop.

Runt held his broom over his head. "Yeah!"

"Penalty. High sticking," teased Boom Chain.

"Whatever," Runt shot back. "That was awesome. Did you guys see Rogue?"

"No, Runt. We're only right here, too," Tuff teased. "That was pretty awesome, though."

"Dude. You did that slide perfectly," praised Boom Chain.

"I think I'll have a bruise, but it was worth it. And my head." Rogan rubbed just above his hairline. "You had that puck haulin'." He smiled at Boom Chain.

"It should've gone in, but you had to get in the way," his stocky friend complained.

"Well, my dad always tells me to use my head."

They all laughed, reset the puck at center position, and resumed play. A half an hour later, they took a break to peel off sweatshirts and have a quick drink and snack break.

"My mom sent some Gold Rush Griddle cookies." Rogan passed a plastic baggie around.

"I love these things." Runt's words crumbled around the cookie he was devouring.

"You love anything as long as it's food," Tuff pointed out.

Runt grinned, crumbs and raisins stuck between his teeth.

"Ew! Gross, man." Tuff opened his mouth to show partially-chewed cookie. "See-food!"

Runt grabbed his arms across his chest and cackled. He couldn't help but snort, but it led to choking. When he had hacked a few, he pounded himself on the chest. "That went down the wrong tube." His eyes were watering.

"Quick, while he can't breathe, let's get back at it," Tuff told Boom Chain with a snap of a punch to his arm.

"Not fair," Runt choked out.

"They can't play without both of us, Runt. I'll wait for you to recover."

The sun snuck out from behind the cloud cover, chasing away the white puffs in the sky. It was still just below freezing, but the boys' activity kept them warm in just their T-shirts.

After a couple of hours of rousing play, they tired enough to switch to a goal-shooting contest, which morphed into a distance-shooting contest.

Happily tired and having taken their dose of competition for the day, they loaded up and headed back to their respective homes.

Rogan had a little time to clean up before their company arrived. "Whew," he told himself. "I definitely need a shower."

The hot water seemed to sting his face more than usual. He was fresh and rested by the time Mr. Hoffman, and then the Petersens arrived.

The smell of the golden-baked turkey had been teasing everyone, so they were happy to crowd around a table laden with homemade delights from both families. Mr. Hoffman had arrived with cans of cranberry sauce and a couple of sticks of butter as his contribution.

"Our tradition is to go around and say one thing for which we are thankful." Jim paused. "I'll go first. I'm thankful for God always watching out for us, from helping us through Peter's death, to Rogan and Ben saving Nico, to giving us a wonderful family and great friends."

Rogan watched as heads nodded, and his parents reached over to clasp each other's hands. He smiled, agreeing.

Lainey was next in line. "I'm thankful for some new strawberry Bonnie Bell Lip Smackers." She smiled down at her younger sister sitting next to her. "It's okay, Peg. I forgive you."

Rogan watched as Peg's face lit up. *Just from being told she's forgiven,* he contemplated.

As it got closer to his turn, Rogan was preparing to keep it light and say he was thankful for the food, but when it was his turn, his voice betrayed that. Instead, what came out was, "I'm thankful that we've gotten to know Mr. Hoffman, and that he is here for Thanksgiving. We went through a tough time together this summer, and I just appreciate him." The end of his impromptu speech trailed off with a self-conscious crack in his voice. He swallowed.

Rogan dared a look at his parents. His mom had put her hand over her heart, and his dad was slowly nodding. His eyes traveled to Mr. Hoffman. He was surprised to see a sheen of tears reflect back at him.

The sharing continued until all had contributed. Jim Chaffey said a prayer, and they all began to pile their plates high with traditional Thanksgiving fare. Rogan turned to Runt, who sat next to him. "It's a good thing we played hockey this morning. I'm going to eat until I can't move."

"Me, too. I was going to say that your face got a little red when you were sharing, but it's still red. Come to think of it, mine feels a little hot."

Rogan hadn't really been paying attention to that detail, but now that he looked, he agreed. "You *are* red. I guess we got too much sun today. We're not used to it." Rogan put a cooling hand up to his own cheek. "Oh, well. I can still eat just as much with a red face."

They dug in like starving animals.

After the meal and cleaning up, the adults went to the living room. Rogan and Runt headed upstairs to Rogan's room to watch a DVD on his computer while their food hopefully settled enough to make room for dessert.

Halfway through the movie, they heard a knock on the doorframe. The door was already open, and Rogan's dad stuck his head in. "I wanted to invite you boys downstairs for a minute. I think you should come." He turned and walked away, not waiting for their reactions.

Rogan looked at Runt and hiked an eyebrow. "That's mysterious."

"Yeah. I guess we'd better go check it out."

They paused the movie and went downstairs. The adults were all quietly sitting on the couches. Rogan noticed tissues in Carol's and in his mom's hands.

Uh oh. He looked at Runt, but his friend seemed oblivious. *What is going on?* he thought, then realized the ladies looked happy, not sad.

Runt flopped down on an open section of the couch, and Rogan sat next to him.

"We thought you might like to be a part of this," said Jim. He glanced at Mr. Hoffman. "Ben here has made up his mind about something."

The boys' eyes swiveled to the old man.

"Well, hmm. I've decided it's time to ask Jesus into my heart."

Rogan gasped. His slightly crooked smile hurried onto his face. "Really?" Mr. Hoffman nodded. "That's awesome."

"We're getting ready to pray the prayer. Ben, you said earlier that you didn't know what to say. If you want, I can pray, and you can just repeat after me."

"Alrighty, sounds good." Their neighbor shifted in his seat.

"All right. Let's bow our heads." Jim led with a thanks to God for Mr. Hoffman and his decision. "Okay, here we go. Dear Lord."

Rogan bowed his head to pray. He couldn't stop smiling.

Ben Hoffman croaked out an echoing, "Dear Lord."

"I admit that I am a sinner in need of Your saving grace."

Mr. Hoffman continued to echo as Mr. Chaffey prayed in chunks.

"The Bible says all have sinned and fall short of the glory of God. It also says the wages of sin is death, but the gift of God is eternal life. I believe that Jesus died on the cross for my sins."

As Mr. Hoffman repeated the prayer, a bubbling joy percolated in Rogan's chest. *Who would've thought, even just this summer, that this would ever happen? Thank you, God,* Rogan rejoiced.

The two men continued, "I ask You to come into my heart and cleanse me from sin. Thank You for welcoming me into Your kingdom as a child of God. Amen."

Rogan opened his eyes to see Ben Hoffman's remained tightly closed. He could see tracks of tears down the old man's weathered face.

"Is that it?" Ben asked.

Jim laughed, full of witnessing new-life joy. "That's it."

Mr. Hoffman opened his eyes. "Well, that was easy."

Everyone laughed as they spontaneously clapped. Ben Hoffman's smile transformed his face. Rogan had never personally witnessed anyone other than his sisters become a Christian. For Mr. Hoffman, it seemed to make him glow. Rogan stared, transfixed. "That was awesome." He and Runt fist bumped.

"Whew. Well, what now?" Ben wanted to know.

"Now you keep learning, reading your Bible, praying, being with fellow believers," Jim explained.

"I feel like I have a lot to learn, but I also feel so light, so happy. I guess I wasn't too bad of a person to be accepted."

"God doesn't work that way, fortunately for us. He forgives us all our sins, no matter how bad we think they are, and then He forgets them." Jim smiled.

"Wow. I get to go to heaven now?" Mr. Hoffman's face had an incredulous expression. His eyes darted from Jim to Elise to Monty to Carol.

"Yes, you do," Elise said with a soft smile.

"Yes, you do!" Jim yelled enthusiastically. Everyone clapped again.

Conversation ceased as everyone seemed to bask in the moment of a miracle. Rogan's chest swelled again with the joy of it.

Elise sighed a happy-sounding sigh and clapped once as she rose onto her feet. "Who's ready for pie?"

Rogan and Runt took theirs, heaped with Cool Whip, back to Rogan's room to finish watching the movie. He had trouble concentrating because he kept thinking about what had just transpired. In a short amount of time, Rogan noticed his eyes were feeling scratchy and they also burned. He reached up and rubbed them, commenting about it.

"Dude. Mine hurt, too. What's up?" Runt was rubbing his too.

By the end of the movie, both boys' eyes were watering and red. They wandered downstairs with their empty plates.

"Mom, Runt and I both have something wrong with our eyes. They hurt." Rogan opened them wide to show his mom.

"Oh, wow. They're really red. Carol? You think it's from the sun today?"

"I'll bet it is. When that sun bounces off the snow and ice…and look how sunburned their faces are," Mrs. Petersen agreed.

"Somebody going snow blind?" Jim had come in on the last part of the conversation.

"What? We're going to go blind?" Runt's voice was a higher pitch than normal.

Rogan shared his friend's worry.

Monty was right behind Jim. "Don't worry, Son. We'll get you a seeing eye dog."

"What?"

"Oh, don't tease, Monty," Carol admonished. "Look at the boys. You've got them worried."

"It's called snow blindness, but it really doesn't make you go blind," Jim explained.

"Usually," Monty cut in with a grin.

"Dad." Runt was exasperated.

"Jim's right. It's like a sunburn on your eyes. Kind of like your red faces. You probably should've been wearing sunglasses while you were playing hockey today. The light reflects off the snow and ice."

"We didn't realize it was going to be so sunny." Rogan reached up to rub his watery eyes.

"Don't rub them. Let's put a cool compress on. I think I have some eyedrops, too." Elise grimaced. "It looks painful."

"It is," Rogan agreed.

"We should call Tuff and Boom Chain and see if they have it too," Runt suggested.

Rogan dialed each of their friends and put the phone on speaker. Tuff reported his face wasn't fried, probably because he had darker skin, but his eyes were. Boom Chain was as miserable as Rogan and Runt.

By the time the Petersens and Mr. Hoffman left for the night, the boys' eyelids were swelling up.

"Great," Runt said. "At least we don't have to go to school for a few days. That would be embarrassing."

"For sure," Rogan agreed. "Good luck getting any sleep tonight. Oh, man. My eyes feel like they've got sand in them."

"Mine, too. 'Night, Rogue. It's been nice knowin' ya. I might keel over from the pain tonight." Runt waved, his eyes squinted and watering, as he headed out the door with his family.

"I'm going to get that cool compress," said Rogan. "Goodnight, everybody."

CHAPTER 15

Flight of the Pink Bird

ROGAN WAS BARELY ABLE TO OPEN HIS SCRATCHY AND gooped-up eyes the next morning. Stumbling out of bed, he headed to the bathroom sink to splash water on his face and squinted at himself in the mirror. He gasped. His face was bright red and swollen like a puffy tomato. His eyes were watering, sending a salty stream down each cheek. He reached up and poked his fat eyelid with a finger. His hand went to his cheek. Unusual warmth radiated onto his palm.

"Oh, man. I'm a sight," he whispered to himself in the mirror. "I hope I didn't damage something." He poked his eyelid again, wanting to rub his eye, but remembering not to.

He padded down the stairs. His mom was cooking breakfast, and his dad was drinking coffee at the table. His dad glanced up as Rogan entered, started to say, "Good morn…" did a double take, and choked out, "Whoa."

Startled, his mom turned around, spatula in hand, and froze. "Oh, Honey." She cleared her throat and used a voice Rogan recognized as trying for diplomacy. "That looks painful."

"It is. Please tell me it isn't irreversible damage." Rogan was concerned, but his dad looked like he was trying to choke back a laugh.

"It's a bad sunburn, but you'll recover. You kind of look like—"

Elise cleared her throat again and shook the spatula at her husband. "Be nice, Jim." Then, to Rogan, "I have some aloe you should put on your face."

"I wonder if the other guys look as bad as I do. I'm calling them." Rogan walked over and grabbed the handset, dialing Runt first.

Runt's mom answered. "Runt's face is all swollen up today, Rogan. Is yours, too?"

"Yep. I'm afraid so."

"Sorry. Well, here he is."

"Oh, man, Rogue." Runt's voice was scratchy like he'd just gotten out of bed. "I look hideous. My face is all puffed up and even redder than last night. What about you?"

"Same. My eyes aren't quite as scratchy, but they still hurt, especially in the light. I just might wear sunglasses today, even in the house."

They conspired to call Tuff and Boom Chain, and then all meet at the Chaffey's for a snow blind face reunion at ten o'clock. When they all arrived, the boys could not stop pointing at each other and laughing.

"You don't even look like yourself, Runt. I wouldn't know it was you except for your hair," Rogan exclaimed.

"And your height," Boom Chain teased.

"You should talk," Runt retorted. He wiped his cheeks. "Ugh. My eyes won't stop watering."

Boom Chain looked at his friends. "Your face isn't too bad, Tuff, but your eyes practically glow red. It's creepy."

Tuff made a scary face, held up his hands like claws, and slowly crept toward Boom Chain.

"We've got to get a picture of this." Rogan turned and headed upstairs to get his camera.

His mom was happy to snap photos of four laughing boys with red, swollen faces, being silly for the camera.

"Well, hopefully we look normal by Sunday. I can hide out until then, so no one sees me like this." Runt looked at his friends, feigned horror, and ran a few steps away, screaming like a little kid and waving his hands back and forth.

"You look like a demented T-rex," Rogan laughed, "But you're right. After church Sunday is the community sledding party. We don't want to miss that."

"I'm going to slather my face with sunscreen this time," Runt announced.

"And wear sunglasses," Tuff added. "My eyes can't take any more of this."

The four boys passed the day commiserating and hanging out, eating Thanksgiving leftovers.

By Sunday, the swelling and redness in their faces had dissipated. During the prayer and praise time at church, Mr. Chaffey stood to share the good news of Mr. Hoffman accepting Jesus. Ben had said he felt more comfortable with Rogan's dad sharing the news.

Rogan felt happy and proud of his neighbor, but the congregation met the announcement with silence. Confused, Rogan looked around. Many people were either staring straight ahead or openly glaring at Mr. Hoffman.

Stunned, Rogan's heart and mind both stuttered. *What is going on?* His mom and Mrs. Petersen must've had the same idea because they both stood and began clapping. The pastor joined in, and then a smattering of applause sounded, hollow in the echo of a sanctuary that should've been filled with celebration.

Rogan watched with consternation as Ben Hoffman slowly stood, eyes downcast and hands gripping his hat. Without a word, he turned and hurried out.

Another silence descended.

Rogan looked over at his dad, wondering if they should go after Mr. Hoffman, but his dad seemed to read his mind and put his hand out in a gesture of "stop" and shook his head.

The pastor was saying something, perhaps admonishing the congregation, but Rogan felt like he was underwater and couldn't quite hear correctly. The top of his head spun like a top, making him a little dizzy. He grabbed the back of the pew in front of him and sat heavily into his seat.

What had just happened? These people are supposed to be God-loving Christians. Anger fell over him like the flakes of snow fluttering down outside.

Church seemed to last forever, and Rogan couldn't concentrate on the sermon. Afterward, his family sat in the car while his dad spoke with Pastor Greg. No one said a word, even Lainey who always had something to prattle on about. When Jim finally joined them in the rig, he looked at Elise, put the 4Runner in gear, and quietly drove home.

They entered their home in silence and went about the task of getting lunch ready in a void of sound.

Finally, when they were all seated and ready to eat, Lainey softly queried, "Are we still going sledding?"

"Yes, Lainey, we are." Jim sighed. "I'm sorry you kids had to witness adults acting that way. It definitely wasn't godly."

"I feel so bad for Mr. Hoffman." Rogan set his fork down. "Why would they do that? Is he going to be okay?"

"I know people still see him as the old him, mean and cranky. But still, we are supposed to forgive as God forgave us. Nobody's perfect and God *has* changed him."

"That's exactly what we have been talking about in Sunday School with Pastor Newby." Rogan sighed. "I hope Mr. Hoffman doesn't change his mind about being a Christian."

His parents nodded, their faces grim.

They gathered their sledding equipment of large, used inner tubes, and this lightened the mood a bit. By the time they were packed up, Rogan was looking forward to the fun ahead, and Lainey was back to her chatty self.

The tubing hill was south of town, and everyone could drive right to a snow-covered parking lot. From there, it was a short hike that seemed longer when carrying tubes, gear, thermoses, and coolers. There would be a huge, shared communal pot of chili over a gas-fueled, single burner as well as a wood fire to warm themselves by and to roast marshmallows over. A few designated community members had brought snow machines so they could haul people up to the top of the tubing hill. It was that or a decent hike. Rogan and his friends usually didn't want to wait around for the ferry service. He was glad he wouldn't have to face some of the churchgoers who had shunned Mr. Hoffman as this was a community-wide event, and he could easily avoid them if he wished. Some of them were older and never came to things like this, anyway.

Rogan quickly found his friends, and they headed up the hill, tubes slung over their shoulders like they were carrying a huge donut. They wanted to be some of the first ones up.

Rogan looked at his friends and chuckled. "Nice shades, guys." He touched the corner of his own goggles.

"There's no way I'm going through that torture again," Runt exclaimed.

"Me, neither," Tuff agreed. "My eyes still hurt a little."

"At least our faces aren't swollen anymore," Boom Chain added. "That was embarrassing."

Rogan stopped, put his tube on the ground, and stepped one foot into the middle of it, so it didn't run away from him. It was lightly snowing, and there was a layer of fresh snow on the tubing run. He knew it would be slower-going the first few runs, and then turn icy-slick by the end of the afternoon with so many people packing it down.

Without waiting for his buddies, he grabbed the inner tube on both sides, ran forward and launched himself down the hill, belly flopping onto his tube. He went about six feet and his tube stopped behind a wall of powdery snow that had built up in front of his tube like a pile from a snowplow. The sudden stopping jolt threw him forward, and he face planted. Rogan didn't have time to recover when Runt and his tube crashed into him from behind, making him face plant again. He heard Runt cackling with laughter and then a snort, but he couldn't see anything. He stood up, removed a glove, and wiped the snow from the lenses of his goggles just in time to see Boom Chain and Tuff headed toward them.

Rogan jumped out of the way as they both crashed into Runt. Runt bumper-car-ed into Rogan's tube, sending it flying down the hill.

"There goes my ride," Rogan good-naturedly complained.

"Too bad," yelled Boom Chain as he picked up his tube, circumvented the pile-up, sat down in the middle hole of the tube, and continued on. He made it a few more feet and then had to pump his legs and scoot the tube, trail-blazing as he went.

"Runt, give me a ride." Rogan didn't wait for an answer but hopped on one side and scooted his friend over, so both of them rode on their stomachs, each on one side. The added weight helped, and they caught up to Boom Chain. They bumped into him, and each grabbed one of his shoulders. They picked up a little speed and made it to the flat area at the base of the hill before Tuff caught up to them.

Tubers were coming behind them already, so they grabbed their rides and got out of the way. Rogan's driverless tube had veered off course, and he had to retrieve it, slogging through knee-deep snow.

The snowplow always scraped the snow into a large pile at the base of the hill as a safety backstop, should anyone overshoot the landing area.

By the third run, the tubes were moving much faster. Rogan was trekking his way up the side of the run, and halfway to the top, came across Lainey and Peg, standing there with one tube they were sharing.

"Not yet," Lainey said to her sister, "But be ready."

"Are you going to tube from here?" Rogan asked.

Lainey looked up at her brother. "Yeah. Will you give us a push when no one's coming?"

"Sure. Hop on and be ready." He handed his tube to Runt.

"What am I, your caddie?"

Rogan gave his friend a quick grin, then bent over and pushed his sisters onto the run. "Have fun," he yelled as they left behind their squeals in the chill air.

On the next run, he was the lead in a train made up of him and his three friends. They sat in the tubes and grabbed the feet of the person behind them, tucking their boots under each armpit and hanging on. They began to slide, four links in a chain.

"Hey, can we join?"

Rogan twisted his head around to see Cory Boots and Thorin Knight.

"Hurry up. Grab on."

The two boys ran and jumped onto their tubes, paddling the snow with their arms on each side. They managed to catch up, and Boom Chain grabbed Cory's feet while Thorin hooked on as the caboose.

Halfway down the run, there was a bump developing. The surface was getting slicker, so combined with the weight of their train, they moved at a good clip.

Rogan saw it coming. "Here it comes."

There was a slight compression of the tube as it hit the front side of the jump. Rogan was momentarily blinded by a spray of snow but felt himself go airborne. He managed to keep hold of Runt's legs as the tube bounced back to earth with a small jarring thump.

"Woohoo!" he yelled.

They floated to a stop at the bottom, laughing as they gathered their blown-up rides. As he moved to the side, Rogan saw the bright pink of his mother's jacket as she made the run with Peg sitting on her lap. His mom had a big smile on her face, but Peg's looked more like a grimace.

It's a little too fast for Peg's liking, Rogan thought. *Someday she'll like the speed. Maybe.*

Ready for the next run, the teenagers stood on the crest of the hill to catch their breath after the hike up.

"Let's go individually, lined up across, and make it a race," Rogan suggested.

Runt smacked the side of his tube, making a wobbly, Jell-O-jiggling *whump* sound. "Game on, Chaffey."

They lined up, holding their tubes in front.

"Hey, step back, Tuff. You're cheating," Boom Chain complained right as Rogan yelled, "Go!"

Rogan was zipping down the run, ice crystals assaulting his cheeks. His tube twisted around, so he was now facing up the hill. He could see he was ahead of most of the boys except Boom Chain, who pulled even with him. He saw Cory and Runt collide, which sent Runt shooting sideways toward some trees that lined the swath where they tubed. Rogan sucked in a quick breath as he saw Runt heading for danger, but the unpacked snow slowed his friend's speed, and Runt rolled off with plenty of feet to spare. Rogan's tube was twisting around again.

A lone figure stood at the bottom with its back to the hill. Rogan was on a trajectory to go near whoever it was. He had a quick thought that the person should have moved out of the way and paid more attention. He yelled, "Look out!"

The figure jerked like he'd been electrified and turned just as Rogan slid past him with barely a foot to spare. The face under the hood was Martin Wolfe. That thought barely registered when Cory, sideways on his tube, barreled into Martin, taking his feet right out from under him and flipping him up and over Cory's tube. Martin spun like a rag doll in the air before landing on his back. His feet came up and over his head and he folded nearly in half.

Rogan jumped off his tube and managed to grab one of Martin's feet, dragging him to the side just as another tuber whizzed by the boy's head.

"Great save," yelled Runt, who had recovered from his own spill and made it the rest of the way down. He kicked his and Rogan's tubes to the side.

Martin moaned and slowly got to his hands and knees, paused to catch his breath, and finally stood. He had snow caked on the hood of his coat and all down his back.

He glared at Cory. "You idiot. Watch where you're going."

"How about you get out of the way, moron?" Cory snapped back. "I can't steer the tube."

Martin sent a pretty strong death glare in Cory's direction. Rogan gave it an eight out of ten, then watched as Martin stalked off, snatching his tube on the way.

Cory waited until Martin was out of earshot. "Couldn't have happened to a better guy."

Most of the boys guffawed at that. Rogan sighed. The boy just seemed to invite ridicule.

Tuff bounced his inner tube. "I'm ready for some chili. What about you guys?"

"I'm first in line." Runt took off running.

There was a rough-hewn log bench, currently unoccupied, so the teens carried their bowls of hearty chili heaped with cheddar cheese and a dollop of sour cream over there to sit down while they ate.

The activity seemed to be winding down. Some families had already packed up and left. The sky softened with waning light. Rogan raised his goggles, perching them on his forehead. It looked a little darker out without the yellow tint of his lenses.

As they ate, they watched other tubers. A train of six tubes was careening down the glassy run, picking up quite a bit of speed. Laughter and delighted shouts wiggled through the air. Rogan saw a flash of bright pink near the front as it whizzed by. He stood, bowl in one hand and spoon in the other. He watched as the train had too much momentum to stop on the flats and hurtled toward the snow berm. The first tubes hit the incline and squirted up into the air, catapulted by the weight of those behind them.

Time somehow slowed for Rogan as a bright pink bird flew for a light moment before crashing down under the frothing wave of people and tubes.

He force-swallowed his mouthful of chili. Someone's laughter echoed. Rogan watched as his dad disentangled from the collision and began pushing people out of the way.

"Move over. Let me through!" Jim yelled. The sound came to Rogan floating in a bubble. He still hadn't moved. His numbed mind and paralyzed body saw his dad kneel before a sprawled-out, unmoving figure in bright pink.

Without conscious thought, his bowl of chili dropped onto the snow with a Styrofoam crack, and he found himself running toward his parents. It was like running with concrete boots, and his lungs couldn't seem to pull in enough air. He faintly heard someone behind him call his name. There was a question mark attached.

Up ahead, some people had run to the bottom of the slope and were frantically waving, trying to get the attention of the tubers waiting to come down. One jumped on a snow machine and headed up the hill.

He was finally almost there. Mrs. Drake, one of his teachers, turned around, her hands over her mouth. She looked distressed.

Rogan dropped to his knees by his mom. She lay on her back, arms and legs lying carelessly on the snow. Her bottom lip was trembling, and tears leaked from the outside corners of her eyes, dripping into the icy snow. His dad was saying something.

Sound came rushing back, attacking his eardrums as he heard his own anguished shout, "Mom!"

Her eyes darted to her son, then quickly returned to her husband. "I…I can't move."

"Everybody, stand back…please. Give us some room."

Behind him, Rogan heard Mrs. Petersen say, "Stay here, Timothy," and then she started praying out loud.

Rogan peered at his dad's face, which looked painted with torment. "Dad, what's wrong?"

Jim spoke to Elise. "Okay. We'll take care of you. We won't move anything yet." He reached up and caressed her cheek, wiping her tears. He tucked a single strand of hair back under her hat. "Does anybody have a blanket or a sleeping bag?"

Someone yelled, "I do," as he raced toward the vehicles.

"Just try to breathe, Sweetheart," Jim encouraged.

Rogan needed the reminder as well, and he gulped some air. He looked down. He was still gripping his plastic spoon in a stranglehold. He tossed it aside.

"Rogan, squeeze Mom's toe on her foot."

As Rogan slid over by her feet, his dad said to his injured wife, "Let me know if you feel it, okay?" He nodded to Rogan.

Rogan flung off his gloves and squeezed. Nothing. He tried the other foot. Nothing.

"Jim, I can't feel it." Rogan had never heard his mom's voice sound panicked before, and it was truly disconcerting.

"How about this?" Jim was squeezing her left hand.

"I can feel it a little, but my arm is all tingly and it makes my hand feel numb."

The helpful man returned with a blanket which they spread over Rogan's mom. Just looking at her lying there burned the back of Rogan's eyes. He wasn't one to cry very often, but he felt the tears coming.

Oh, Lord. Please, help my mom to be okay. Please, help my mom to be okay. His shocked brain could only pray in a repetitive loop.

"Dad, what can we do?"

"I saw Sam here earlier. Does anyone see him?" Jim inquired of the concerned crowd. Sam was one of the town's first responders.

"Oh, he was over getting some chili. I'll run and get him," said another helpful citizen.

God, we've already had one tragedy. Please, don't let it happen again. Rogan felt a wave of nausea filtrate his torso. He was afraid he was going to puke.

Mrs. Petersen came closer. "I'm taking the girls home with us. Just let us know what else we can do, besides pray."

"Thank you, Carol," Rogan's mom choke-sobbed. "Tell them I'll be okay, so they don't worry."

"I'll stay and help," Monty told his wife, and to Runt, "You go with your mom."

Rogan felt totally helpless, just sitting there. It seemed to take an eternity for Sam to arrive, but when he did, he was carrying a backboard and a cervical collar so they could immobilize her spine. Just a few short months ago, Rogan had watched them place one on Mr. Hoffman after his four-wheeler wreck. Now they did the same for his mother.

While they packaged her up, Sam asked, "Do you want us to call the chopper?" He looked at Rogan's dad. "They may not come now that it's almost dark and snowing harder."

Indeed, the flakes were large and falling quickly. Rogan hadn't noticed the light of day sneak away. His stomach churned and twisted. He had the rancid taste of fear filling his mouth. An involuntary hiccup of grief escaped.

Elise's eyes had been closed, but she now gazed at her son. "Be strong, Rogan. God will help us."

All he could do was nod, unable to trust his voice to not shatter into a million pieces if he tried to use it. *Please, God. Please.*

"I think it will be faster getting her to the clinic if we load her up in our 4Runner. We'll put the seats down, and we can fit her in on the backboard. Rogan and I will drive her to the clinic. It will take the helicopter at least an hour to get here if it can come at all. By that time, we'll be more than halfway there. It would take another hour to fly her there, so I think this will be faster."

Rogan heard his dad almost whisper, "I hope I'm making the right decision."

His dad looked around. "Rogan, go put the seats and tailgate down. I've got plenty of help to carry her." Jim tossed him the keys, and Rogan took off running, glad to finally take some action.

He had things ready by the time the litter bearers arrived and gently placed his mom in the back. He felt like his heart rate would never return to normal, it was thumping so fast. Dread squeezed his chest, and he felt the unreality of it all trying to trick him as he clambered into the passenger seat and they took off for the almost two-hour drive, especially in these conditions, to town.

Rogan twisted around in his seat. "Mom, we're going to get you help. Hang in there. Do you need anything?"

Her voice seemed weaker and floated forward to him. "I'm okay, Rogan. Thanks. I'm just going to rest. And pray."

"I'm praying, too."

"I know you are. Thank you."

"We never should have had so many in the train that late in the day when it was so slick. How could I have been so stupid?" Jim punched the steering wheel. "I'm so sorry, Elise." Even his voice cracked, and that shot a new arrow of pain through Rogan's heart.

He had to turn away from his father's anguish or he was really going to lose it.

"It's not your fault. We were all just having fun." A pause. A sob. "I'm scared, Jim. What if I'm paralyzed?"

At that, Rogan lost the fight, and the tears flowed down his face. He kept himself turned to the passenger window and tried to sniff quietly. Rogan felt a comforting hand clamp onto his shoulder. He looked over to see silent tears tracking down his father's face, too. They shared a knowing look, and Rogan nodded, understanding his dad felt the same fear. He also knew by silent pact that they were going to be brave for his mom. He sucked in a deep breath.

Black darkness was coming. The headlights shone ahead of them, reflecting off the compact snow and ice on the roadway. Flakes fell in a crowd, making an optical illusion like they were moving through a tunnel with shots of snow streaming at them.

Rogan looked at his dad again. His knuckles were almost white, he gripped the steering wheel so tightly. He was gritting his teeth so hard Rogan could see his jaw muscle stand out in a ridge. Rogan's stomach cramped anew.

"Mom, how's the temperature? Are you hot? Cold? Can I get you some water?" He wanted to say something to divert the path of his thoughts.

"Water would be nice, thanks."

Rogan unbuckled his seat belt and awkwardly maneuvered himself between the front bucket seats and into the back without stepping on the supine figure. He grabbed a plastic bottle of water from the stash they always kept in the rig and twisted off the cap. He paused, considering.

"This might be tricky, Mom. I'll try not to spill it all over you. Between the bumpy road and you strapped to the backboard…"

She smiled. "I won't hold it against you." She opened her mouth. "Cheep, cheep."

Rogan had to smile at that. "You're amazing, Mom. All of this going on and you're cracking jokes."

"I have to, or I'll go crazy if I dwell on it."

They sobered up again. Rogan carefully tilted the container and dribbled some water into his mom's mouth. She swallowed, and they repeated the process, not spilling too much. Rogan used a towel to dry the droplets that got away.

"Thanks, honey." She let out a sigh. "I'm going to try and rest now."

"Okay, Mom. I'll just stay back here in case you need something."

The silence that followed seemed to suck everything into a black hole, only broken by the thunking of the wipers. The snow fell, and the tension coursed through their bodies. Rogan kept staring at his mother's face, looking for signs that she was still breathing.

About half an hour into the interminable trip, Mr. Chaffey released a soft, "Whoa." Rogan felt the 4Runner slide sideways. Their progress slowed.

Rogan leaned forward and whispered, "Slick roads?"

"Yes, and it keeps getting worse. As if we didn't have enough going on. Lord, help us." The last part was a fervent prayer.

The stressful drive went on and on, but they stayed on the road-way. Elise dozed fitfully, woke, drank, cried, and went back to dozing. Rogan did what he could to help her. She tried not to complain, but the backboard was quite uncomfortable on her shoulders and neck where she still had some feeling.

Finally, peeking out of the snowstorm, they could see the lights from the houses on the outskirts of town. Minutes later, Jim pulled into the parking lot of the health clinic. "Oh, no."

"What's wrong, Dad?"

"I forgot to have someone call ahead, since it's after hours."

Thoughts of running through the storm to a stranger's house and asking to use the telephone flew through Rogan's mind, but as they pulled under the awning, a warm yellow light cut through the dark. A man wearing sea-green scrubs exited, propping open the door. He was followed by one more man and two ladies, rolling a transport stretcher.

When questioned, the man said, "Someone named Monty called to let us know you were coming."

With everyone helping, they efficiently unloaded Elise, scared and in pain from being strapped to the backboard, and wheeled her inside. Rogan listened to his dad give the medical staff a run-down of what had happened. All the while, his dad had his hand on his mom's head, comforting her. Rogan watched as tears again leaked down the sides of her face.

Rogan choked out, "Bathroom?"

Luckily there was one close by. Rogan ran in, shut the door, and barely made it to the toilet before his heaving stomach let loose. After he repeatedly retched, Rogan had the exhausted thought that he was glad he hadn't eaten much of his chili. He leaned over, both hands on the sides of the sink, and glanced in the mirror. He was a bit shocked at his appearance.

Despite the sunburn from a few days ago, his skin had a pale, greenish cast. He had dark circles under his eyes and a strange tint in his chocolatey-brown eyes. The steely squeeze of his heart created a pain. A pain from his past. A pain from losing his brother, Peter. A pain he couldn't endure again.

What if Mom is paralyzed and never walks again? He couldn't help the traitorous thought. Rogan hung his head. *Please, Lord. We need a miracle. I'm here again, begging you.* More tears leaked out.

When he'd splashed water on his face and rinsed the acrid taste out of his mouth, he walked back out into the hall. The exam room was empty. He felt a jolt of panic. *Where is everyone?*

One of the nurses found him, offered some 7UP for his reeling stomach, and took him to a more comfortable waiting room where he joined his dad. He found out that they were taking his mom in for x-rays, checking for damage to her spine. Jim reached out and pulled Rogan into a hug. They stood like that for a long minute. Rogan felt more tears escape and melt into his dad's sweatshirt.

His dad tightened his grip on his son and began to pray out loud. "God, we really need You, here. Please, help Elise to recover from this accident with no damage to her spine. We may be asking for a miracle." His dad's voice cracked. Rogan squeezed him tighter. "But if we need a miracle, that's what we're asking for. Please."

Time stretched out, each minute lasting way too long. The nurse practitioner finally came with news. "The x-rays all look good. There aren't any broken bones in her spine or neck."

Rogan felt like he was floating, pumped up by relief.

"Is she still paralyzed?" Jim asked.

"She is."

Rogan crashed back down to earth.

"We are pretty sure she has cervical radiculopathy, or a pinched a nerve in her neck, and that's what's causing her numbness and paralysis. She's already beginning to feel pain in her shoulder and down one arm, so that is encouraging. We would need to do an MRI to be sure, but of course, we don't have one on the island. The closest medical facility that does would be in Ketchikan."

"So, what do you recommend?"

"Right now, we have given her some muscle relaxants, anti-inflammatory medicine, and she needs to rest. We aren't a hospital, as you know, but with our unique circumstances of serving the island, we do have rooms for overnight stays. I think she should remain here for at least three days so we can monitor her progress. We'll most likely end up giving her some steroid injections at some point, but right now it really is a 'wait and see' situation."

Rogan watched his dad's face as he nodded. "Thank the Lord she didn't break her neck," he said to no one in particular. He turned to the nurse practitioner. "Thank you. That sounds like as good of news as we can be hearing right now. Is she settled in yet? Can we go see her?"

"Almost. I'll have the nurse come get you when your wife is ready."

Jim reached out and shook his hand. "Thank you so much, again."

When they were alone again, Jim wiped his hands down his face.

"So, she'll be okay, Dad?"

"It sounds promising, Rogan. We'll just keep praying her through it."

"That's good news. I was so worried."

"Me too, Son. Me, too."

After more waiting, they were allowed to see her. It was another shock to see his mother lying there, looking helpless. She was no longer strapped to a backboard, but still wore a white cervical collar around her neck, and she had an IV in her arm. It went against how he usually saw her, which was active, strong, and independent. It felt good, however, to be able to talk with her. She looked tired and needed rest after a crazy day, so they left her sooner than Rogan wanted.

"Where are we going to go for the night, Dad?"

"Good question. I hadn't thought that far ahead. Let's see if we can get a hotel at this late hour. I'd also like to call the Petersens and update them; see how the girls are doing."

A fitful night's sleep and six inches of fresh snow later, Rogan and his dad were back at the health clinic. They were relieved to hear that

Elise had regained feeling in both arms and legs, though her hands and feet were still tingly, and she was very weak.

"I'm just so thankful to be able to wiggle my toes again," she admitted to her family.

"We're praying that it just keeps on improving." Jim reached down and hugged her.

Rogan grabbed her hand until it was his turn for a hug.

"I can feel that!" She smiled.

After speaking with the nurse practitioner and having a family discussion, they decided that Rogan and his dad would head back, get the girls from the Petersens, and go home. Jim would pack up some clothes and necessities for his wife and head back to town. Rogan would watch his sisters, and they could all go back to school. Elise was expected to be released in three days.

Around two o'clock, Rogan reluctantly said goodbye. They gassed up the 4Runner and headed home in a light snow. The roads around town had been plowed since last night's snowfall, but the farther they drove, the more the roads deteriorated. The 4Runner had been in four-wheel drive all winter so far, but the roads were slick under the fresh covering of white.

The trip passed mostly in silence. Rogan thought he should probably let his dad concentrate on driving with the roads being so squirrely. Rogan's mind was lost in thoughts and prayers, anyway.

Suddenly, his head bobbed forward, hitting his chest, and waking him up. "Whoa. I didn't realize I'd fallen asleep."

"It's okay. I'm sure you're tired. I am, too."

"Where are we? It's hard to tell with the snow making it dark a little early."

"It's taken us longer to get home than it did to get to town. The roads are really slick, so I've had to go a lot slower."

Rogan leaned forward and peered into the fading light. "Oh, wow." He yawned.

"We are only about three miles out now."

"That's not too bad," Rogan said just a split second too soon.

His dad barely had time to utter an exclamation of surprise when the back end of the 4Runner swept around to the driver's side. His dad tried to turn into the slide, and Rogan gripped the armrest on the door with his right hand, reaching forward to brace against the dash with his left. All vestiges of sleep ran screaming from his mind.

The fishtailing rig couldn't stop on the compact snow and ice. Rogan felt disoriented in the dark and couldn't tell where the ditch was as the 4Runner slid. There was an abrupt sideways jolt as the rear end gave up what tentative grip it had on the road and dropped into the ditch. The suspension creaked from the compression. They kept going for another couple of feet and then struck something hard and stopped. Rogan's adrenaline tingled as the vehicle tipped precariously, carried by its sideways momentum. He felt suspended in space and time until the rig decided to remain upright and settled back down on all four tires. The headlights pointed straight ahead into the forest on the opposite side of the road. Incongruously, the snow still fell peacefully.

"Rogan, are you okay?"

"I am, Dad. Are you?"

"Bumped my noggin on the window, but other than that, I'm good." Jim sighed. "Great. This is just what I want to deal with right now."

"I'm sorry, Dad." Rogan's stomach was churning again. He pushed a fist into his midsection, trying to stem the nausea.

"Well, I always try to teach you kids to adapt and overcome, so let's step out and see what we've got." Jim turned off the engine but left the headlights on.

Rogan donned his coat and opened his door. He couldn't quite tell how far down the ground was, so he eased himself out carefully. He must've landed on one side of the ditch because his feet slipped downward. Luckily, he was still holding on to the doorframe. He was now up to his knees in snow.

I should've worn my ski pants for the trip home, I guess, he thought as the wet and cold seeped into his blue jeans. Too late now.

"What does it look like on your side?" his dad hollered across.

"The back tire's on the ground, pretty much in the bottom of the ditch. It looks like we're high centered on the edge of the road."

"Yep. That's what it looks like from over here. We ran into a big rock. That's what stopped us. Looks like it dented up the rim a little but hopefully the wheel is okay, and the tire can still hold air. Let's get back in the rig."

It was difficult to reenter the 4Runner due to its position and the snow. Once inside, Mr. Chaffey admitted to Rogan that there was no way they were digging out of this one. He decided they'd wait and see if someone else came along who could give them a lift.

"We'll have to bring someone back who has a winch to pull us out. Let me know when you start to get cold, Rogue, and I'll turn on the heater for a while."

"Sure, Dad."

They passed the time talking about Mrs. Chaffey, school, plans for future adventures, and more. Time seemed to go backward instead of forward. No headlights in shining armor arrived to rescue them.

"Well, it's been an hour and a half. I hate to say it, but I think we get to hike home." Jim looked at his son.

"Good thing we have a flashlight and some water," Rogan stated. "I think I'll put my ski pants on over my wet jeans. It'll keep me warmer."

They gathered clothes and supplies and prepared for their trek. Rogan saw his dad grab his .45 from the console and shrug into the shoulder holster before putting on his jacket. They each armed themselves with a flashlight or headlamp and set off down the snowy, icy road.

Rogan was grateful he had on his warm winter gear. The night was still and crisp. Their boots crunched on the road. Their breath puffed out, lingering in the beams of light.

Rogan had to hurry along to keep up with the brisk pace, even on the slippery ground, set by his dad. He gave himself a pep talk. *You can do this. You won't complain, and you'll keep up.*

The faint outlines of the trees were eerie shadows lined up to stare at them as they strode along. Rogan tried to do some calculations in his head. *Let's see. If we can walk a ten-minute mile, and we have three miles, that should only take us around a half an hour. Okay, that's not so bad.* He picked up his pace a little.

Rogan's next step reminded him of when he was playing hockey on the frozen lake. He arched his back then windmilled his arms, trying to stay on feet that refused to find traction. Rogan hit the ground hard, cracking his elbow on the unforgiving ice.

"Ow," he moaned, grabbing his elbow.

FORGIVENESS AT SKELETON COVE

Mr. Chaffey stopped and turned, slipping himself and falling to his hands and knees. "I think we found another icy spot on the road. You okay?"

"Yeah. Hurt my elbow, but I'll live."

They both gingerly regained their feet. Rogan pushed up the sleeve of his coat and consulted the glowing hands of his wristwatch. "I think we've probably come a mile."

"Only two more to go." Jim grinned, but Rogan didn't see any humor in it.

They had taken two cautious steps when a most unwelcome sound reverberated through the woods.

CHAPTER 16

Primal Symphony

ROGAN'S HEART STOPPED. *KA-THUNK*. HIS HEART THEN surged ahead, pounding heavily throughout his whole body. His wide-open eyes cut to his dad, but his dad was scanning the woods with the hazy beam of the flashlight, trying to pierce the heavy darkness. The darkness that now felt menacing and dangerous.

A lone howl, long and eerie, again shattered the silence. Other yips, whines, and moans joined in to produce a cacophony of an ancient, primal symphony that floated around them. Rogan couldn't tell which direction it all came from, but it seemed to be from every-where. The noise changed to something akin to the evil laughter of many voices bent on sinister actions.

He felt the back of his neck prickle like there was electricity in the air. His breathing was rapid and shallow. Rogan couldn't help but imagine glowing red eyes and sharp white fangs dripping saliva, or blood, on large-pawed wolves circling him and his dad. He didn't know if he should speak or not, but the whisper came out of its own volition.

"Dad. What do we do?"

His dad unsnapped the strap on his shoulder holster and unsheathed his pistol, pointing the barrel down at the ground. Rogan was still looking for an answer. His dad put a finger to his lips, then put his hand palm up in a motion that Rogan recognized as telling him to stay still.

Rogan complied, but he could feel the panic tingling his muscles, telling them to run. There was no way to determine how close the pack was, but the noise was thunderous. He had the impractical urge to slap his hands over his ears to make it go away. He couldn't help it and scooted over next to his dad.

The discordant concert kept on, bouncing off the walls of blackness. Finally, his dad practically yelled at his son, "I can't tell where they are, but they know we're here, so we're going to make some noise. We'll keep walking home and watch all around. If you see a couple of rocks you could pick up, so you have something to throw, grab them. I know most of them are buried in snow, but the vehicles might have kicked some out. Whatever we do, we don't want to turn our backs to them or run." Jim paused and took a hard look at his son's tight face. "You okay?"

Rogan took a deep breath and nodded three times, quickly. "Yeah. Fear but fear not, right?"

He was referring to a saying his dad had taught him, "Fear but fear not, for fear is your greatest weakness." This had been very meaningful to Rogan toward the end of summer, during his ordeal at Dead Man's Hole. He knew firsthand now that it meant it was all right to feel afraid, but it was important to face the fear calmly and intelligently, so it didn't make matters worse.

His dad grabbed Rogan's shoulder in a firm, encouraging grip. "You got it, Son." Jim straightened up. "At the first lull in the howling, let's yell and whistle as loud as we can. For now, let's start walking."

Rogan's headlamp didn't do enough, in his opinion, to illuminate what was hidden out there. He swung his head back and forth, searching for the telltale sheen of light reflecting off animal eyes. He could hear the individual voices now. One had a sharp yip, one howled deep and low, one whined like something caught in a trap, and one chuckled evilly like a demented hyena.

Quiet suddenly descended, and Rogan jumped, cringing, as his dad let out a shout behind him. He felt foolish for being so jumpy and covered up by adding his voice to the yelling.

"Hey, Mr. Wolf. We're over here, so you stay over there!" He felt silly again.

His dad sounded like an auctioneer behind him, just making some nonsense noise. Rogan took off his glove and put his fingers in his mouth. His first attempt at producing a shrill whistle fell flat, probably because he was shaking with nerves. The next one came out loud and clear.

They continued walking as their noise-making was paused. Rogan thought he could hear the padding of wolf paws in the woods, but he tried to reassure himself that it was all his imagination.

At least they've stopped howling. Oh, wait. Not sure if that's a good thing or not. Where are they? His brain churned out desperate thoughts.

His dad began shouting again at the same time as the pack resumed their ruckus. Rogan joined in, deciding to stick with, "Hey, batter, batter!" which somehow popped into his mind. It sounded better than what he'd hollered before. He soon found a couple of rocks and picked them up, striking them against each other to make additional noise.

Not knowing where the wolves were, or how close, frayed Rogan's nerves. He worried that the howling animals might jump out at him and his dad at any second. He second-guessed what he thought he was seeing in the dark. His racing heart needed a break. He gulped some cold night air that burned his lungs.

Ten minutes and hopefully close to another mile later, the humans and canines were still keeping pace with each other and serenading each other. Rogan felt a deep weariness from all that had been going on over the past couple of days. He forced himself to not think about being home and in a warm, safe bed. He sent pleas heavenward in between tortured thoughts and shouting or whistling at the wolf pack. His throat was feeling the strain.

The echoing clamor stopped abruptly. Father and son stopped, by unspoken agreement, and listened. Nothing. Just a slight stirring of a biting breeze.

"Let's keep making noise for a while," Jim instructed.

In response, Rogan burst out singing, "The ants go marching one by one, hurrah, hurrah…"

He could hear a laugh from his dad who then joined in.

For the longest last mile home, they didn't hear any more of the wild predators. Rogan still felt like he was being watched and followed, but he never saw the evidence to prove his theory. His feet felt like lead weights as he slogged up their driveway. The house was going to be dark and cold. Jim grabbed the front doorknob and paused.

"Thank you, Lord, for getting us home safely. Please continue to watch over Elise."

Rogan agreed. "Amen."

"Let's build a fire and maybe sleep in the living room, since it will take too long to heat the house," his dad suggested. "It's too late now to call the Petersens. We'll go get your sisters in the morning. It won't kill you to miss one more day of school, I suppose."

"Sounds good, Dad." Rogan was bone-weary tired. He could only drag his feet across the threshold. His snow boots were so heavy.

To their surprise, there was a banked fire going in the Franklin and a note on their table from Monty explaining that the girls were fine spending another night, the chores were done, and to please call them, regardless of time, when they arrived home.

"What good friends." His dad rubbed his face. "I'm tired. How're you holding up?"

"Super tired. I'm happy the house is warmed up, and I get to sleep in my own bed." He smiled a sleepy smile and gave his dad a hug. "I'm glad we weren't wolf dinner."

His dad chuckled. "Me too, Son. Go get some well-deserved sleep. I'm proud of you, how you handled everything today, without complaining or freaking out."

The warm glow from his dad's praise followed him upstairs.

Throughout the night, Rogan tossed and turned as he dreamed about snarling wolves running at him, teeth bared and dripping slobber. The next image was a group of them ripping and tearing at something, shaking their heads from side to side while holding it down with their paws. In his dream, Rogan inched closer, needing to see what was at their mercy. As Rogan got closer, one massive wolf raised his furry head. Rogan saw strips of bright pink material stabbed onto the wolf's teeth. Rogan stared. He couldn't find his breath.

Rogan suddenly found himself sitting straight up in his own bed with blankets and sheets in a careless pile or wrapped around his legs. He was breathing rapidly. He wiped a forearm across his forehead, smearing droplets of sweat.

He decided it was time to get up, so he headed downstairs, still in his pajamas, and found his dad already up and stoking the fire.

"Sorry, but you look like you slept about as well as I did." His dad closed the latch on the black metal stove.

"Bad dreams. You?"

"Some. Worrying about your mom. I'll call in a little bit to see how she's doing. It's only six, so it's a little early for that. I wonder if I should've called last night?"

"I guess you'll find out when you call today." Rogan couldn't hide the amusement in his voice. He and his dad shared a chuckle.

"Well, here's the plan. Carol will get the girls to school. Monty and Timothy will drive us to the rig and help us hopefully get it back on the road. I'm going to pack a bag for your mom and leave from there if there isn't any damage to the 4Runner that I need to be concerned about. You'll come home with the Petersens and be here when Carol brings your sisters home from school. Then, you're in charge until your mom and I get back."

"Sounds good, Dad. Make sure and pack Mom's Bible and the latest book she's been reading."

"Already on it, but good thinking."

By eight-thirty, they were ready for Monty and Runt to pick them up. Monty had put chains on the Jeep, hoping to keep his vehicle on the slippery roads. On the trip there, Rogan recounted their experience with the wolves. Eyes wide, Runt declared he wanted to go look for tracks. The fathers reminded him that their main priority was getting the 4Runner out of the ditch so Jim could get back to the clinic and Elise.

They pulled up a little way past the wounded Toyota.

"Wow. It seemed so much farther away last night," Rogan told Runt as the men got out to inspect and strategize.

The boys were put to work shoveling snow away from the front of the tires, and then digging through snow to find rocks and sticks to lay down in the cleared path. Jim and Monty hooked a chain to the hitch on the Jeep and then hooked the tow hook under the front bumper of the 4Runner.

It would be a bit tricky pulling the rig out as it was perpendicular to the road. They also had to contend with the large rock by the back tire. When things were all hooked up and ready, they had the boys move out of the way. Monty got in the Wrangler and Jim was driving the Toyota.

"You ready?" Monty yelled out his open window.

"Ready," Jim yelled back.

Both engines revved. The rear end of the Jeep swung side to side, and the Toyota's tires jerkily spun, but it didn't make any progress. The chained tires of the Jeep chipped away at the icy road. They tried again with the same results. Both men got out.

"Something feels stuck." Jim got in the ditch on his hands and knees in the snow to peer under the vehicle. His muffled voice announced, "It's on a log with a branch that's sticking straight up and catching on the bumper."

"I'll get an ax and chop it off, Dad." Rogan was eager to help.

He grabbed the tool from the 4Runner and jumped into the ditch. Sliding under the vehicle, he had to lay on his side. It was an awkward position for chopping, but it was the best he could do. He hacked at the branch which was about as big around as his upper arm. After several swings, he stopped to rest and readjust his grip.

"Hey, slacker. Do you need a real man to take over?"

Rogan looked across the undercarriage and saw Runt's grinning face peeking at him. Rogan snorted. "You *are* talking to a real man. Stand back." He began swinging the ax again. The branch separated from the log after three swings.

"Timber," Runt announced.

Both boys crawled out and stood back. "Try it again, Dad." Rogan was wiping off the snow from his snow pants and jacket.

The wheels of the 4Runner dug through the boughs they had placed, spitting them out behind, but still couldn't find traction. Rogan noticed what was happening and hollered for the men to stop.

"The log is in the exact wrong spot," he explained. "The tires just spin on it, and it's too big to move. It's actually a tree. You spun off all the bark."

"Well, shall we go with plan B?" Jim asked.

"Yep. Let's use the chain and anchor the Jeep to a tree behind it. Then we can use the cable to, hopefully, winch the Toyota out. What do you think?" Monty looked at Jim.

"I like it."

They unhitched the chain, wound it around a suitable tree, and then backed up the Jeep until they could attach the chain back onto the hitch. Next, they pulled to unwind the cable, which was on free spool, and hooked that to the Runner's tow hook. Everyone took their places and hoped it would work this time. Rogan thought the trick would be for his dad to not slide into the front of the Petersen's rig once he was up on the road as there wasn't much leeway. He saw that at least Monty had a remote control, so he wouldn't have to stand sandwiched between the two rigs.

There was a soft whir as the winch's motor tightened the cable, so there wasn't any slack. Monty paused. "Here we go."

The cable retracted, and the Toyota's back tires slunk their way over the slippery log. The rig lurched as it dropped down off the log and deeper into the ditch. The back bumper scraped on the tree. Rogan winced. He looked at Runt. "The ditch is deeper than I thought."

"Yeah. I hope the winch is strong enough."

Both boys watched as the almost-rescued vehicle slowly rose over the edge of the road and finally settled on the flat surface, mere inches from the Jeep's grille.

After disconnecting the cable and chain, Monty was able to back up a foot, which was enough for Jim to maneuver his rig around it with help from the teens spotting and giving directions. He thanked his helpers, did a quick inspection, and determined things looked undamaged for driving back to the clinic. He then transferred the things he needed to take with him from the Jeep, said goodbye to Rogan, and headed down the road.

Rogan felt a twinge of concern as he watched him drive off, knowing his dad would be traveling alone on still-slick roads. *Please keep him safe, Lord. And help Mom to be okay.*

The three who were left loaded up the gear and headed in the other direction. When they got to the spot in the road where Rogan and his dad had first heard the wolves, Rogan pointed it out.

"I remember that big boulder on the side of the road."

Monty found a wide spot in the road that the plow had made and pulled over. "I'd like to see if we can find some sign. You boys up for it?"

They both enthusiastically agreed. Monty was packing his handgun, and since it was daylight, Rogan was more curious than frightened.

Monty stood in the middle of the road, hands on his hips. "Could you tell which side they were on?"

Rogan contemplated his answer. "It was really hard to tell. The howls seemed to come from everywhere, but…I'm not sure why, but I feel like they were over there." He pointed to the left of the road.

"Okay. Let's see if we can find anything and if not, we'll try the other side. Everyone stay together and keep your eyes peeled."

They headed out through the wintry trees, sweeping snow-laden boughs aside with their hands. Rogan wished he had on snowshoes. It was difficult walking as he didn't know what lay underneath the blanket of white. They crossed a line of deer tracks heading parallel to the road. Rogan wondered if the deer were around when he and his dad heard the wolves. Rogan estimated they'd come about fifty yards from the road.

Monty stopped. "Well, will you look at that."

Rogan and Runt hurried to Monty's side and looked down. The tracks sank down enough into the snow that in between the deep imprints, Rogan could see marks where a paw or a furry stomach had grazed the top layer, leaving a mark.

They squatted down to examine it closer. The actual tracks had a glaze of ice over them like a slight melting had occurred and had then frozen over again. Many of the tracks were trampled by the paws of the followers in the pack, but right in front of them was a very distinct one. The four toe pads curved slightly inward and sat above the heel pad. Curved points tipped the track. Rogan imagined the sharp claws that had pierced the snow like needles.

"Wow. How many do you think there were?" Rogan looked at Mr. Petersen as he asked.

"It's hard to tell, but there seems to be quite a few. I guess I'd estimate twelve to fourteen." Monty said it with a question in his voice.

"I'm glad I didn't know how many there were when we were out here in the dark. It was pretty creepy," Rogan said.

"I wish I would've been there to hear them. I've only heard one or two howling at a time." Runt sounded slightly jealous.

Rogan extended his arm and put his hand next to the track of the grey wolf, his fingers splayed out.

"Yikes! That track is almost as big as your hand," Runt exclaimed.

Mr. Petersen sat back on his heels and surveyed the area. "That's a big one, all right." He pointed to the right. "The tracks go that way for as far as I can see."

Rogan felt a shiver ripple up his back. "Do you think they were following us?"

Runt chose that moment to grab Rogan's shoulders and let out a loud growl. Rogan startled, half turned, bent slightly forward with his shoulders, and lost his balance. He toppled over in the snow. Runt's snort echoed in his ears.

"Got ya. You should've seen the look on your face, Rogue."

Rogan rapidly regained his feet, grabbed a handful of snow as he did so, and lunged at Runt. He was quick enough to grab the front of his friend's jacket with his free hand. He pulled Runt toward himself and smashed the snow onto the top of his head, rubbing it in for good measure.

"Ah! Cold. Cold." Runt wiggled around, trying to free himself, but Rogan's grip was firm.

"I think I'd like to follow the tracks a little way. You two hooligans up for it?"

They laughingly gave each other a friendly shove and then turned and followed Monty. Walking to the side of the wolf pack's trail, they slogged on for another half a mile or so. At this point, Rogan could see the tracks suddenly take a sharp ninety-degree turn to veer toward where he figured the road was.

"That's weird. I wonder why they all of a sudden turned so sharp?" Rogan wondered out loud.

"Curious," was all Mr. Petersen said.

Runt tapped the fingertips of his gloves together. "Curiouser and curiouser."

The tracks ended at a patch of forest where the sign showed the wolves had milled around, sat, and had lain in the snow.

"It looks like they decided to hang out for a while," Runt observed. "Watch out for that pile. You wouldn't want to step in that. Ew."

"Let's keep going a bit more," Monty suggested.

Twenty more yards, and they stepped out of the forest and onto the road.

"Oh, man. They were so close. Were they waiting for us?" Rogan was served a slice of fear he'd felt last night as they hiked home in the dark.

"They certainly paralleled your position and then turned for some reason. But yeah, I wonder why they held up back there?" Monty scratched his head.

"Man, you're lucky you weren't dinner." Runt grabbed Rogan's arm and pantomimed eating it like corn on the cob.

It broke the tension Rogan was feeling, and he laughingly pushed his friend away. The trio headed back down the road to the waiting rig, loaded up, and continued driving home. Rogan had a fire going and the house warmed up by the time Mrs. Petersen brought his sisters home from school.

When it was dinner time, Rogan stood looking over the food options in the pantry. "How does mac and cheese sound?"

The girls liked the idea, and Rogan felt confident in his boxed dinner culinary skills. He dug through the freezer and found a package of hot dogs to go along with the pasta. Peg came out of the pantry carrying a jar of applesauce. Rogan decided it was a dinner close enough to having the four food groups.

Their dad called shortly after they'd eaten to let them know he'd made it there safely and to give them an update on their mom. "She can feel everything again and move all her arms and legs now, thank the Lord. She's having some pretty bad headaches. They've got her on muscle relaxants, and the doctor just gave her a steroid injection. Because we live so far away, they want to keep her here a few more days to see how she reacts to the steroids, so we won't get to come home tomorrow. She really misses all of you."

Rogan had put his dad on speaker phone, so they could all hear. The girls got teary-eyed saying how much they missed her, too.

"I know Rogan is taking good care of you. Be sure and be good listeners and help him out, okay?"

After saying their goodbyes, it was bedtime. Rogan knew his mom always tucked in Lainey and Peg, and then prayed with them. He decided to do the same.

"I'm glad Mom's getting better. I wish she could come home tomorrow," Lainey lamented.

"Me, too. I miss her," said Peg.

"So do I, but she needs to rest and get better. We can make it a couple more days, right?" Rogan smiled at his sisters.

After performing the bedtime routine, Rogan went down the hall to his bedroom.

"Rogue," Peg's voice was plaintive. "Will you leave the hall light on?"

"Sure, Peg. Get some sleep."

Rogan was exhausted emotionally and physically. It had been a couple of crazy days. He flopped down on his bed and stared at his ceiling. The wooden beams morphed into dark tree branches that created a dense canopy, blocking out any light from the stars or moon. Rogan heard a quiet, panting breath behind him. He whirled around, searching the inky blackness. Even though he couldn't see anything, he knew something dangerous was stalking him. He tried to calm himself, so he could hear over the roaring of his pulse in his ears and the thundering of his agitated heart. There was a slight noise, again behind him. He spun around in time to see a massive wolf with glowing red eyes and huge shining fangs make a leap straight at him. All Rogan could do was throw his hands up to shield his face. He couldn't even suck in enough air to scream. The wolf's open maw floated closer, droplets of saliva shining like demented dew drops.

This time, he did yell.

Rogan found himself sitting up in his bed, fully clothed, with his hands thrown up in front of his face. He was practically hyperventilating.

"It was just a dream," he reassured himself, patting his chest and legs to make sure he was unscathed. He got up, trying to shake it off, got dressed for bed, brushed his teeth, and checked on his sisters. They were both sound asleep. *Hopefully, I can sleep now with no more bad dreams*, he thought as he climbed into bed, this time under the covers.

CHAPTER 17

Homecoming and Going

ROGAN MANAGED TO GET HIMSELF AND HIS SISTERS ready for school on time for the next three days. Mrs. Petersen gave them all a ride to and from school. Rogan felt the burden of doing all the chores and tasks his parents usually took care of.

The bags under his eyes grew more pronounced as the week dragged itself to Friday. One night he'd been up with Peg having nightmares, and he'd felt completely unqualified, not knowing what to do to make her feel better. He ended up sitting in the kitchen with her, mixing some powdered Ovaltine into her milk to make it chocolate-flavored. He'd put his head on the table and watched her take twice as long as he'd thought she should have to drink it.

In the mornings, he had to do most of the chores even though Lainey helped some. He had to haul firewood and make a fire every evening when they got home from school. He had to make dinner and do his own homework after he helped his sisters with theirs. They didn't often let the dog come into the house, but Rogan had been letting Sitka come in to keep him company. She usually lasted a couple of hours and then whined to get let out, panting from being too warm indoors. With all that, Rogan found himself nodding off during his classes. He was ready to not play the parent anymore.

Friday night's dinner was Hamburger Helper and a can of green beans. Rogan went to bed feeling hopeful, glad that tomorrow was Saturday, and his parents would finally be home.

Rogan and his sisters spent the morning cleaning the house and making a welcome home sign. Lainey and Peg made a batch of chocolate chip cookies with some help from their brother. The cookies ended up a little lopsided, but they tasted good. Rogan knew because they had all sampled a few.

Time stretched out like taffy. It strung them along, sticky with the waiting. Lainey and Peg were camped out by the bay window, watching. The blue 4Runner finally crawled up the driveway. Everyone ran outside to greet their parents. Rogan had reminded his sisters to be careful when hugging their mom, so they wouldn't hurt her. Rogan thought it wasn't difficult to remember as Elise cautiously emerged from the vehicle, holding Jim's arm for support, her neck stiff in the cervical collar. She couldn't turn her head but had to turn her whole body to look at something not directly in front of her.

When she was settled on the couch with a cookie, everyone crowded around to hear what had been going on with their parents. The kids told their side of the experience as well. Elise had given many hugs and was holding each girl's hand. Rogan saw his sisters didn't want to be even a few feet away from their mom.

Smiling warmly, Elise thanked Rogan for holding down the fort, as she put it. "You look tired. Are you doing okay?"

"I'm okay, Mom. I don't know how you do it all the time. I had no idea."

"Well, you're a teenager, and I've had lots of experience. I'm really proud of you, Rogan. Girls, don't you have a great brother?"

"Yes!" Peg yelled. "He helped me when I had a nightmare, and he let me drink chocolate milk."

Lainey perked up at that. "Why didn't I get any?"

"Sorry, Lainey. It was the middle of the night, and you were asleep."

"Unfortunately," his mom said, "I'm still going to need some help for a while. In fact, Peg, will you please get me a glass of water? The muscle relaxers make my mouth really dry."

Peg jumped up. Rogan could tell she was eager to help. They spent the rest of the day hanging out, letting their mom rest, and watching a movie.

Before going to bed, they all decided to skip church the next day. Rogan was grateful for a chance to sleep in.

Sunday evening, as Rogan was heading outside to do chores, he opened the door to find Mr. Hoffman standing there with a covered Dutch oven in one hand, the other raised in a fist. Rogan had caught him just before he knocked. The teen invited him in. Mr. Hoffman noticed they weren't in church but had heard Jim and Elise were back, and he had made them some chicken and dumplings.

Rogan's family expressed their gratitude and invited him to stay to share the dinner. There were also a couple of casseroles in the refrigerator that Carol Petersen had brought over.

The day passed pleasantly, and Rogan felt a little refreshed for the start of another round of school. It turned out to be a demanding week with homework and projects due. Rogan was up late Thursday night working on an essay for English when he heard a crash from downstairs. He hurried down to see what was going on. It apparently hadn't been loud enough to wake his sisters, since they were still slumbering when he peeked in their room.

At the bottom of the stairs, he halted. He could hear his mother sobbing. She sounded almost hysterical. Rogan could hear his dad's voice, soothing but firm, explaining that it wasn't a big deal. This was so uncharacteristic of his mom that he wasn't sure what to do.

Should I go down, or should I go back to my room?

He made a quick decision to go down. The scene that met him in the kitchen was his dad holding his mom in a wrap-around hug, pieces of a ceramic mug and some kind of liquid splayed across the floor. She was still crying.

"Is everything okay?" Rogan's voice squeaked a little.

His mother's hair was unbound from her usual ponytail and was a disheveled mess. Her face looked pale.

"Everything's okay, Son. Your mom dropped her mug of tea, but we'll clean it up."

"I can help." Rogan stepped forward, bent down, and began collecting the scattered pieces.

"Rogan! Your dad said we'll take care of it. Leave it alone." His mother was almost growling at him. Her eyes were red from crying, and Rogan had a flash of the images from his recent nightmares.

He rose slowly, staring at his mom. *What is wrong with her?* His eyes flicked to his dad, questioning.

Jim kept his tone of voice calm and kept hold of his wife. "Thanks anyway. We'll take care of it. Go on up to bed. I'll come check on you later."

Rogan took that as secret code for his dad coming to explain what was going on. The pieces of the broken mug he'd already collected were on the open palm of his hand. He wasn't close enough to the counter or trash can to put them there, so he tipped his hand and let them fall to the floor. This elicited another wave of sobbing from his mom. Rogan flinched. He turned and hurried back upstairs, his thoughts colliding with questions. He had never seen his mom lash out at anyone before, and it was unnerving.

He sat at his desk, and his fingers traced the carved name of his older brother, Peter. The desk was previously Peter's when he was young, but after his death, Rogan inherited it. There was zero likelihood he could concentrate on homework anymore.

Rogan's world felt unbalanced. He reached for his Bible and set it on the desk in front of him. *Where should I read? God, I don't know what's going on, but I sure don't like it. Please help Mom.*

His fingers slowly flipped through pages, looking for something, but he didn't know what. He registered that he was in the book of John. He turned one more page, and his eyes were drawn to a verse he had highlighted years ago. It was John 14:27. He murmured the promise, "'Peace I leave with you; my peace I give you. I do not give to you as the world gives. Do not let your hearts be troubled and do not be afraid.' I definitely need some peace in my life right now."

He was still sitting, elbows supporting a bowed head in his hands, when his dad came into his room half an hour later. Rogan had been staring at blurry words on a page, and a few salty drops had plunked down onto the thin pages of his still-open Bible.

He sniffed. "Hey, Dad. What's going on?"

The bed creaked as Jim sat, putting his hands on his knees. "I'm pretty sure it's the muscle relaxants. The nurse practitioner warned us some side effects could be dizziness and irritability. I'm going to call the clinic in the morning and see if I should stop having her take them.

She certainly isn't acting like herself. She got dizzy and dropped her cup of tea, and then just fell apart over it. Sorry she snapped at you. I know she didn't mean it."

"I know that too, Dad." Rogan sighed. "I feel so bad for her."

His dad nodded wearily, like his head was almost too heavy for him to move. He looked at the bedside clock. "Oh, wow. It's later than I thought. You should probably get some sleep."

They both stood. "I'll bet you're pretty tired too, Dad. Goodnight. Love you."

"Love you too, Rogue."

Rogan's brain lingered in a foggy state all the next morning. He told himself he just had to survive this Friday. Distracted, he kept wondering what his dad had learned from calling the clinic, and he worried about his mom.

In the noisy lunchroom, he got in line behind his friends. Boom Chain was right in front of him, and he did a double take as Rogan walked up. "Are you okay? You look terrible."

"Thanks for the compliment," Rogan halfheartedly teased.

This caused Runt and Tuff to peek around Boom Chain. They agreed. They all grabbed a divided melamine lunch tray from the stack. Rogan explained that his mom wasn't doing so well and that the drugs were likely the culprit. "It's been rough. I was up really late last night."

His friends looked sympathetic, and Tuff opened his mouth, presumably to say something, when Rogan jumped at a loud, "Ha!" from behind him.

He turned enough to look over his shoulder. Martin stood a foot away. His rancid smell assaulted Rogan's nose.

"Your mom's gonna get addicted to drugs, 'cause that's what happens to moms. She'll keep getting weirder with her behavior, and then she'll leave. You'll see."

Rogan felt Boom Chain's presence next to him, but he was laser focused on Martin's smirking face and his ridiculous red bandana.

"Hey, you'd better watch it," Boom Chain growled.

Martin raised his hands and wiggled his fingers. "Ooh. I'm scared."

Boom Chain's voice sounded to Rogan like it was a long way away as he snarled, "You'd better be," which was clearly heard in the abrupt silence of the cafeteria. The high schoolers had an uncanny ability to home in on a potential fight.

Something foreign and powerful exploded in Rogan's chest. He was gripping his as-yet empty lunch tray with white knuckles. Slowly and deliberately, he turned the rest of the way, so he was facing the boy who dared disrespect his mom like that. All of the stress and fatigue of the previous week turned up the heat in Rogan's body. He was only aware of his anger and greasy-haired Martin.

His words began low but increased in volume with each one that came spitting out of his mouth without any self-control to police them.

"How dare you. My mom is not like that. You take that back, or I'll punch your snarky face." His words were a fire that first sputtered weakly, then caught tinder, building in intensity until the flames began to consume him.

Martin just looked at Rogan. "Ooh, ooh. Somebody's having a bad day."

The anger ripped through Rogan's heart like it was tearing a flimsy piece of paper. "You're about to get a worse one," Rogan snarled.

A ring of curious students was closing in. Martin became shifty-eyed.

"You are a terrible person. Did you ever wonder why no one likes you?" Rogan was full-on yelling and jabbing the tray in Martin's direction. Martin began backing up.

"You scumbag!" Rogan was completely out of control now. "You don't have any friends because you're mean and you're an idiot."

Rogan advanced; Martin retreated.

Martin morphed into his whipped dog persona and turned to flee as Rogan yelled one parting shot. "And while you're at it, take a bath. You stink!"

There was a collective pause while Martin's departing footsteps echoed in the lunchroom. A raucous roar returned with scattered applause, laughter, congratulations, and the chatter of excited witnesses. Rogan stood frozen, nostrils flared, breathing heavily.

Boom Chain clapped him on the back. "Way to give it to him, Chaffey. What a piece of work. He deserved it."

The rage sloughed off, and Rogan felt like he suddenly became himself again. He lowered the tray. He looked at his friends. "I gotta go home."

Runt said, "I'll walk with you to the office."

Rogan placed his tray on the empty table as he passed and woodenly went through the motions of retrieving his things from his locker. They continued to the office. Runt waited while Rogan told the secretary he wasn't feeling well, and she let him call home.

"I can't come to get you right now, Rogan. I'm in the middle of helping your mom."

"It's okay, Dad. I'll walk."

"If you're okay with that. Let me tell Mrs. Kapinsky you have my permission."

Rogan handed over the phone.

Runt walked him to the front door. "I'm really sorry for what Martin said about your mom. He shouldn't have done that. It was really low."

"Thanks, Runt. Catch you later."

"You going to be okay, man?"

"Yeah," Rogan sighed as he went out into the cold.

Walking home, jacket zipped up, hunched against the bracing wind, Rogan had ample time to reflect on what had just occurred.

Why did I say all those things? I was so mean. I don't think I've ever felt so angry in my life. But he was such a jerk.

Guilt and regret quickly invaded, a platoon of soldiers who emerged out of the darkness, fanning out to all corners of his soul, weapons drawn.

On one hand, Rogan just wanted to be home to sleep it off, but on the other hand, he dreaded what he would say to his parents.

I'm not going to lie to them, but maybe I'll just stick with not feeling well. They don't need another problem to deal with. He gave a cynical chuckle. "That's my story, and I'm sticking to it," he muttered.

It felt good to occasionally swing his leg back, hauling off and kicking an undeserving clod of ice or snow.

I just want to go to bed and forget everything, was the thought loop that accompanied him all the way home.

By the time he stomped off his boots and entered the mud room, he was truly feeling ill. He got his wish to head to his room after a quick conversation with his dad. He didn't see his mom anywhere and assumed she was napping.

Awakening in a dark room hours later, Rogan felt a little better. He headed downstairs with the thought of dinner as his number one priority. He was surprised no one was around. The kitchen was quiet and dark except a soft light glowing from the hood over the stove. He glanced at the microwave.

Ten o'clock. Wow. I really slept.

He headed for the refrigerator. There was a sticky note addressed to him. He reached up and fingered it, eventually pulling it off. There was a plastic-wrapped plate made for him on the top shelf. Rogan gratefully heated it up in the microwave and sat at the lonely table to eat.

Saturday morning dawned dark with ominous-looking storm clouds that hung behind the mountains surrounding the bay. Everyone was present for Saturday morning breakfast. After praying over the food, Mr. Chaffey wanted to fill his children in on Elise's condition.

"Your mom is doing a lot better now. Yesterday I talked to the nurse practitioner, and he told me to discontinue the muscle relaxants. Like we suspected, they affected her negatively."

Mrs. Chaffey piped up, "They made me crazy. I feel much better today. Sorry you had to see me like that, Rogan."

"It's okay. You couldn't help it." Rogan smiled at his mom.

Inside his head, he considered how he had also lost it, but he couldn't blame it on a medication reaction.

"Are you feeling better, Rogan?" His dad's question broke into his thoughts. "You look better than when you got home from school yesterday."

"I'm feeling a lot better."

"I did your chores last night." Lainey sat up straighter.

"Thanks, sis."

"She didn't want to," Peg revealed. "Dad made her."

Everyone laughed.

"If you kids will please all pitch in and help clean up, I'm going to help your mom with her stretches."

Elise grimaced. "Yay. I know they're helpful, but they really hurt."

Jim took her hand. "I know, and I'm sorry."

* * *

Rogan popped the last bite of his afternoon sandwich into his mouth and wiped his hands on his napkin after hesitating over the temptation of wiping them on the front of his jeans. He wadded up his paper napkin and threw it at the trash can at the end of the counter. It hit the rim and bounced off.

"Oh, I was robbed."

"Or, you just missed," his mom teased.

Rogan was formulating a hopefully witty reply when a loud crackle of radio static belched out from the home base VHF.

"Emergency. Emergency. Emergency." Rogan jumped to his feet at the same time as his dad. "Attention, everyone. This is Sam. We have a situation with a missing teen and need everyone who is available to come to the Community Center ASAP. We'll have a briefing followed by a search. Please come prepared. I repeat, come to the Community Center right away for a briefing. We have a missing teen."

Rogan and his parents all looked at each other, shock showing on their faces.

"This doesn't sound good," Jim said.

Rogan agreed. "Yeah. Man, I wonder who it is?"

His dad was heading to gather his cold-weather gear. "I'm heading over. Rogan, can you grab my backpack from the floor of the hall closet, please?"

"Sure, Dad. Can I come?"

Jim pushed an arm into his jacket. He paused briefly. "I'd say yes, but I think I'll have you stay here in case your mom needs something. I'll see what's going on, and we'll go from there, okay?"

Rogan was disappointed that he'd miss out on learning about what was going on, but he also wanted to help his mom. "Sure thing, Dad. I'll go get your backpack."

Every person in their family had what they called a "go bag" which was kept handy and fully stocked in case of an emergency where they had to leave quickly and needed the essentials for survival. Each backpack had a flashlight, multi-tool, fire starting paraphernalia, a basic first aid kit, extra clothing, food, water, a GPS system of some sort, rain gear, and an emergency blanket. Rogan's also had cordage, a water filtration system, a saw, extra batteries, and a few more items. He knew his dad had even more in his and that Peg had snuck a stuffed animal into hers. His dad's go bag was heavy as he hefted it, slinging the strap over one shoulder.

He handed it to his dad who had just kissed his wife goodbye.

"Good luck, Dad."

"Thanks, Rogue. Hold down the fort."

"You know I will."

There was a silence after the door shut. Rogan sat with his mom in the living room, talking about this new turn of events. Rogan's curiosity was on high alert. He was anxious to hear who it was who had gone missing.

"This is a terrible time of the year to go missing," his mom stated, then amended, "Well, it's terrible to go missing any time, but especially in the winter."

Rogan nodded.

"Let's start praying," his mom suggested.

They said a prayer for the missing youth, that God would keep him or her safe and that the rescuers would not only stay safe themselves but would find the teen quickly.

One o'clock rolled around, and they still hadn't heard any news. It was time for Elise to do some stretches and then apply cold compresses to her neck and shoulders. Rogan had watched his dad help her but still had to rely on his mom telling him what to do. He assisted her in removing the c-collar. There were two Velcro straps, one on each side, but she still couldn't reach up and across to do it herself without tingling sensations and pain.

She instructed him on how to help with the stretches which were also painful. By the end of the fifteen minutes it took them to complete the exercises, Elise had unbidden tears dribbling down her cheeks.

Lainey walked in at that moment. "Mom. What's wrong? Rogan! You're hurting her." Lainey started crying, herself. Rogan stood still, at a loss about what to do.

"It's okay, Sweetie. Rogan isn't hurting me. He's helping. It just hurts when I do my exercises. Can you please go get the ice pack the clinic gave me from out of the freezer? That would be a big help."

Lainey nodded, sniffed up her tears, and went to fetch it.

Elise looked at her son. "This is what really hurts, having the cold on there." She sighed.

"Sorry, Mom." Rogan felt empathetic.

She smiled. "I know. Thanks, Lainey. Now Rogan, I'm going to scoot back against the couch, and if you'll put it across my shoulders but also part way up my neck, please."

Rogan did as instructed. "How long?"

Elise closed her eyes. "Twenty minutes."

Rogan set his watch, troubled at the pain etched into his mother's face. He picked up a magazine, thumbing through the pages to pass the time.

The phone rang. His dad's voice was on the other end, so Rogan took the handset over near his mom and put it on speaker mode.

His dad asked how Elise was doing, and then told them how they'd set up a grid around the town and which section he'd be searching. "No one has a clue where he might have gone, but he's been missing since Friday after school."

"That's terrible," said Mrs. Chaffey.

"Dad, who is it?"

"It's a boy named Martin Wolfe. I'm assuming you know him, Rogan. He's also a ninth-grader."

Rogan managed to choke out, "Yeah, I know him." His head spun, and there was a loud ringing in his ears. He felt like he'd just been hit with an imaginary cement truck, and it had crushed his chest. It was so hard to suck in air. Fuzzy noises floated around his head.

"Rogan. Rogan?"

He slowly turned his head to stare at his mom.

"Are you okay? I've been trying to get your attention." Rogan noticed his dad was no longer on the phone. The handset was lying face down on the couch. "I remember you telling us about a Martin who caused trouble at Survival School. Is that the same boy?"

"Sorry, Mom. I'm just shocked. And yeah, it's the same Martin. I wonder what stunt he's pulling this time?" The last sentence came out weakly. Rogan felt a sickening lump forming in the pit of his stomach. He was trying to deny it, but guilt was forcibly squeezing its way in.

Is this my fault? Did he take off after I yelled at him in front of everyone at school? What have I done?

The alarm on his watch blared harsh beeps that the twenty minutes of icing therapy was over. Glad for the distraction, Rogan took it off his mom's shoulders and replaced the cervical collar. After that, his mom felt the need for some rest and headed to her room.

Rogan sat heavily on the edge of the couch and dropped his head into his hands. He tried to reason with himself, rationalizing that Martin was a bit of a loose cannon and could be hiding out to get back at his parents, or maybe he ran away for whatever reason. But where would he go in the dead of winter? A heavy sigh whooshed out. He ran his fingers through his thick brown hair.

I'm sure this isn't my fault.

He tried to placate the regret that had already constructed a rock pile in his gut. He slapped his thighs and stood, pacing around the living room, gazing out the windows but not really seeing anything.

Time didn't just crawl; it went as fast as the large, bright yellow and brown-spotted banana slugs that oozed along their slimy trails without much discernable motion. Rogan's opposing thoughts—guilty, not guilty—swirled in his head, plopping one at a time into the blender of anxiety. They became a sludge-like stew until his head felt like it was going to explode.

The day dragged on. Rogan could barely eat anything for dinner. His chatty sisters had perhaps distracted his mom enough that she didn't comment on the unusual behavior her son was exhibiting. Whatever the reason, he was grateful.

The evening wore on and still there was no radio chatter or word from Mr. Chaffey about how the search fared. Finally, after everyone but Rogan had gone to bed, he heard his dad get home.

From the look on his face, Rogan figured things had not gone well. "No luck?"

"We didn't find Martin, no." His dad sighed.

Rogan just stood there, worried and hopeless, and silently encouraged his dad to say more.

"Come into the kitchen with me, and I'll tell you more. I want to eat something."

Jim described Martin's dad, Stu. "I've never formally met him, but I've heard rumors, and apparently at least some of them are true. He showed up to the search meeting, drunk. He totally reeked of alcohol. He was belligerent and insisted we find his son and practically accused us of making his son disappear. That was ridiculous, of course, because we were there to help find him."

Rogan forced a swallow. "Why do you think Martin took off? Was he running away from his drunk dad?" This seemed a hopeful and logical theory.

"Nobody knows, apparently. There's no clue as to where he'd go. I hate to think of him out there overnight in this weather."

"Is everyone giving up?" Consternation filled Rogan. He was feeling ill again.

"We've done all we can for today. It's midnight, and it's cold. We're going to start back up in the daylight tomorrow. We didn't quite make it through every search quadrant." His dad wiped his hand down his face. "It's so hard, not having a clue about where he might be." His voice trailed off. Jim sat motionless for a few seconds and then seemed to shake himself awake. "Let's hit the hay. Did your mom do okay this afternoon?"

Rogan quickly filled him in, said goodnight, and headed upstairs. He lay there with guilt-laden insomnia pecking at his brain until he finally drifted to sleep.

Rogan drove his family, minus his dad, to church the next morning. The men of the community were back out, searching. Service had just finished, after a long prayer time for Martin's well-being and rescue, when one of the searchers entered the sanctuary.

"I have an update," he announced. Everyone was quiet as he made his way to the front of the church. "One of the groups came across evidence that someone had broken into a shed that is rarely used on the Roberts' property. That's only half a mile from the Wolfe's place. There were some empty cans of food on the floor and some empty, used chip bags scattered around. They were able to follow footprints in the snow for a while and those were headed away from the Wolfe's house. They lost the trail when they hit the road." He lifted his shoulders in a shrug. "It's not a whole lot, but that's what we found."

"So, hopefully, he's still around town. We should spread the word for everyone to keep their eyes out," one of the congregation's members commented.

"Yes, we are sending out that message."

"Are the volunteers still searching?" another asked.

"We are, and hopefully he'll be spotted soon. We have called the State Troopers and the Coast Guard. They should be arriving to help this afternoon."

There were murmurs of affirmation and some speculation with the person sitting nearby.

Rogan felt slightly less guilty because it sounded like Martin hadn't gone very far and was pulling a bad stunt. *Maybe it has nothing to do with what I did,* he thought.

The gut bomb returned when Jim Chaffey arrived home, again after dark, with news of another unsuccessful search, even with help from the recently-arrived authorities.

The next day at school, all anyone wanted to talk about was Martin's disappearance. Rogan heard comments ranging from, "He's probably back home, but his dad wouldn't know because he's too drunk," to, "Good riddance."

Rogan was up late again, wanting to hear the news when his dad got home, wet and cold. He and his mom waited while Jim went to change into dry clothes. Returning, he plopped on the couch.

"Well, this is unbelievable. Stu showed up to the briefing this morning, acting totally unconcerned for his son's welfare, and announced he was done with the search, that as far as he was concerned, Martin is dead."

"What? How can a parent do that?" Elise looked distressed.

Rogan shook his head. "What about his mom?"

"Apparently, she left them both about five years ago and moved down south somewhere. The troopers are trying to locate her, but it's doubtful Martin's trying to head to see her, because he has no clue where she is. According to Stu, Martin has not had any contact with her for years."

"That is so sad. That poor boy." Elise's mother's heart showed in her words.

"Wow," Rogan murmured. "Maybe that's why he's so messed up."

Jim arched an eyebrow. "Messed up, how?"

Rogan explained what he knew about the teen, from his reeking body odor to his behavior at school. He didn't say anything about their confrontation on Friday.

I'm not lying. I'm just leaving something out. It was an attempt at justifying his omission.

His dad commented, "Well, I guess OCS has been called a couple of times, but they never removed Martin from the home."

His dad was referring to the Office of Children's Services that existed to support the well-being of Alaska's children and youth. "The, I guess, good news is that we found another outbuilding that had been broken into, so if it is Martin, he's staying out of the weather. In this one, he used a propane tank that was in there and hooked up the radiant propane tank top heater, so he probably stayed warm."

"Why isn't anyone seeing him?" Elise sounded frustrated.

Rogan spent another restless night, trying to convince himself Martin's disappearance had nothing to do with how he had treated the boy. He wasn't being very persuasive with himself and felt the load of secret guilt.

Tuesday, he was with his group of friends at lunch, whispering, "Do you think Martin took off because of me? I feel so terrible. What if it's my fault?"

His buddies tried to be helpful. "Dude, you're one of the few people who have tried to be nice to him. You put up with a lot," Boom Chain tried to reassure him.

"Yeah, and look at all the people at school who teased him all the time," Tuff added.

Rogan appreciated the gesture, but it didn't ease his mind. When he was at his locker after lunch, grabbing his things for the next class, it was only him and Runt.

"I'm sorry you feel like Martin running away is your fault, Rogan. That's one thing I admire about you is how you always try to do what's right."

Rogan stared at his best friend. "Well, I sure didn't this time."

That evening, his dad received a phone call from the trooper in charge of the search operation. He hung up and turned to his family. "They're calling another briefing at the Community Center. I guess they have some new information. I'll see you later."

"Can I come, Dad?" Rogan wanted to be involved somehow.

Jim looked at Elise. "Will you be okay while we're gone?"

"Yes, I'll be fine. You two go."

CHAPTER 18

Return to Skeleton Cove

THE COMMUNITY CENTER WAS PACKED, BUT EVERYONE came to attention quickly when the trooper stepped onto the stage and walked to the podium. Rogan and his dad found a seat in plastic folding chairs next to Monty and Runt.

"Thank you all for coming and thank you to those of you who have been tirelessly and selflessly helping in the search. We, uh, had some investigators go to the Wolfe residence to speak with Stu and to search for any clues in Martin's room. There was a note..."

The audience buzzed.

"There was a note on Martin's bed. We did a comparison with his schoolwork, and it appears to be his handwriting."

Someone behind them shouted out, "Was it there the whole time, and Stu just didn't see it in his drunken stupor?"

The audience buzzed again.

Trooper Milliken put up his hands, pleading for quiet to return. "Please, at this point, it doesn't really matter because we just now have the information, so we need to focus on moving forward."

Rogan was flabbergasted. He whispered to Runt, "Do you think it was there the whole time?"

Runt's ice blue eyes seemed to spark. "What a rat. He doesn't even care about his kid enough to look in his room? I'm betting it was there all along."

"I'm starting to really feel sorry for the guy. Now we know why he's so messed up."

"For sure."

Rogan felt his dad elbow him to be quiet. The trooper was speaking again, reading from a copy of Martin's note. "'Dear Everybody, ha ha. Not that anyone will care that I'm gone, but just in case you want to know, I'm leaving. I can't take it anymore. Everyone hates me, and I'd rather take my chances somewhere else. You shouldn't look for me. I doubt that it matters, anyway.'"

With every word, Rogan sank down farther in his chair. His dad threw a few glances his way. Rogan could feel his face flushing. His leg jiggled, bouncing up and down. Runt cleared his throat and wiped his palms on his thighs.

"And here's the cryptic part." Trooper Milliken paused.

"It's signed Martin, but then it says, 'P.S. I didn't really mean it. Your mom's cool.' Does anyone know what that means?"

Rogan felt like he was going to throw up. His stomach rolled and rumbled. He couldn't bring himself to say it in front of everyone. He looked up at his dad, feeling the imagined disappointment, and choked out, "Dad, I need to talk to you. Now, please."

Rogan stood on wobbly knees. Runt's eyes were wide and worried. Jim followed his son outside.

The days of shouldering the weighty guilt came crashing in. Rogan blurted out about the fight at school, what Martin had said, and what he'd done in response. "I'm so sorry, Dad. I should've told you. I knew what I'd done was wrong, and…I've been asking myself if it was my fault he left. I'm so sorry." He stuffed his hands in his jeans pockets and began to silently weep. He couldn't bring himself to look at his dad.

He was surprised when his dad pulled him into a hug. "Oh, Rogan," was all he said for a few moments. He pushed his son away, grasping both of his shoulders. "We need to go talk to the trooper and tell him that, okay? I'll be right there beside you."

Rogan nodded and wiped the tears that had betrayed him with the sleeve of his hoody. He was startled when the door flung open, and meeting-goers began to exit. When they had the opportunity, they went inside. There were still a few people milling around. Rogan caught Runt's eye as he continued walking forward. He told his story once again, this time to the trooper.

"Thanks, son, for the information. That clears that up. Listen, I don't think this was your fault if that's how you're feeling. I think Martin felt bad about badmouthing your mom and just wanted to apologize before he left. It sounds like he was bullied a lot at school, but not by you."

"Except Friday." Rogan felt regret and remorse oozing out of his pores.

"Don't beat yourself up about it." Someone redirected the trooper's attention, and Rogan was left standing there with his dad. Monty and Runt joined them.

"Runt filled me in," said Monty.

Jim nodded. "Well, I don't know what's next. They have residents checking their outbuildings tonight. I guess we'll see what happens by morning."

They said their goodnights. The drive home was a silence heavy with things not yet spoken. Rogan felt like he did when he was little, knowing he'd done wrong and waiting for the looming punishment. His dad parked the 4Runner and turned in his seat to face Rogan.

"I kept a secret once when I was about your age. I knew I should've said something, but I didn't. Because of that, a nice old lady was injured when some high school punks broke into her house. I felt terribly guilty for a long time."

Rogan looked at his dad in the dim light. All he saw was compassion, not condemnation. The tears again burned hot in his eyes.

"God forgives us when we ask, Rogan. Then, we just have to learn from it. I'll let you talk to God about it."

Rogan nodded, unable to trust his voice. They sat in a more comfortable silence until they were ready to head in. Rogan went straight up to his room, avoiding everyone. He sat on his bed in the dark, his door closed.

God, please forgive me. I know I keep asking, but I still feel terrible. I'm sorry I didn't treat Martin right. I'm sorry he has such a crummy home life. I'm sorry I yelled at him instead of showing him Jesus. I'm sorry I cared about what other people thought. I'm just so sorry.

His prayers were silent admissions. He was afraid if he said them out loud, someone would find out what a bad person he had been.

Overnight, no one had spotted Martin breaking in to find shelter. Mr. Chaffey told Rogan this after he woke his son in the early morning hours. "There is, however, a boat missing from the harbor. It's the Roberts' Lund."

The remnants of sleep slid off Rogan. "The sixteen-foot Fury?"

"Yes, and there's more. They found a dirty red bandana knotted to the mooring ring on the dock."

"That's Martin's for sure, Dad. He always wears that."

"Get dressed in your warmest. I'd like you to come with us today. You can miss school. We'll take the *Coho Cora*, and Monty and Timothy will take their boat. I already made us a lunch. The search is now concentrating on all the little islands around us. The Coast Guard Search and Rescue is in charge now." His dad reached over and ruffled Rogan's hair, which was already standing straight up after a night of tossing and turning. "Did you have a good talk with God?"

"Yeah, I did. I still feel terrible, but I *think* I'm forgiven."

Jim smiled. "You are." He turned to leave, stopped, and turned back. "Oh, and make sure you bring your go bag, too. The seas are supposed to be calm today, but it's always good to be prepared, right?"

Rogan gave him a thumbs up and hurried to get ready.

The volunteer sea rescue fleet met at the town's dock. Rogan let the excitement of the mission overrule his guilty burden for a few moments. He spotted Runt and hurried over. He greeted Runt with, "This is awesome that we get to go. How crazy is he, stealing a boat and going who knows where in this cold?"

"He is crazy, all right. Did you hear he left his grungy bandana behind? I've never seen him without it."

"Me neither. Yeah, my dad told me. Think we'll find him today?" Rogan certainly hoped so. In his estimation, this had gone on long enough.

"I hope so, and I want to spot him first, so I can be the conquering hero. The girls would all like that, for sure."

Rogan grinned his slightly crooked smile.

After a quick briefing, the chief petty officer handed out assignments for the search grid. He reminded everyone to be on channel sixteen but to not contribute to radio chatter. Everyone needed to keep it clear for emergencies and for if someone spotted Martin.

Motors purred to life, bubbling seawater as props, anxious to speed through the gray-green water, whirled below the surface. The day was overcast and gloomy. Rogan huddled next to his father by the steering console, wrapped in an emergency blanket to ward off icy winds that bit with sharp fangs at any exposed skin. Rogan was thankful he'd worn his balaclava to somewhat protect his face.

It took ten minutes to get to their first designated island. By then, Rogan's eyes were watering from the cold breeze. He'd been swiveling his head, looking in every direction as they traveled, hoping to catch a glimpse of the stolen Lund, or better yet, of a lost boy standing on a lonely beach.

"At least the Lund is part red. Maybe that will show up better than just silver." Rogan yelled at his dad so his words wouldn't fly away in the sea breeze, and so he was heard over the noise from their motor.

His dad eased up on the throttle. "Yes, I hope so. I'm going to stay out a way and circle the island. Let's make sure to look under the trees, too, not just on the water or the beach. He or the boat may be hiding there."

"Aye, aye, Captain."

"Do you have the binoculars handy?"

Rogan grabbed them with chilly fingers. "Right here."

"Good."

They slowly motored about twenty yards from shore. Rogan knew his dad was also watching the navigation system, a Lowrance that was a depth finder and GPS combo. They had downloaded Navionics marine charts onto it, thus ensuring they didn't run too shallow or hit an underwater rock or structure. Eyes straining, Rogan wish-prayed he'd see Martin, and this would all be over.

They circled the first island with no success and motored a couple hundred yards to the next one, a small brushy knob with stubby waves crashing on a steep shore.

"Not a likely place to beach a boat, but we'll check it out," his dad commented.

The excitement of being a part of the search, and hopefully rescue, soon gave way to shivers, dashed hopes, and monotony. Rogan could feel a headache creeping up the back of his tight neck. Despair tapped him on the shoulder, trying to get his full attention, but he ignored it like it was an annoying stranger.

Or, like it was Martin.

If he was honest with himself, he'd pretended at trying to be nice to the kid, doing the bare minimum to be civil.

I'm sorry, God. Please help us find him, and I promise to be nicer. Rogan realized he was praying a sort of foxhole prayer, but he couldn't seem to help thinking the words over and over.

After motoring around the perimeter of their sixth island with no luck, Jim picked up the Motorola handheld radio. It was set to channel seven, so he could communicate with Monty without hogging the airwaves of the VHF.

"*Tide Runner*, do you read?" Rogan heard his dad use the name of the Petersen's boat to hail them.

A tinny voice responded. "Go ahead, *Coho Cora*. I copy."

"Any luck? We're batting zero."

"Same here. Nothing."

"All right. Just checking."

Rogan looked out across the ocean. "Dad, what if no one finds him?"

"I don't know. It would be hard for him to survive. But...there's still hope. Let's get back at it."

Find the next island on the search map. Circle the island. Look through the binoculars. Listen for the VHF to bring good news. Stomp freezing feet to get back some circulation. Scan the sea. Move on to the next island. Repeat.

Rogan felt time blob and morph around him. His mind quit hoping. His eyes kept searching.

By the time they motored back to the dock, they were low on fuel and high on the exhaustion meter. There had been no sightings. Cold and tired men and boys shuffled to their rigs to drive home. Rogan almost fell asleep on the ten-minute drive around the bay to home. They took five-gallon gas cans and filled them up from the large storage container they kept on hand. They would take them to the dock tomorrow to fill up the *Cora* for another day of searching.

It will be Thursday tomorrow, Rogan thought. *Martin's been gone almost a week.* He practically ate dinner in his sleep, and then crashed.

Mr. Chaffey told Rogan he could help search for one more day. He told his son that he understood the need to be involved since Rogan had confessed his feelings of guilt. Thursday morning arrived with light snow flurries. Rogan managed to drag himself out of bed, stiff

FORGIVENESS AT SKELETON COVE

and sore, and head down for breakfast. He was surprised that his mom had cooked a hearty meal.

"I'm getting my strength back and wanted to celebrate," she explained. "Most of the tingling is gone, too."

"Just don't overdo it, Hon. Take it a little easy," Jim reminded her.

She smiled. "I will."

Back to the dock, get assignments, head out.

Runt had to return to school today, and Monty had Old Man Tate with him for his extra set of eyes. Rogan thought of him as a salty character. He knew the white-whiskered man had been on the ocean for most of his life.

Rogan and his dad had listened to the marine weather forecast before launching. The voice from the National Weather Service out of Juneau gave the forecast. "A low, south of the Gulf of Alaska, will bring snow flurries over southeast Alaska through Thursday night. Northwest winds becoming ten knots in the afternoon. Seas three feet or less."

The day was shaping up to be much like yesterday. There still wasn't any happy announcement over the radio. Things were looking bleak. Searchers were weary.

Monty called on the Motorola radio that they were pulling into a cove on the island marked number twenty-four. Jim had Rogan check the map. They were near and decided to join them for a leg-stretching break. They soon caught up to their friends. Rogan's legs felt a bit wobbly after being in the boat for so long. As they debarked, Rogan saw Old Man Tate sitting on a rock part-way up the beach.

He looks a little green. I can't believe he'd be seasick, Rogan pondered.

Rogan walked down the beach and picked up a couple of snow-capped rocks. He threw them one at a time into the sea that was self-ishly holding its knowledge as to where Martin had gone. A few lacy crystals floated from the cloudy sky, but it seemed to be lightening up a bit.

"Rogan!" He heard his name yelled; a sense of urgency wrapped up in it. He turned to see his dad beckoning him to come with a wildly waving arm. Monty was bending over the wriggling form of Old Man Tate, who was on his back on the crusty, cold rocks. Slipping, Rogan raced back.

"Pretty sure he's having a heart attack, Jim," Monty panted. "We've got to get him back."

A loud groan was Old Man Tate's answer.

Jim looked toward the boats. "I guess let's leave the *Cora* here, so one of us can drive, and one can do CPR if it's needed. Rogan, help me beach it."

"Dad. You go with Mr. Petersen. I can drive the *Cora* back. I know how to follow the track back on the nav system. You know I can do it."

A gurgling sound from the elderly man sealed the deal.

"Okay. Help us get him into Monty's boat, and then you head home behind us."

Wrangling Old Man Tate up and over the side of the boat wasn't pretty, but they finally managed. They laid him down on the floor. Monty had a covered cockpit that would be an asset in the race back.

"We'll call for a first responder to meet us at the dock. See you soon and be careful," was his father's parting remark as they sped off.

Rogan's stomach was rolling again from the stress of it all. *Can anything else go wrong?* He took a moment to say a prayer for Old Man

Tate and then untied the moorage and shoved off. As he began to turn toward home, following the line the Lowrance had paved for his road back, the low cloud cover lifted enough for him to see an island he hadn't noticed earlier. He throttled down and let the boat drift, grabbing for his binoculars. It took a moment to zero in on the distinctive rock columns, since he was bobbing up and down with the waves.

He lowered the binoculars, peering into the distance. It was a little too far away to make out details with the naked eye, so he looked through the binoculars once more.

"That's our Survival School Island," he mused out loud. "I can see Martin going there. Should I check it out?" His question floated away, unanswered except for the shrill cry of a gull. He looked at his watch. It was two o'clock. He didn't have much time before it started getting dark, and his dad was expecting him to motor back as he'd promised. On the other hand, this may be his only chance to find Martin. He felt a deep need to right his wrong.

"Uuh!" His frustration echoed in the solitude.

He picked up the binoculars again, changed his mind, and quickly exchanged them for the VHF radio.

"*Tide Runner*, this is *Coho Cora*. Do you copy?" He emulated his father's radio conversations. Nothing but static answered him. He tried again, repeating the summons. He turned the squelch down to get rid of the static.

"Okay, here's what you'll do." Talking out loud to himself helped calm his nerves, somehow. "We'll zip over to the island and see if we can see Martin or his boat." He paused. "Not sure who 'we' is. It's just me. Great."

Another heavy pause and a sigh. "I'm going."

It only took five minutes to get to the side of the island where they'd made camp by the tall rock spires. Rogan went up the length of the beach, driving the boat twenty yards offshore like his dad had, without spotting any sign of human life. He cupped his hands by his mouth and yelled, "Martin!"

"Okay, now do I go all the way around the island, or…" He was talking out loud to himself again. "Skeleton Cove. I'm betting he's in Skeleton Cove."

Rogan drove the *Cora* around the north end of the island. Things looked a bit different with a covering of snow. The beach had a few feet right next to the water that was cleared of snow from the rising and falling tides.

"Speaking of tides…" Rogan grabbed the tide book. "Okay, high tide was at eleven-ten, and it's two-twenty. I hope the tide is high enough." Rogan remembered how the passageway into Skeleton Cove got shallow during low tide. That was, he assumed, how the whale was trapped in the cove. He didn't want to scrape bottom, get stuck, or damage the motor because he wasn't supposed to be doing this in the first place. He knew he was going to try, though. He felt the pull of it like the tractor beam that caught Han Solo's spaceship in *Star Wars*.

"Sorry, Dad. I have to."

Spotting the almost-hidden opening to Skeleton Cove, Rogan carefully maneuvered the skiff, going at the slowest speed possible and still maintain functional steering. He sat on the edge of his seat in case he needed to quickly flip up the motor. He looked over the gunwale on the starboard side, hoping to see the bottom, but the waters were stormy. He looked back at the depth finder.

"I've still got four feet. So far, so good."

The *Coho Cora* rounded the tight corner. There, at the far end of the cove, the red color somehow bright in the gloom of the afternoon, was the missing Lund. Its bow was pulled part-way up the beach but not tied off. Rogan figured it was enough to secure it in the protected confines of the cove. He scanned the beach and tree line, which were blanketed in winter white.

No sign of Martin.

Rogan gave the motor a spurt from the throttle and then quickly raised it. The forward momentum would be enough to carry him to shore. Hopping off the bow, he pulled the skiff up a little higher onto the rocky beach.

He turned his head from side to side, scanning. There! It appeared that Martin was using the whale's rib cage for his shelter. He had a brown tarp draped over the bones, now a support for his make-shift camp.

Rogan headed that way, hoping Martin wasn't lying in there injured, or even worse… He refused to let his mind go there. He caught a whiff of smoke. Relaxing a little, he figured the boy was well enough to keep a fire going.

Rogan was almost there when Martin flipped open the tarp and crawled out. They stood there, staring at each other. Rogan had dreamed of this moment but never beyond it.

Martin spoke first, and it seemed to Rogan that his usual defiance and bravado were gone. "Well, I see you found me. I'm surprised you're alone, though. Where is everyone else?"

"It's just me." Rogan decided to save the particulars for later.

Martin cocked his head. "Well, I'd say make yourself at home, but I'm not sure I want you here. You yelled at me in front of everyone. I'm not leaving. I've got enough food to last me a while. I'm not sure what you're going to eat, though."

Okay, he still has the attitude, Rogan thought.

"I've found you, and you have to come back. Everyone has been out looking for you. They're worried about you."

At this, Martin snorted. "Yeah, they're real worried."

"It's true, Martin. People are putting themselves in danger to find you. The reason I'm alone is because Old Man Tate had a heart attack. He's too old to be out here in the cold. My dad and Mr. Petersen took him back. I was supposed to be following them. We need to go home."

With the mention of Old Man Tate, Martin's countenance softened. "I'm sorry about the old guy. I hope he's okay. But, it doesn't change anything. I'm still staying."

"Fine. I'm going without you." Rogan turned to leave.

"I know what you're thinking, Chaffey. You'll go back and tell everyone where I am, so they can send the Coast Guard, or something. I won't be here, and you won't know where I've gone."

Rogan stopped and looked up, his shoulders lifting and then slumping with a heavy sigh. He turned back to the rough-looking boy, only now noticing Martin's jacket had strips of duct tape here and there, and he had socks on for mittens. The would-be rescuer watched as Martin shrugged as if to say, "Do what you want, but I'm forcing your hand," then bent over and re-entered his tarp tent.

What to do? That was the question of the hour. Rogan had a growing unease about not heading straight home. His dad would be worried. He had probably also broken, perhaps irrevocably, the trust his dad held toward him. Rogan mentally kicked himself for deciding to look for Martin on his own.

Right now, he really wanted to leave, tell everyone where Martin was, and let them come back to get him, but as Martin had just told him, he'd probably be long gone.

If I left now, I'd only be about half an hour behind schedule. What should I do?

Rogan realized he was pacing back and forth. He stopped. His arms reached up as if trying to grasp an answer from the steel-colored heavens, and then he let them fall, empty. His hands slapped the sides of his thighs.

"Fine," he huffed. "I'm going back and hope it all works out." A feeling of dread was slithering around in his chest, waiting for the next thing to go wrong.

He pushed on the bow of the boat and was surprised to find it heavily beached. He let go and walked to the side. Shocked, he noticed how far down the tide had gone out in such a short time.

"Oh, snap," he muttered. The back third of the boat was all that was in the water. Rogan dug his feet into the rolling pebbles that constituted the composition of the beach and strained. The boat reluctantly inched back into the sea. A few more pushes, and he was able to jump in and start the motor.

As he rounded the corner that led out of the cove, the alarm on the Lowrance blurped out its shallow depth warning. He hastily shut off the motor and raised it. He could both feel and hear a light scraping of rocks on the aluminum hull.

Rogan looked around. The tide had already gone out too far for him to escape the cove. He grabbed the wooden paddle secured to the inside of the boat, below the gunwale, and gently dipped it into the water at the bow, pushing to guide his boat back into the cove. As much as he hated the prospect of going back, getting the boat grounded would be a terrible idea. It was his only option. Once he was in the deeper water of the cove, Rogan plopped down on the seat and put his head in his hands.

Great. I'm stuck here until the tide comes back up. By then it will be after eleven and completely dark.

A new revelation crashed into the first one, causing a casualty of hope. *If high tide is at eleven tonight, that means low will be around five in the morning, so I'm stuck here until almost noon tomorrow.*

Regret wrapped around him like a coat of ice. *I'm so sorry I'm letting you down, Dad.* Rogan knew how much his family would worry, and his dad would come back looking for him, even in the dark when it wasn't close to safe conditions. He thought about how much his mom had gone through recently, and he felt shame fill up the void in his stomach.

What have I done? Lord, I really need some help right now.

Hiking to the other side of the island was out because what would that accomplish? He couldn't get the boat over there. Rogan felt an overwhelming sadness and despair. He sat in the *Cora*, adrift in the middle of Skeleton Cove, his head in his hands, wanting to cry.

His father's voice, perhaps a gift from The Father, echoed in his brain. "Adapt and overcome."

He sat up straight, staring into the darkening sky. "Thank You."

Why he hadn't thought of it before was a mystery. He grabbed his go bag, pulling it near his feet and unzipping one of the front pockets. His hand fumbled around, seeking what he hoped was the solution to his problem. There! Hope came knocking on his heart, and as soon as he had his SPOT satellite GPS messenger in his fist, he welcomed hope back in.

"Okay, I hope I remember how this thing works," he muttered to himself.

The device was a black plastic contraption with an orange stripe that looked similar to a pager. It was a modern invention made for situations such as this one. It would determine his GPS location. He could send that, plus one of his pre-programmed messages, to his parents' email and to the GEOS Rescue Coordination Center. The Center would also call his home phone, which was fortunate since his dad wasn't home to get an email, and who knew if his mom would be checking. Cell phones did not work in his small island community.

The SPOT was completely independent of any land-based coverage, since it used satellites. All he needed was a clear view of the sky, which he had from where his boat sat. If he was on the beach at Skeleton Cove, it might not have worked as well. He pressed the power button, briefly holding it down. Instead of blinking green, it began blinking red.

"No, no, no."

It was low on battery power. He set it down on the gunwale and dug into his backpack again, searching for his spare batteries. His hand closed around the baggie, and he pulled it out, turned to grab the SPOT device, and promptly knocked it overboard. It landed with a small splash that felt more like a death sentence than a ripple effect.

Hurrying to peek over the side, his heart unclenched as he saw it floating nearby, but out of reach. He grabbed the paddle and used it to gently draw the GPS unit back to the boat.

"No more idiot moves, Chaffey." He took a few deep breaths, hoping to reduce the shaking of his hands.

Rogan managed to change the batteries without further mishap. The power light was now blinking green, as it should be.

Whew. Okay, now I hold it with the logo facing up.

He held it aloft in the hopes that the slight elevation gain would be beneficial. He brought it back down in front of his face after about a minute, hoping it would have acquired the satellite, not certain how long it would take. The GPS button was blinking red.

"Grr," he growled. "I'm getting tired of red blinking lights. What is it now? I need some help here, Lord." His frustration delayed his next word. "Please."

He was stymied. *Why isn't it working?* He moved to the back of the boat, staring at the device, and willing it to work. The GPS began blinking green. The message-sending light soon joined it.

Ecstatic, he returned to the bench seat by the steering console and sat, preparing to send his message.

Wait...what? The message light and GPS had both returned to red warning flashers. He felt like chucking the thing overboard again. He knocked on it a few times with his knuckles. No change.

Rogan reminded himself to take a deep breath and think calmly. If he could. On the third breath, his eyes landed on the Lowrance right by him. *That's right! It can't be so close to another GPS.* He returned to the stern, and the friendly green lights were reinstated.

He breathed a "Yes." He quickly went to the message function and chose the "I'm okay but send help," preloaded communication.

He sat on the back near the motor and felt a sweet relief. Both his message and GPS location had gone out. Now he just had to wait.

Looking over at Martin's shelter, he knew he needed to try and make things right between them. He was reluctant to do so and realized he felt justified in some of his actions. Martin was not likable. In fact, he could be downright mean. Rogan thought of the lessons on forgiveness Dexter Newby had been teaching them. He needed to forgive the sulking boy.

God has forgiven me, even though I still don't feel pardoned from my actions.

God wanted him to forgive Martin.

Why is life so hard?

Deep down inside, Rogan had always wanted to do the right thing for as long as he could remember. *I try hard to be a good person, well… to live by what the Bible says to do.*

He felt badly when he messed up and usually tried to correct it right away. This situation had been eating at his conscience for too long.

Rogan used the paddle to get to the beach, and then set up a bungee mooring system so the skiff would stay farther from shore, going up and down with the tide, but not grounding. Once that was set up, he pulled on the bow rope until he could jump off onto the rocks. The bungee tied to the stern and anchor pulled the *Cora* back out, while the bow line kept it moored to the shore.

Reluctantly, Rogan walked over to Martin's shelter. He stood there, not sure how to proceed. Finally, he cleared his throat and said, "Knock, knock."

Martin poked his head out. "You're still here?"

"Uh, yeah. It's too shallow to get out, so you're stuck with me for a few hours."

Martin just stared at him and said nothing.

"Can I come in, so we can talk?"

"I guess." Martin's head disappeared.

Rogan's eyes involuntarily rolled. He pulled the tarp flap aside, bent over, and crawled in. It was a little smoky inside but warm and dry.

"Nice shelter." Rogan went for the compliment first.

Martin said a seemingly grudging thanks. Rogan did a quick sweep with his eyes. Martin had a sleeping bag, a couple of camp pots and pans, a tote where Rogan assumed he had some food stored, and a collapsible water bucket. Rogan bought himself more time by taking off his jacket, folding it, and placing it in his lap.

He felt quite awkward but decided to jump in. "Look, Martin, I wanted to tell you I'm sorry. I shouldn't have yelled at you in school." He looked at the other boy, but Martin was back to staring with a mostly blank face. Rogan forged ahead. "I was tired and stressed out because of everything going on with my mom, and I'm embarrassed and disappointed that I lost it. So…" It was hard to say the words. "Please forgive me. It's no excuse. I shouldn't have reacted that way." Rogan cast a humble glance at Martin.

Rogan wasn't sure what to think at first. Martin had a strange, almost puckered look on his face that Rogan couldn't read.

It was Martin's turn to clear his throat. He also turned his head away to the side and took a quick swipe at his eyes. Turning back, he croaked out, "No one has ever apologized to me before or asked me to forgive them. What does that even mean?"

"It means I'm sorry, and I want you to know I'm sorry. Also, well, it's like I owed you money, and you canceled my debt?" Rogan was thinking of the parable from Sunday school.

Martin just said, "I'm confused."

"I don't think I'm explaining it very well," Rogan agreed. "I guess it means I want you to stop being mad at me and…well, maybe we can start over and be more like friends."

Rogan thought Martin looked like he felt suspicious. The feeling was confirmed when Martin asked, "Are you being serious or just jerking my chain?"

"No, I'm totally serious."

"Why would you want to be my friend? Aren't you worried about what everyone would say?" Martin's chin began to quiver. Before Rogan could witness the tears, Martin covered his face with his hands. His shoulders shook.

Unsure of how to proceed, Rogan kept talking. "I found out about your mom leaving and your dad drinking, and I can't imagine how hard that must be." He had to admit to himself that Martin was right. He did worry about being ridiculed by others—guilt by association. *But I shouldn't be.*

The other boy had pulled himself together somewhat. He sniffed and wiped his nose. "I loved my mom and don't even know why she left. She wasn't perfect, but she was my mom. I think things were bad for her and she started taking some drugs. That's why I said what I did. She was just gone one day, and my dad would never talk about it. I barely remember what she looks like."

"Do you know where she lives now?"

"No clue." A thoughtful pause. "Then there's my dad. What a jerk."

Rogan felt the pain radiating off Martin like shimmery heat waves, and he suddenly realized how lucky he was to have the wonderful, godly family he had. Sure, he had been grateful for them all along, but Martin's agony brought the depth of it into sharp focus.

"Did he even show up to help search for me?"

"Yes, he did."

"I'm actually surprised he even figured out I was gone. He's so drunk all the time."

Rogan willed his tongue to not reveal that Mr. Wolfe had not only given up the search early on but hadn't even noticed the note his son had left behind. *How hurtful would that be?* Instead, he offered, "I heard the P.S. about my mom on your note. Thank you for that." He picked up a nearby twig, broke it into pieces, and slowly tossed them, one at a time, into the fire.

Martin chewed on his lower lip. "I should man up, too. I'm sorry about saying those things about your mom. I was just being a jerk. Will you…forgive me?"

Rogan smiled. "Of course." He reached out a closed fist, an invitation for a first bump, which Martin accepted.

After that, the conversation felt more natural. Rogan felt his disgust slip away. Martin seemed more like a regular kid, and he didn't notice Martin's body odor as much as before. The smoke swirling in the air also helped to mask it. Outside, evening laid itself out under the blanket of steel-gray clouds. They added more wood to the fire.

At a pause in the conversation, Rogan announced he wanted to go check on the boat to make sure the moorings were holding. Martin offered to tag along, explaining, "I'm going to bring Mr. Roberts' boat back sometime. Not sure when, but I feel kinda bad for takin' it. I didn't know what else to do."

Rogan nodded. "I hope he's understanding."

Two boys stood on the dark beach, windswept and icy, and stared out into the inky night. Even without moonlight, the snow glazing the tree branches gave off a dim glow.

A sharp crack from the black woods beyond the whale skeleton sounded loudly in the crisp stillness, making both boys jump.

CHAPTER 19

Hoffman's Redemption

ROGAN GRABBED MARTIN'S UPPER ARM AND DRAGGED him along as he sprinted for the boat. Hands shaking, he grabbed the bowline and pulled, hand over hand. Both boys scrambled onboard, puffs of air shooting like a steam engine into the darkness indicative of how fast they were breathing.

"What was that?" Martin whispered. "A bear?"

"They're usually hibernating by now. I don't know," Rogan whispered back.

They both hunkered down to be less visible, straining their eyes to see what monster would creep or crawl out of the forest. For a few ticks of time, all Rogan could hear was his pulse whooshing in his ears. Another sharp crack rent the air. Then…voices. The boys looked at each other quizzically.

"Rogan, can you hear me?"

He recognized that voice! Rogan popped to his feet. "Over here, Dad. I'm in the boat."

Cleansing relief washed over him. A big grin couldn't help putting in an immediate appearance. He reached over and clapped Martin on the back, forgetting for a second that the other boy wouldn't be excited about a rescue. Martin, however, was grinning back at him.

Maybe he was just trying to be brave, Rogan thought. *Maybe he really does want to go home.*

The boys jumped out onto the beach and ran to meet Jim and Monty. Rogan kept running, right into a bear hug from his dad.

"I'm so glad you found us. You must've hiked overland from the sea's side of the island?"

"We did." Jim looked around. In the gloom of night, the boats were faintly outlined on the water. "How did you get the boats in here?"

Rogan and Martin took turns explaining about the entrance to Skeleton Cove and how they were trapped by the tide until around noon tomorrow unless they tried it at midnight, which wasn't appealing.

"So, this is Skeleton Cove from Survival School. From what I can see in the dark, I understand why you boys liked it," Monty observed.

"Well, young man," Jim was speaking to Martin, "A lot of people are worried about you. A lot of people have been searching for you."

Rogan thought Martin had the good sense to look chagrined. His own guilt was resurfacing.

"Dad, I'm sorry I didn't follow you right away. The clouds lifted, and I saw this island, and I just knew that was where Martin was. I tried calling you on the radio." His voice lamely trailed off as Jim put up a hand.

"We'll talk about that later."

Rogan dropped his chin to his chest, feeling ashamed.

"How is Old Man Tate?" Martin inquired. "I feel real bad about that."

"We're not sure," said Monty. "We got him back to the dock and handed him off to the Coast Guard's Health Services Technician. He's taking care of him."

"That's like a medic," Jim explained. "We're just praying he'll be okay."

Martin nodded. "I hope he is."

They discussed their next steps. Everyone agreed it was too dangerous to leave at midnight, so they would all spend the night and leave when the *Coho Cora* and the stolen Lund could motor out of the cove. Rogan was instructed to stay with Martin in the tarp shelter, while his dad and Monty would hike back to the boat and attempt to radio the Coast Guard or a nearby vessel to get the message to Elise and the searchers. Rogan figured Martin shouldn't be left alone, and that's why his dad told him to stay here. No one would be very comfortable, since both types of sleeping quarters would be crowded.

Rogan retrieved his go bag so he could use the emergency blanket to stay warm and also use it for his pillow. Even without the usual comforts, he fell into an exhausted sleep.

They woke to snow that drifted down gracefully and daintily. The tops of the trees that grew along the upper shore of the cove began swaying back and forth, performing their own waltz to partner with the snowflakes.

"I hope this storm that's rolling in holds off until we are able to get out of the cove," Rogan told Martin.

"Yeah. Could make it tricky."

As they disassembled the tarp structure, Martin said, "I think I've decided to try and find my mom. I'd rather live with her than with my drunk dad. She's got to be better than him, right?"

Martin's hopeful look stabbed Rogan in the heart. "I'm sure it will be. Maybe she didn't really want to leave you." Rogan thought it could be true and was trying to be positive for Martin.

"I wish I had your mom. She seems really nice. I've seen her when she's at school for stuff and at community events. Does she cook dinner for you and everything?"

Taken aback, Rogan realized he'd taken his whole family for granted. Not everyone had what he had.

Wow. Thank you, Lord, for my amazing family. We're not perfect, but they love me. He looked out across the cove. *Even when I mess up,* he thought. *Speaking of messing up, I just added one more thing for You to forgive me for, God. Why didn't I just follow them back and tell them about Survival School Island?*

With those thoughts firing through his neurons, Rogan answered Martin. "My mom *is* really nice. And yes, she cooks me dinner."

Martin nodded and licked his dry, cracked lips. "Dinner sounds really good right now. What's your favorite food she makes?"

"Oh, boy. That's a hard one. I love her barbecued venison, her sourdough bread, and…oh, I know. Probably her homemade mac-n-cheese." Rogan sighed, imagining a delectable bite of the creamy pasta.

"That sounds amazing. I'm pretty hungry right now."

"Yeah. That granola bar didn't last too long, did it?"

Martin's camp was packed up and in the Lund. Rogan wondered when his dad and Monty would be there. Knowing they were close gave him comfort, but he also felt a niggling of anxiety about the unknown. *Was everything okay with them? Shouldn't they be here by now?*

They stood next to the campfire, which they had kept burning, holding their hands out to the warmth, and watching snowflakes disappear into the flames. Rogan was starting to forget how it felt to be warm and dry and comfortable.

The two men soon appeared, tramping through the wet brush. While waiting for the tide to rise, they decided Martin would ride with Monty in the *Tide Runner*, Jim would drive the Roberts' Lund, and Rogan would captain the *Coho Cora*. His dad gave him a pointed look.

"Don't worry, Dad. I'm not going anywhere but home. I promise."

His dad continued to pierce him with a stern gaze for a second or two, then transformed when a grin erupted. "I believe you, Son."

Rogan encouraged Martin to share his plan for changing his living arrangements, and the spotlight shifted its focusing beam to the other boy. While they were talking, Rogan excused himself to answer the call of nature. On his way back, he was passing the whale skeleton and saw a slab of rib that had been broken off. He was bummed, but then decided to snag it. The bone was flat and wide, about six inches in length. He put it into the cargo pocket on the side of his pant leg.

When it was time and they figured the tide was high enough, Martin followed Monty overland to his boat. Jim and Rogan shoved off in the other two vessels.

"You go first, and I'll follow you," his dad instructed.

Rogan gave a thumbs up and motored out of the cove, saying a silent goodbye to the stark whale skeleton. He hoped he could come back someday under better circumstances.

Leaving the protection of the cove, Rogan was buffeted by winds and angry-looking swells. The skiff rode the upside of the swell before slapping down the other side. Rogan's recently overworked adrenaline kicked back in. Dark, somber-looking clouds were low in the sky. His mind tried to remember everything he knew about how to drive the boat in these conditions. He would've felt safer if his dad could take over, but that wasn't going to happen. It was up to him.

I'm not alone, he told himself. *I can do it.*

His eyes continually scanned the water for debris, floating chunks of tree, or patches of kelp. It was difficult to tell in the stormy light and with the rolling sea. He also paid close attention to the navigation on the Lowrance, following the return path leading to home, warmth, and food.

Ten minutes into the trip, Monty caught up to them and passed the two smaller boats. Rogan was slightly jealous that Martin got to sit in a covered cabin while he and his dad were exposed to the elements, and all because of Martin.

Oh well, forget about it, he chastised himself.

Not long after, the clouds had waited long enough and let loose, shooting icy pellets of rain. They hit Rogan's cheeks, stinging. He pulled down the face mask part of his balaclava and squinted his eyes against the onslaught. Deciding which speed was best for the three-foot swells took some practice, but Rogan felt like he was getting the hang of it. He looked over at his dad, sitting in the stern of the red Lund. His dad pointed at him, then made the "okay" sign with his hand. Rogan gave him a thumbs up.

The trip felt interminable. There was nothing to look at except the color gray. Gray ocean, gray clouds, gray sky, gray raindrops. No birds were flying, and the seals and sea lions must have been hiding in the gray depths. Rogan knew they were almost to their home bay when he entered the more element-protected waters and the swells calmed considerably. He and his dad were able to increase their speed.

Finally, Rogan caught sight of the north entrance to the bay. He felt like cheering. He felt stiff and cold and wet. He felt a great weariness throughout his body.

The Chaffey's boat slip was vacant, even with the extra Coast Guard boats and activity surrounding the search and rescue effort. Rogan saw Monty in his boat, and it looked like he was heading back out. Jim waved at him, and the *Tide Runner* turned around when Monty spotted the two strays.

Once everyone was back on land, they hustled Jim and Rogan up the dock's ramp to the Community Center. It was crowded with townsfolk and rescuers who had heard the news of Martin's return. As Rogan walked in the door, following his dad and Monty, everyone began to clap. Runt ran up and punched his best friend on the shoulder.

"Man, I wish I could've been out there, too. But, no, I had to be in boring old school while you get to be the hero again." Runt was grinning.

"I'm not a hero. I just happened to find him. He was at Skeleton Cove!"

"No way."

"Way. We've got to go back there this spring—with permission, of course, and do a campout. That place is so awesome."

"I'm in."

Someone grabbed Rogan from behind, spun him around, and pulled him into a fierce hug. "Mom, you're here."

She released her son and cupped his face in her hands. "You're okay?"

Rogan smiled, nodded, and said, "I'm so sorry for worrying you."

"The center called with your message, so I felt a little better. I radioed your dad, and he and Monty came to find you. This whole thing has been a horrible ordeal. I'm so thankful Martin is alive and well."

People were shaking Jim's and Monty's hands, and excited chatter filled the hall. Rogan looked around and saw Martin sitting near the stage, a wool blanket around his shoulders and a cup of hot something in his hands.

Rogan looked at Runt. "Let's go talk to Martin."

Runt tweaked an eyebrow but nonetheless followed his friend.

"Hey, Martin. Glad to be back?"

"Yeah, I guess." He shrugged. "OCS talked to me already, and I don't have to go back with my dad. They're going to try to find my mom for me."

"That's great news. Where are you going to stay in the meantime? I mean, until they find your mom?"

Runt's eyes were wide, darting back and forth between Rogan and Martin, like he couldn't believe what he was hearing.

Rogan chuckled. "Runt, Martin and I had a good talk while we were on the island. We forgave each other."

"Yeah, we did," said Martin as his hand peeked out of the blanket, offering a fist bump, which first Rogan and then Runt accepted.

"That's cool," said Runt.

"Anyway, they want me to go to the hospital in Ketchikan to get checked out. I'll stay at a place over there, kind of like a temporary foster home, for a few weeks, anyway."

"I'll be praying that they find your mom and that you get to live with her, and that it will be a good thing."

"Thanks, Rogan. I hope so, too."

Rogan was glad it was Friday, so he didn't have to worry about going to school tomorrow. His body ached, and he felt like he'd never be completely warm. At home, he went through the refrigerator and ate most of the leftovers like a human garbage disposal, then headed for a hot shower and bed. He felt a great relief that the situation had worked out favorably and that he was home. That night's sleep was deep and peaceful.

Everyone in the Chaffey household was a little slow getting up and going Saturday morning. They all congregated in the kitchen, enjoying being a family. Elise was making huckleberry pancakes, and the conversation was about the plans for the day. It was snowing again and with all the recent excitement, Elise still recovering, and Rogan having missed school, his parents thought it should be a stay-at-home-and-get-caught-up day. Lainey and Peg wanted to play with their Lego Friends Forest House set. The only thing tainting the happy morning for Rogan was he knew he'd be having a talk with his dad about his disobedience.

Breakfast was cleaned up, and Mr. Chaffey looked at his son. He tipped his head toward his home office, and Rogan knew it was time. Inside he grimaced, but outwardly he tried not to betray his anxiety. He turned to follow his dad.

The radio crackled.

"Emergency. Emergency. Emergency. We have a missing toddler. Everyone available, please meet at the Community Center. Time is of the essence. Repeat. Toddler missing. Meet at the Community Center."

Everyone had a stunned look on their face.

"What in the world? We've never had a missing person call, and now we've had two in one week?" Jim shook his head.

"A toddler," cried Mrs. Chaffey.

"Let's go, Rogan." His dad was already heading for the door, grabbing his emergency bag.

Rogan hurried to grab his, which he hadn't even restocked and put away yet, and ran to catch up.

When they arrived at the Community Center, the briefing had just started. The toddler in question was the Roseberry's two-and-a-half-year-old son, Warren. The parents, as per the report, were frantic. They'd looked all over the house and couldn't find the tot. They and the closest neighbors were beginning to search outside. This was a concerning prospect as it was only twenty degrees, snowing, and the boy had been wearing only a diaper.

Sam was just beginning to assign searchers to their areas when the door burst open and banged against a chair behind it. All heads turned in that direction. There stood Ben Hoffman, holding a bunched-up wool blanket. Two miniature XTRATUF boots dangled below the blanket, and a head with red curls popped out the top.

"I found him! I found him!"

The Center resounded with shouts of joy and applause. Everyone gathered around, patting Mr. Hoffman on the back, and touching the boy on the head, perhaps to solidify that he really was alive and there.

Sam called the parents, and when they arrived, Ben had to retell the entire story as they held their son tightly and cried tears of joy.

Ben had been answering the call for help from the radio, heading for the Community Center, when he rounded a corner and saw the strangest but most welcome sight. A red-headed little boy was waddling down the center of the road in the almost off-balance gait of a two-year-old.

"He had nuthin' on but his boots and a soggy diaper. I was like to run over him but managed to stop in time. I got out, and he just reached his little arms up at me like he was sayin', 'Pick me up.'" Ben wiped a tear. "I thank the Lord he was found. It was the Lord who brought me to find him. It truly was, because I was so prayin'."

"You saved him, Ben," said Jim. "He wouldn't have lasted too long in the cold."

The parents hugged Mr. Hoffman, thanking him profusely. "I don't know how he got outside. I didn't think he could reach the door-knob yet," explained Mrs. Roseberry.

"Good job putting your boots on first, Son." Mr. Roseberry ruffled Warren's hair.

Everyone laughed.

Rogan soaked in the joy like it was a tropical sun. On the drive home, he admitted to his dad that he'd had enough of search and rescue practice for a while. They chuckled about that.

"Well, Son, I've been thinking about how to handle your disobedience."

Rogan nodded, looking down at his shoes.

"I know you tried to radio us, but at that point, what better choice could you have made?"

"To follow you back and tell you about the island and my suspicions that Martin might be there."

"Yes. It could have turned out very differently if you'd run into trouble or didn't have your SPOT GPS."

"I've thought about all of that too, Dad. I went back and forth, trying to decide, but it just seemed like an emergency at the time. Now, I can see better what I should've done, and I'm sorry. I know I worried you and Mom."

"We forgive you, of course, but I think there will be some consequences. I'll talk to your mom about it, and we'll let you know what we decide. I'm just very thankful it all turned out fine."

"Me too, Dad. I'm sorry I broke your trust. I feel really lousy about that."

Rogan felt relieved to have talked to his dad and surprisingly wasn't nervous about the punishment, whatever it may be. He knew he deserved it, and he vowed to try to make better choices in the future. His dad and mom forgave him, and God had forgiven him. It was time to move on.

Funny how I can let that go, but I'm still feeling unforgiven about how I yelled at Martin, Rogan thought.

"Oh, I almost forgot to tell you." His dad's words broke his reverie. "Old Man Tate is going to be okay. It was something with his heart they could fix with medication. He should be home soon."

"That's great news, Dad."

* * *

The church sanctuary that Sunday was upbeat with joy and celebration over the two young lives that were saved. The Roseberrys weren't normally church-goers, but they showed up toward the end of service with their escape-artist toddler in tow. Pastor Greg prayed a closing prayer. The congregation began to gather their things.

Mr. Roseberry's voice rose above the chatter. "Everyone, may my wife and I please have a moment of your time?"

"Of course. Everyone, please be seated. Mr. and Mrs. Roseberry, the floor is yours." Pastor Greg swept his arm and bowed slightly.

Rogan thought the couple looked a little nervous, but they headed up front.

"We just wanted to say thank you so much for everyone showing up to help look for Warren." Mr. Roseberry ruffled his son's red curls. They bounced around like metal springs.

Mrs. Roseberry smiled up at her son. "He's a little mischief maker."

Her husband nodded and continued. "We don't know all of you, but I know many of you were also praying for us, and that means a lot. I think it worked. It was a true miracle that he was found so quickly. He could have wandered off anywhere, but he was right there in the middle of the road."

"He could have frozen to death or gotten run over." His wife now had tears shimmering in her eyes. Someone in the front row handed her a tissue.

Mr. Roseberry continued, "I guess we'd like to especially thank the hero of the hour, Ben Hoffman."

All eyes turned to Mr. Hoffman. Rogan knew the old man certainly deserved the accolades, but he wouldn't necessarily like it. He was easily embarrassed by attention since he had been the town's recluse until recently.

The congregation was clapping, and many were crying. The applause lasted a long time and echoed in the rafters of the sanctuary. Rogan heartily clapped along. He was surprised that Mr. Hoffman, usually so shy, was smiling and looking around. People began shaking his hand or slapping him on the back with an "atta boy." Some even gave him a hug.

When the celebration died down some, Pastor Greg stood up again. "I think I need to say something here. I feel like the Lord is telling me that we need to repent and ask Mr. Hoffman for forgiveness."

A solemn silence descended.

"Many of us have not been Christ-like in our attitudes and actions toward you in the past, Ben. For that…" Pastor Greg's voice cracked. He took a deep breath. "I am so sorry. Please forgive me."

Rogan was flabbergasted, but a warm feeling also swelled in his chest. It looked like the town was finally accepting Mr. Hoffman. Rogan had gotten to know him over the past few months, and he thought he was really a likable guy. Now that "Crazy Hoffman" had given his life to the Lord, he was much kinder and more open, less crazy.

His mother's arm crossed Rogan's shoulders and gave him a squeeze. He turned toward her, and they shared a smile.

"Finally," he said.

Others followed suit, asking Mr. Hoffman for forgiveness. Rogan thought Ben was awfully gracious and accepting, given the way some of them had treated him. *He's able to forgive,* thought Rogan.

Eventually, everyone headed home. The Chaffeys and Ben were the last ones left, besides Pastor Greg, who was straightening things up. They stood on the front steps of the church. The world was clean, white, and beautiful.

Jim smiled. "Well, that was quite the service."

Mr. Hoffman smiled back. Rogan had the sense that their neighbor was also feeling clean and new.

"I can't thank you folks enough. You showed me Jesus. It's changed my whole life. You accepted me when no one else did." Tears unashamedly bubbled from his eyes.

Rogan, his parents and sisters, and not-so-crazy Hoffman all reached out and took each other's hands.

CHAPTER 20

Healing Flames

CHRISTMAS WAS ONE WEEK AWAY, AND THE CHAFFEY children were newly on break from school. Excitement was building for their favorite holiday. Rogan walked by as Lainey and Peg gazed intently at the few presents tantalizing them from under the tree, speculating on what they could be.

"Remember, no touching," he reminded them with a smile. There was a family rule that they could look but not touch. Rogan recalled struggling with that when he and Peter were young.

Ah, the delicious anticipation, he reminisced.

Rogan had been hard at work, carving a scene onto the flat piece of whale rib he had brought back from Skeleton Cove. It depicted the whale skeleton, the curve of the shore with the Lund beached nearby, and a few trees in the background to represent the forest. In the lower-left area, he had etched two hands in a handshake and the word, "forgiven." "From, Rogan," went in the lower-right. He was making it as a gift for Martin.

He held it at arm's length. "Not too bad if I do say so, myself."

Remembering that he'd come downstairs to show it to his dad, he went to find him. "Hey, Dad. Did you get Martin's new address from Trooper Milliken yet?"

"I did." Jim paused. "I'm going to tell you this in confidence, Rogan. You can't spread it around to your friends, okay?"

"I won't, Dad." Rogan was curious about what the big secret would be.

"They found Martin's mom. She's living in Oregon. I guess the reason she left was that Stu was abusing her, beating her up. She claims she tried to take Martin with her, but Stu threatened to steal their son back and hurt him if she tried to get custody. She was emotionally wrecked and scared enough to not try taking Martin. Plus, she had started taking drugs to help her escape her situation and she was afraid if the authorities found that out, she couldn't have Martin anyway, so she just left. She told OCS she wishes she would've gone to the authorities back then."

"Wow. That's rough. Are the authorities going to go after Mr. Wolfe now?" Rogan thought the man should be locked up in jail for how he treated his son and wife.

"I'm not sure. They didn't tell me that."

"I sure hope his mom is nice and they can be happy." Rogan also hoped Martin could start fresh down south.

"Here's his address. Did you finish?" Jim pointed at the piece of whalebone.

"I kind of did, but it's a little hard to see the picture." Rogan turned it so his dad could inspect it. "That halibut hook I modified worked great for an etching tool."

"That's really nice, Rogan. I see what you mean, though, about it not being as visible." His dad paused. "You need some kind of dye or ink to smear into the cracks."

"I could use a Sharpie?"

Snapping his fingers, Jim appeared to have thought of something. "I have an idea. I remember seeing some native Tlingit art that used squid or octopus ink. They drew the picture with it, but I wonder if it would work to stain your carving?"

"Oh, cool. That's a great idea, Dad. Hmm...duh. I'll ask Tuff if his mom or grandma knows anything about it or where to get some. Thanks, Dad."

A phone call, waiting time, a phone call back, and a couple of hours later, Rogan and Tuff were knocking on the door of his friend's grandmother. Rogan had met her a couple of times and she seemed like a sweet lady. She was stooped with age, and her smiling face was quite wrinkly, but she had a musical voice when she greeted the two boys.

"Come in, come in."

"Yak'éi yagiyee, Léelk'w." Tuff gave her a hug.

She welcomed them in, giving Rogan a hug as well. He looked over at Tuff. "That sounded cool. What did you say?"

"Good day, Grandmother."

She shuffled over and sat at her dining room table, her hand inviting the boys to do the same.

"Like I explained over the phone, Rogan has a whale rib he carved, and he needs some octopus ink to rub in the cracks, so they show up."

His grandmother's eyes seemed to twinkle and spark as she grinned like a toddler reaching for a toy. "May I see it?"

Rogan passed it over. "I'm not any kind of expert. I just wanted to make a memento for a friend."

Tuff's grandmother held the rib in one hand while the other hovered over the carving. Her hands were wrinkled like her face, and her skin was translucent. Her hand swam in the air gracefully.

"No, young man. You did just fine. I can feel the love that went into this." She touched the word "forgiveness." "This is powerful. Have you forgiven?"

Rogan was surprised she'd ask. "Yes, I have."

She leaned forward, and in her lilting voice asked, "Have you been forgiven?" Those dark eyes seemed to look inside him and know.

Feeling his face flush, Rogan squirmed in his chair. "I've asked, but yeah...I guess I am."

Tuff's grandmother nodded, a wise look on her aged face. "Keep seeking. It will come to you soon."

She set the rib down and abruptly stood, then shuffled into a back room.

Rogan wiped his sweaty palms on the front of his jeans. He let out a whoosh of air and looked over at Tuff.

"Sorry, man. I didn't think she'd ask you personal questions like that. Then again, I don't know why I'm surprised. She does that to me all the time." His voice dropped to a whisper. "It's like she can see right through me."

"I hear ya."

Tuff's grandmother came back with a small bottle of black liquid. "Here you go. Octopus ink. I'll get a sheet of plastic to put down, and you can do it right here."

"Let me get it, Grandmother." Tuff sprang up to help her out.

When it was all set up, Rogan used a soft cloth and dipped it into the ink. He then spread it over the entire carving, wiping back and forth. The ink settled into the etched trenches, creating dark lines that highlighted the art. The ink dried fairly quickly. The last step was to use a fine-grit piece of sandpaper to go over the rib, sanding off the ink that had dried on the surface, but leaving the ink in the carvings.

Rogan blew off some dust from the sanding and held it up. "That looks great. You can see the picture and how cool is that to use octopus ink. Thank you so much."

Tuff grabbed the whale rib. "Nice job, Chaffey. If Martin doesn't keep this forever, he really is a loser." Tuff sent a guilty-looking glance toward his grandmother. "Not that he is a loser. Not that anyone is a loser."

The look of consternation on Tuff's face as he tried to dig himself out of a hole was too much, and first his grandmother, and then Rogan began to laugh. Tuff looked relieved as he joined in.

"Yeah...sorry."

The boys cleaned up the mess, then brought in a few armloads of firewood to stack near her stove. They went outside and burned the elderly woman's trash in a rusty fifty-five-gallon drum used for that purpose before saying their goodbyes.

Rogan thanked Tuff again and, as he prepared to head home on the Ski-Doo, hollered out, "See you soon at youth group."

After dinner and chores, it was time to head back out.

"Dad, Mom. I'm going to youth group," he hollered as he walked back out to the Ski-Doo.

"Have fun," his mom yelled back.

When he arrived at the church, Runt and Tuff were already there and helping Dexter Newby build a roaring fire.

"Please tell me you brought marshmallows," Runt pleaded.

"I think I have some around here, somewhere."

"Yes!" Runt looked over at Tuff. "Sorry, but they're better than Pop-Tarts. Roasted to a light-brown perfection. Mm."

"They're good, but they're not that good," Tuff countered.

"Whatever. I'll eat your share."

"No way. I didn't say I didn't like them, just that Pop-Tarts are a more intricate taste for a discerning palate."

"What are you even saying?" Runt gave him a friendly shove.

Rogan just shook his head.

More of the youth arrived, and it was a fun evening of singing, roasting marshmallows, and hanging out.

The fire burned low. Dexter waited until there was a lull in the conversation. Rogan was staring into the flames, watching them pulse and flicker orange and yellow, the coals glowing hot.

"I'm going to give each one of you a piece of paper. We've been learning about forgiveness, and tonight we're going to wrap up what we've discovered about God and His forgiveness." He stood up and walked around the fire ring, handing out a small piece of paper to everyone. "I'm going to ask for five whole minutes of silence. Think you can handle that, Runt?"

"It'll be hard, but I'll manage," Runt teased.

"In those five minutes, I want you to pray and to think of what you feel you need to be forgiven for, or if you need to forgive someone. Maybe you've asked for forgiveness, but you still feel the burden of it weighing you down. Maybe you haven't been able to bring yourself to ask for forgiveness yet. Maybe you feel like you don't deserve it. Maybe you have a spirit of stubbornness. Whatever the reason, I want you to pick the one thing related to forgiveness that is most on your heart after talking to God about it. Everybody good?"

Everyone nodded.

Rogan fingered the slip of paper and bowed his head as Dexter told them to begin. At first, he just closed his eyes and felt the warmth of the fire on his face. Then, he began to pray. Right away, he knew what he was going to write down on his paper. He still felt terrible about how he'd treated Martin, especially after learning about the other boy's home life.

Lord, help me learn to be more like You. I did a crummy thing to Martin. I didn't want everyone to see me all mad like that. It was a bad example, and I'm sorry. I know I've asked for forgiveness from both him and You. I just want to let go of the guilt and regret. I hope I've learned my lesson, and I'll sure try better from now on.

The silence of the atmosphere, the crackle and pop of the comforting fire, and Rogan's thoughts all twisted together like the spirals of smoke wafting up in a column, reaching for the night sky.

When the time was up, Rogan spread the paper flat on his knee and wrote, "I was a jerk to Martin. I didn't show Christ's love to others. I'M SORRY. Rogan." The pencil poked a few small holes in the paper as he wrote.

Pastor Newby waited until everyone had finished writing, then he instructed them to fold it over once. "I'm going to go inside, and when you're ready, please step up to the fire and throw in your paper. You've already asked for forgiveness. Just as you see it reduced to ashes,

God promises to remember our sins no more." With that, he headed inside the church.

Rogan looked around. His youth group mates all seemed deep in thought. One of the girls walked over, threw it in, and quickly walked away, not seeming to care to watch it burn. Two more youth quickly followed suit, leaving Rogan and his three friends.

Boom Chain spoke up. "Can we all do ours together?"

Without answering, they stood and stepped up near the fire pit, one on each side, forming around the circle.

Rogan threw out, "On three?" and held his arm straight out, the paper dangling from his fingers over the low flames that seemed ready to ingest his wrongdoing. It seemed to him that it was like poison that would not affect the consumer but would free the original owner. Forgiveness shuffled up next to Rogan, available to shake hands and seal the deal if he would make the first move. He wanted it, desperately needed it.

He began the countdown. "One. Two. Three."

Each boy released his paper. The four scraps spiraled down, fluttering like ugly, beautiful butterflies heading for the cleansing flames. The papers landed gracefully, caught fire, and were obliterated in only a few seconds. The boys all remained silent and still, staring. Even Runt.

Rogan felt strangely released from his burden. *God remembers it no more.*

Boom Chain was on Rogan's left. Rogan heard him softly weeping and reached over to clasp his friend's shoulder. "You okay, man?"

Boom Chain looked up to the sky and inhaled deeply. "Yeah. I think I really am. It's crazy. This thing worked."

"I know what you mean," Rogan agreed.

Tuff and Runt added affirmation with nods. They stayed like that for a few contemplative minutes until heading back in, thanking Dexter before they dispersed and left for their respective homes.

Rogan walked into his house to find his parents sitting on the couch, Jim's arm around his wife, and only the warm glow of the Christmas tree lights illuminating the room. They looked peaceful and content, and Rogan was feeling the same.

"How was youth group?" his dad inquired.

"It was really good." Rogan joined them on the couch and told them about burning their forgiveness issues in the fire. "I want to ask you and Mom to forgive me for my bad choices. I've learned from it, for sure, and want you to be able to still trust me."

"Of course we forgive you, Son." His dad smiled, and his mom nodded. "And I *do* trust you."

"One thing I love about you, Rogan, is that you try to do the right thing. Please don't ever change that." His mom reached out and took his hand.

"Well, I must've had good parents who taught me right," Rogan half-joked. He was rewarded with chuckles. "Seriously, though, you are amazing parents. I couldn't imagine having ones like Martin's. And thanks, you guys. That means a lot." Rogan felt the residual weight he'd carried take wings.

"Oh, so I'm a guy now?" his mom teased.

The lighthearted question brought humorous relief.

* * *

Christmas Eve in the Chaffey home was admittedly everyone's favorite holiday. There was no formal dinner, just snacks and munchies—traditionally, the same menu every year since Rogan could remember. They gathered in the living room when the setting sun had left it dark enough for the Christmas tree to show off its brilliance. Snow gently drifted from unseen clouds, the flakes peeking through the windows as they twirled by. The fire roared in the Franklin stove, and Christmas music played softly in the background. Sitka was snoozing on her doggy bed. They had moved the rawhide bone from under the tree to up on the counter. The dog was as impatient for presents as Lainey and Peg.

Taking turns with who read the Christmas story from Luke chapter two was also a tradition, and this year was Rogan's turn again. He had his Bible ready, his finger on verse one. He would read through verse twenty.

When he finished, he closed the Bible. "You know, I never really thought about it until this year with everything going on about forgiveness, but Christmas is about forgiveness almost more than Easter is. If Jesus wasn't sent to earth, being born as a baby, then He never would've been able to do His thing of dying on the cross for our sins. We wouldn't be able to just ask for forgiveness and get it. That would stink."

"You're right," his dad agreed. "That's insightful of you to realize that."

"I'm glad we have both holidays." Lainey was bouncing up and down on the end of the couch. "Can we open presents now?"

Jim and Elise chuckled.

"Okay, Lainey. Find one present for everyone," Elise ordered.

Peg clapped her hands, a huge grin on her face as her sister shot to her feet and skipped over to the pile of presents.

Rogan let the excitement, contentment, and love swirl around him. His heart felt full of thankfulness for his imperfect, yet perfect, family, for living in the wilds of Alaska and all that came with that, for his mom's healing, and for feeling that forgiveness had set him free.

He felt at this moment that he didn't need anything else.

His life was complete.

Except...maybe he needed that six-and-a-quarter-inch satin finish, stainless steel, straight-back bowie blade Buck knife with a black Micarta handle in a genuine leather sheath he'd hinted that he wanted for Christmas.

GOLD RUSH GRIDDLE COOKIES

Recipe from my mom, Marilyn Lusby

These are great camping, hiking, and hunting snacks!

3 ½ cups sifted flour	1 cup shortening
1 cup sugar	1 beaten egg
1 ½ teaspoons baking powder	¾ cup milk
1 teaspoon salt	1 ¼ cup raisins**
½ teaspoon baking soda	

Mix dry ingredients together in a large bowl. Cut in shortening until mixture is mealy. Add egg, milk, and raisins. Mix until all ingredients are moistened, and dough holds together. Roll out on floured board to ¼ inch thickness. Cut with a two-inch round cookie cutter. Heat griddle to 275 degrees. Place cookies on the griddle. As the bottoms brown, the tops become puffy. Turn and brown the other side. Makes approximately four dozen.

**I hate to even mention this, but my daughters like to substitute chocolate chips for the raisins.